Dark Ruby

"A true gem—a medieval masterpiece. Wonderfully compelling, filled with adventure and intrigue, sizzling sexual tension and a to-die-for hero, this one has it all."　　　　　　　　　—Samantha James

"Rich, mysterious, passionate. It's a winner."
　　　　　　　　　　　　　　　—Alexis Harrington

"Fast-paced and fun from the start . . . a high-action adventure that will keep you turning the pages."
　　　　　　　　　　　　　　　—Kat Martin

"A rich, unforgettable tale."　　　　—Stella Cameron

WILD
AND
WICKED

Lisa Jackson

A SIGNET BOOK

SIGNET
Published by New American Library, a division of
Penguin Group (USA) Inc., 375 Hudson Street,
New York, New York 10014, USA
Penguin Group (Canada), 90 Eglinton Avenue East, Suite 700, Toronto,
Ontario M4P 2Y3, Canada (a division of Pearson Penguin Canada Inc.)
Penguin Books Ltd., 80 Strand, London WC2R 0RL, England
Penguin Ireland, 25 St. Stephen's Green, Dublin 2,
Ireland (a division of Penguin Books Ltd.)
Penguin Group (Australia), 250 Camberwell Road, Camberwell, Victoria 3124,
Australia (a division of Pearson Australia Group Pty. Ltd.)
Penguin Books India Pvt. Ltd., 11 Community Centre, Panchsheel Park,
New Delhi - 110 017, India
Penguin Group (NZ), 67 Apollo Drive, Rosedale, North Shore 0632,
New Zealand (a division of Pearson New Zealand Ltd.)
Penguin Books (South Africa) (Pty.) Ltd., 24 Sturdee Avenue,
Rosebank, Johannesburg 2196, South Africa

Penguin Books Ltd., Registered Offices:
80 Strand, London WC2R 0RL, England

First published by Signet, an imprint of New American Library,
a division of Penguin Group (USA) Inc.

First Printing, February 2002
First Printing ($4.99 Edition), January 2008
10 9 8 7 6 5 4 3 2 1

 REGISTERED TRADEMARK—MARCA REGISTRADA

Printed in the United States of America

This book is dedicated to my editor, Cecilia Oh,
not only because of the title, though that may
be appropriate, but because she's hung in there
with me and helped me stay the course,
being my champion as well as my conscience.

Prologue

November 1283
Castle Serennog

"You ask the impossible!" Apryll stared at her brother as if he'd gone mad. She slapped the reins of her listless mare into a stable boy's hand and frowned as she glanced up at the foreboding sky. Dark winter clouds, swollen with rain, moved slowly across the heavens as a keening wind tore through the outer bailey of the castle she'd called home for all of her twenty-two years.

Mud spackled her skirts and gusts of the blasted wind snatched at her hair as she strode toward the great hall. Payton, her half brother, marched at her side and she was certain he'd gone daft. "I cannot sneak into Black Thorn Castle and dupe the lord with my . . . charms—is that what you said—you want me to . . . 'charm' the beast of Black Thorn while you . . . you . . . what? Steal his jewels and his horses? 'Tis madness."

"You will not need to sneak. During the Christmas Revels the portcullis is raised and the doors of Black Thorn are thrown wide," Payton assured her, his jaw set, determination etched in his bladed features. He took a quick step in front of her and, grabbing both her arms, forced her to stop just as the first drops of rain began to fall. "Look around you," he ordered, desperation and a need for revenge carved into his features as he insisted she take a harder look at the once-beautiful castle now falling deep into ruin. Thatching had blown from the roofs of some of the huts in the bailey, beams had rotted, even the mortar in the thick curtain wall surrounding the keep was giving way, pebbles littering the dead grass. Winter apples hanging on leafless trees were shriveled and wormy. Sheep were huddled against the wind, their coats black with mud and dung, their bleats pathetic.

"You can't be so blind as not to see that there is not enough wood in all of the forest to get us through the winter, the stock is sickly, the grain supply infested with rats, the horses already showing bones. The stores of wheat and spices are nearly empty, the wool to make new clothes in scant supply as the sheep are dying. You're the lady here," he reminded her roughly as she threw off his hands and began walking again, hurrying through the inner bailey where chickens scattered, their tattered feathers flying into the puddles that had collected in the rutted pathways. "'Tis your obligation to help those who serve you."

"Aye, Payton, I must do something," she admitted with a heavy sigh. Few hammers were banging as carpenters labored against impossible repairs and though the blacksmith's forge was glowing bright, the bellows hissing, 'twould only be a short time before the castle was depleted of steel. Boys ran carrying sacks of acorns they'd gathered for the pigs, but soon what meager stores of feed that had been harvested and gathered would be drained. Gripping her cloak more tightly around her, Apryll bit her lip and hurried up the chipped steps to the keep.

A rail-thin guard with a pockmarked complexion and sad eyes opened the door. "M'lady," he said with only a shadow of a smile.

"Geoffrey." She paused before entering and felt rain seep under her hood to run through her hair and down her face. "How is your wife?"

He glanced to the ground and clamped his lips together, then cleared his throat. "Mary—she be fine. As soon as the babes—twins they be, the midwife says—arrive, she'll be back on her feet, mark my words. A strong lass Mary is." But his gaze belied the courage in his words.

"I'll see that the physician stops to see her and that Cook makes her best soup. I'll bring it to your hut myself."

"'Tis kind ye be, m'lady." Geoffrey nodded, managing a grateful, snaggletoothed smile as he shut the door behind them. Apryll felt cold to the bottom of her soul.

"His wife will be dead within a week," Payton predicted. The tables within the great hall had been pushed against the aging walls. He rubbed his gloved hands together. "As for Mary's unborn babes . . ." He clucked his tongue and shook his head in dire prediction. "'Tis a pity."

"They're not yet born, for the love of God. Mary has already birthed two fine, strong sons, so don't be placing the twins in their graves already." She refused to believe there was a grain of truth in his words. Mary, with her flaming hair and wide smile, was a big-boned, strong woman. The twins would survive. Somehow.

But the gloom of the castle with its cracked walls and cobweb-dusted rafters couldn't be ignored. *And if those babes die, and other children as well, who will be to blame?*

You, Apryll.

A fire burned within the grate and yet the cavernous room was as chilled as if a ghost had passed behind the ragged curtains. There had been a time when the whitewashed walls had been covered by colorful tapestries, the rushes had been fresh and sweet smelling, the enticing aromas from the kitchen had been ever present. Apryll remembered the smell of roasting pork as it turned on the spit, fat dripping into the coals, or the sweet scent of fruit tarts, or the smoky tang of charring eel flesh. Delicious scents had mingled and swept through the corridors and tunnels, sweeping through the great hall and filling the secret nooks and crannies where Apryll had played with the castle dogs or other children. But that had been long ago in a time when it had never seemed to grow cold, a time of laughter and songs and freedom. A time when her mother had been alive. Apryll had been her father's pet, a spoiled child who had easily weaseled sweet tidbits before dinner from Cook, or been allowed to play seek-and-hide in the hay stored for the winter, or who had been dressed like a small princess for every festive occasion. She'd sat on her father's knee and tugged on his thick reddish beard. It had been long ago, of course.

Before the curse of Black Thorn had been cast upon us.

Wrapping her arms around herself, she rubbed her sleeves, as if warding off a chill.

Payton had never known the happiness that had once spilled like sunshine through this very hall.

"The treasury be nearly empty," he reminded her as Apryll tore off her riding gloves and, ignoring the hole in one finger, stuffed them into her pocket. Tossing off her hood, she warmed her palms by the fire. Piled high with ashes, the iron dogs supporting the burning logs seemed to glower up at her with their tarnished and blackened eyes. "The stores of feed are lower than they have been in years."

She bit her lip and braced herself, for she knew what was to come. Always, after Payton prophecied doom and disaster for the keep, he came up with suggestions on how to improve things. She wasn't disappointed this afternoon.

"'Tis simple, Apryll. Either you marry and marry well, or we will not make it through the winter. Your subjects will starve."

"I'll not marry—"

"Lord Jamison asks for your hand," he cut in.

She shuddered at the thought of the rheumy-eyed baron. His girth was equal to his height and he had a cruel streak she'd witnessed while hunting. Angry that the quarry, an impressive stag, had escaped, he'd raged and sputtered and whipped his dogs and steed with a fury that had brought a gleam to his eye and spittle to his lips. Apryll didn't doubt for a second that his brutality had extended to his wives. "He has been married four times, brother. None of his wives lived longer than three years. Think you I should be the fifth?"

"You are strong . . ."

"Nay!"

"Fine, fine. But if not Jamison, why not Baron William of Balchdar? He asks of you often and would make a fine husband."

"Then you marry him," she snapped angrily, shaking the rain from her hair. "I detest him."

"You detest all men." Payton raised a dismissive hand.

"Not true."

"Then all suitors. 'Tis long past the time when you should marry. By now, you should be wed and have two or three babes."

"Not Lord William," she said angrily. William was a handsome man with crafty eyes and a prideful stance. He looked down his straight nose as if everyone he came upon—peasants, servants, knights and even other lords—were beneath him, were put upon this land but to serve him. There were secrets hidden in his dark, arrogant eyes, secrets that sent a shiver down Apryll's spine, secrets she, nor anyone else, dared unveil.

"What of—?"

"Say no more," she ordered. "You need not remind me of each and every baron who would deign wed me and save Serennog. By the saints, I know well who they are!"

Payton laid a brotherly hand upon her shoulder as the fire crackled and smoke spiraled to the patched ceiling. Raindrops found their way inside, running down the walls or plopping in ever-growing puddles on the stone floor. "I know you want not to marry them and so I am offering you another answer." Her half brother's voice was soothing and sincere, yet she told herself he had his own reasons for scheming against Black Thorn.

The wind whistled eerily through the cracks in the walls, muting the sound of a baby wailing, sobbing pitifully in some distant part of the keep. Payton, curse his sorry hide, was right. Soon the sickness that had infected a few would spread throughout the castle and village, killing many and leaving those who were strong and lucky enough to survive the illness to face starvation.

"'Twas grim."

"Listen, Apryll, 'tis your sworn duty to protect and care for these people," her half brother reminded her as he spied a page huddled in a corner. "You there, boy!" Payton snapped his fingers. "John—wine for the lady and myself!" he ordered and Apryll cringed inwardly, for in light of their conversation, the wine seemed frivolous, best saved. "And see that it is warmed, as we be chilled to our bones." The wool of his cloak was steaming, giving off an odor from the heat of the fire, and his eyes, usually as blue as a summer sky, had darkened. "All the trouble that has come this way can be laid at the feet of those who rule Black Thorn. 'Twas Black Thorn's army and its lord that brought a curse upon Serennog. 'Tis only justice that we return the favor."

"Or revenge," she said, eyeing her half brother and wondering how deep his hatred ran.

He lifted a shoulder. "As I said, you, *m'lady*, have an obligation to those who serve you, and, as I see it, you can either marry some rich baron or partake in my plan."

She dropped into a chair near the fire. Neither option was acceptable, both left a bad taste in her mouth. "And if I were to agree to your plan, I would need clothes . . . a fine gown and jewels . . . as well as an invitation."

"I have considered all this."

"Have you?" There was more to her brother than

she knew, a side far more shrewd and deadly. She would have to tread lightly.

"Aye, and I've found all but the invitation, which will not be necessary."

"*Found?*" She laughed hollowly and rolled her eyes. "You *found* a gown? We have no grain for the livestock, little food and not even a scrap of cloth large enough for Cook's apron, as you so just warned me, but now, *now* you claim you've got a gown and gems fine enough to wear to the revels at Black Thorn?" She shook her head at the folly of it all. "Now, Payton, 'tis no longer a guess. Now I *know* you be daft."

"Trust me." Payton's face was sincere, his brown hair glinting red in the light from the fire. "There are treasures within this very castle that were hidden away—our mother's bridal gown and her jewels, all packed and wrapped carefully with dried herbs and flowers, then hidden deep within a crypt, untouched by the castle rats or moths or mold."

"And you just happened to find them."

"Father Hadrian and I."

She scowled a bit. The priest was new to the castle, a seemingly pious man whose kindness seemed forced. Apryll wasn't sure she trusted the man. There was something very amiss here, something wrong. "Even if you did have these things—"

"I do."

"Then bring them before me and . . . nay! 'Tis foolishness. There must be another way," she said, drumming her fingers on the smooth arm of her chair. Stealing from the Lord of Black Thorn would only spell deeper trouble.

"Mayhap." Payton scowled and shrugged out of his

mantle, draping it on a stool by the fire. "But I know not of it and we have little time."

As if on cue, one of the servants who had been hiding behind the thin curtains began coughing loudly, the sound rattling in the poor man's lungs and ricocheting through the rafters and ceilings of the drafty castle.

"Geneva has had a vision—"

"Hush! I'll not trust the prophecies of a woman who claims to see spirits and casts spells and practices the dark arts!" Apryll quickly made the sign of the cross over her chest, for, in truth, the sorceress was a kind yet disturbing woman.

"Did Geneva not foretell the death of the miller's son?" he asked, and she refused to think of the poor boy drowning in the millpond just this past spring. Payton lowered himself into the chair next to hers. "And what of the loss of Father Benjamin's eyesight? Did not Geneva predict 'twould be so?"

"Aye, aye." Apryll's eyebrows pulled into a knot of concentration. Because of the rotund priest's blindness, Father Hadrian had been sent to Serennog. "'Twas happenchance."

"I don't think so."

John, the nervous page with hair that stuck out like dirty straw, entered quickly and poured two mazers of wine from a jug.

"Even Father Benjamin, a true man of our Lord, now believes that Geneva is blessed by God with the sight to see what is to come," Payton insisted, taking his cup from the table and dismissing the page quickly with an impatient snap of his wrist. "Geneva has seen prosperity for Serennog again."

"Because of your plan against Black Thorn?"

"Aye." He crossed one booted leg over his knee and took a long swallow of wine. Firelight reflected in his eyes and the edges of his mouth curved ever downward. Deep in the rushes, the sounds of tiny claws, mice and rats, scraped against the stone floor.

Apryll sensed a half truth hidden in her brother's plan. "There is more you have not told me."

Payton lifted a dismissive shoulder. "Mayhap."

"What is the rest of it?"

He hesitated. Buried his nose in his mazer.

"If I am to be a part of this or give your scheme any merit, I must hear it all."

"So be it." He set his cup on the scarred planks of a small table. "Geneva . . . she . . ." He sighed, clenched and opened a fist, and shook his head as if he were unable or unwilling to say the rest. Turning his head slightly, he called. "Geneva. Be you here?"

Apryll felt a tingle on the back of her neck, the fine hairs at her nape raising one by one. 'Twas as if Satan himself had breathed upon her.

Appearing on silent footsteps, Geneva rounded a pillar where, Apryll surmised, she'd been lurking and listening—at Payton's behest.

Tall and slender, wearing a faded green gown and an expression of abject serenity, Geneva observed Apryll with eyes a pale watery blue. Her skin was without a wrinkle and so white it was nearly translucent.

"M'lady," she said with a half curtsy.

"What do you know of this?" Apryll demanded, but Geneva's gaze was turned toward Payton.

"You were to tell her the truth, Sir Payton." Reproach edged the deep clarity of her voice.

Payton's Adam's apple bobbed. He didn't meet her

eyes. The wind whistled and the coals in the fire glowed bright.

"What is it?" Apryll demanded. A frigid chill seeped deep into her skin and she knew in a heartbeat that whatever it was, she would not like what the sorceress had to say. When Payton didn't answer, she turned her question to Geneva. "Tell me."

A second's hesitation.

"Now," Apryll ordered. "What is it you see?"

Geneva lifted an elegant eyebrow. Her gaze fixed deep in Apryll's. "In order for there to be peace and prosperity at Serennog again," she said, "you will marry the Lord of Black Thorn."

Apryll's blood turned to ice. "Never," she said in a hoarse whisper that was far from her normal voice. Her stomach clenched in repulsion when she thought of the powerful, brooding baron and the rumors that had swirled around him. Cruel. Without a heart. Feared rather than loved, Lord Devlynn of Black Thorn was known throughout Wales for his unbending will. "Did he not kill his first wife and unborn babe?"

"No one knows that for certain." Geneva's demeanor remained unmoved, expressionless.

The wind seemed to have died. Apryll's heart drummed a furious, denying tattoo. "And yet you think I would agree to marry him?" 'Twas absurd. Swiveling her head, she asked, "Payton? You knew of this?"

He nodded stiffly, then snapped his fingers for more wine.

"'Tis not about choice," Geneva said with quiet conviction as she stepped closer, and Apryll was drawn once again to those unblinking pallid eyes. "'Tis about destiny, m'lady. Your destiny."

Chapter One

Black Thorn Forest
December 1283

"Happy Christmas," Lord Devlynn muttered without a trace of a smile. Tossing a sprig of mistletoe onto the grave where his wife and unborn daughter were buried, he couldn't ignore the remorse that lay heavy upon his soul, nor the bitterness that had festered deep in his heart. He stared at the graying tombstone, fingered the rosary deep within his pocket, but could conjure up no prayer to ask God's forgiveness.

A raw December wind, promising snow, blew across the hillside. Frosted blades of grass crumpled beneath his boots. Two horses pawed the hard ground. Astride the bay, his brother sat, gloved hands over the pommel of his saddle, a long-suffering expression on a face considered handsome by nearly every woman in the barony. "Come along, *m'lord*," Collin mocked. "'Tis time to put away the ghosts and leave the dead buried where they belong. There is living to be done and now 'tis the time. Like it or not, the revels are upon us and soon the keep will be filled with guests and laughter and celebration." In the coming darkness, Collin slanted a wicked grin, the likes of which had melted the ice around more than one young maid's heart. "'Tis time to forget the past, get drunk, raise a skirt or two and make merry."

"Is it?"

"Aye." Deep lines of frustration furrowed across Collin's brow. He rubbed his hands together and his breath fogged in the air. "Mayhap you fancy a tongue-lashing from our sweet sister but I, for one, would like to forgo that supreme pleasure at least for this night."

"Ride ahead."

"Nay—"

"I'll be along! Tell Miranda to heat my mazer and fill it with wine." Mayhap his brother was right; 'twas time to look forward rather than back.

Collin hesitated, then glanced across the stream and tops of the forest trees to the hill upon which Castle Black Thorn rose, a massive stone and mortar fortress with towers spiraling heavenward. The main gate was thrown open, the drawbridge lowered and portcullis raised, while high on poles above the watchtowers, twin standards emblazoned gold and black snapped in the harsh winter breeze.

"Have it your way, then. After all, you be the lord."

"Forget it not," Devlynn suggested, striving for humor and failing miserably. His brother sent him a look of pity, reined his stallion and, shaking his head, slapped the beast on his broad rump. With a snort the steed bolted, and Collin, fur-lined mantle swelling behind him, rode furiously down the hillside. The horse's hooves thundered against the frozen ground. Overhead a startled hawk flapped its great wings as it soared toward the woods.

Devlynn watched horse and rider splash through the stream at the base of the hill, then disappear into a thicket of naked-branched oaks on the far side of the creek. Waiting until the echo of hoofbeats had faded into the low moan of the wind, Devlynn turned back to the grave. His jaw clenched so hard it ached. 'Twas time to let all the old pain die. Banish the guilt. He pulled off a glove with his teeth, then, reaching beneath his mantle, he wrapped chilled fingers around the black ribbon he'd worn around his arm, the reminder of the tragedy that had claimed his wife and unborn daughter's lives, the symbol of the guilt that was forever carved into his heart.

"'Tis over," he growled, stripping the band from his arm and dropping it onto the dead grass. The first flakes of snow drifted from the dark sky as he strode to his horse and swung easily into the saddle. With thoughts as black as the coming night, he yanked on the reins and urged his barrel-chested gray. "Run, you devil," he growled.

The stallion shot forward. Sleek muscles moved effortlessly, long strides tore over the open fields and ever downward to the creek. On the near bank, the steed's gait shifted, his muscles bunched, and Devlynn caught his breath. Phantom sprang, catapulting over the gurgling stream where ice had collected between the rocks. Devlynn felt a surge of power, a freedom as the raw wind pressed hard against his flesh and stung his eyes.

This night he would bury all thoughts of his wife and daughter. By the grace of God he still had his son. A hint of a smile tugged at the corners of Devlynn's mouth as he thought of the boy. A strong, smart boy nearing ten, Yale was as quick with a dagger as he was with a roll of the dice. Quick with a bow and arrow, sly and bullheaded, Yale eagerly argued with the castle priest, defied his teachers and often escaped from beneath his nursemaid's wary eye. He rode the finest steeds without a saddle alone in the forest, was known to shimmy up a tree or down a rope faster than the most agile knights, and promised to be a handsome man in time. Gray eyes, thick black hair, a dusting of freckles and a bravery that bordered on recklessness. Aye, the lad was trouble, but also Devlynn's pride and joy. Soon Yale would grow tall and strong, and Devlynn never once doubted his decision to keep Yale here, at Black Thorn, rather than send him to be a page at another lord's castle.

The boy would someday be Lord of Black Thorn.

There was no reason for Devlynn to ever marry again; he had his only son and heir.

Hours later, aided by warm wine, a long, hot meal and the crackling yule log burning in the grate, the chill had drained from Devlynn's bones. Holly, mistletoe and ivy had been draped throughout the great hall, where hundreds of candles burned, their flames flickering brightly.

As part of the festivities and feast a boar's head, replete with sprays of laurel and an apple stuffed into its mouth, had been paraded through the guests upon a silver platter, then consumed along with great trays of eel, pheasant, salmon and crane. Wine flowed. Music trilled. Laughter rang. Dozens of finely garbed guests, resplendent with jewels, were dancing and making merry, laughing and drinking as if they had not a care in the world. Half of them he'd never met.

The spirit of the season was lost on the Lord of Black Thorn. Slouched against the small of his back at the head table with the rest of his family, Devlynn had no interest in the festivities, nor had he paid any attention to more than one fetching young maid determined to catch his eye.

"You break more hearts and dash more hopes than 'tis wise," Collin warned his brother after Yale, uncharacteristically drowsy, had been hauled off to bed. "There be skirts to be lifted tonight."

"So lift them," Devlynn replied, drinking heartily and motioning to a page to refill his cup. "All of them."

"Some of the maids have eyes only for you."

Because I am the lord, he thought cynically as the yule candle burned bright before him. He had no interest in foolish, ambitious women. The page refilled his cup and he wondered when the evening would end.

"By the saints, 'tis an angel," Aunt Violet whispered almost reverently as she gazed upon the guests.

Devlynn slid a glance in the older woman's direction and saw her pale lips quiver in awe. Hurriedly, with deft be-ringed fingers, she made the sign of the cross over her ample, velvet-draped bosom. 'Twas as if she were warding off evil spirits rather than embracing a divine being cast down from the heavens.

Devlynn paid little mind to the old woman and swallowed another gulp of wine.

Though her once-clear eyes had clouded with age, Violet was always seeing spirits and ghosts. Now, during the holidays, his aunt was forever searching for some sign of heavenly intervention—conjuring up a miracle to lift what she considered a dark, gloomy pall that had fallen upon the Lord of Black Thorn's shoulders.

'Twas foolishness.

A scamp of a child, the daughter of his sister Miranda, screamed gleefully as she dashed past.

"Hush, Bronwyn, off to bed with you," Miranda ordered.

"Nay, mother, not yet," the girl cried, brown curls bouncing around her flushed eight-year-old face. "We've not yet played hoodman's-blind or bob apple."

"But soon, the nurse will take you upstairs."

"Where be Yale?" she asked Devlynn.

"Already abed," her mother said sternly. "Where you should be."

"Why? 'Tis not like him," Bronwyn sniffed.

"Nay, 'tis not," Devlynn agreed, wondering if the lad was becoming ill.

"Mayhap he is only pretending sleep and he is even now escaping the castle, as he has before!" Bronwyn said, her eyes glittering at the thought of her adventurous cousin.

"Nay. 'Tis only too much merriment and festivities," Miranda said and Bronwyn, as if realizing she was in danger of being hauled off to bed this very minute, tossed her dark ringlets, then scampered away, chasing after a servant carrying platters of jellied eggs, tarts and meat pies.

"Violet is right. She *is* a beauty," Collin whispered under his breath. There was awe in his voice, but Devlynn refused to be infected with the rapture his brother felt for females.

"All women are beauties to you, brother." Devlynn tossed back his mazer, wiped his mouth and, bored by the conversation, searched the milling crowd with his eyes.

Then he saw her.

Unerringly.

Knowing instinctively that it was the "angel" of whom his aunt had murmured in awe. Mayhap his doddery, ancient aunt was right for the first time in her seventy-odd years, that the unknown woman was a magical being sent straight from the gates of heaven.

She certainly was like no other Devlynn had ever seen.

Tall and slender, bedecked in a dazzling white gown, she moved through the crowd with an easy, elegant grace. Her dress was embroidered with silver and gold thread, intricately woven, and her hair, as pale as flax, was threaded with silver and gold ribbons. Her eyes sparkled from the reflection of the hundreds of candles within the room, her cheekbones arched high above rosy spots of color on flawless skin.

Devlynn's heart thumped in his chest. He silently called himself a fool. Took another swallow of wine.

Who the devil was she?

"You told me not that you had invited divinity," Collin teased, leaning closer to his brother, one side of his mouth lifted in cynical, wicked appreciation.

"I knew not." Devlynn couldn't pull his eyes from the curve of her cheek, nor the lift of her small, pointed chin.

Christ Jesus. The air stilled in his lungs.

"I think I might ask her to dance." Scraping his chair back, Collin lifted an eyebrow in his brother's direction, as if in challenge. 'Twas his way these days. Collin seemed restless and bored, ready for a fight, always daring his older brother.

A spurt of jealousy swept through Devlynn, but he raised one shoulder as if he was not interested in the woman. Not at all. Yet he couldn't stop following her with his eyes and felt the muscles at the base of his neck grow taut as Collin strode to the woman and, with only the slightest bit of conversation, began dancing with her.

She smiled radiantly, and slid easily into his brother's arms.

Devlynn's gut clenched. He feigned interest in the conversation around him, drank heartily, but the truth of the matter was that he could barely drag his eyes from the elegant woman draped in white as she swirled past lords and ladies festooned in purple, dark green and scarlet.

When the dance was finished, Collin bowed and she inclined her head, then turned to yet another man, a burly knight, who swept her into his arms. For a second Devlynn thought she cast a quick glance in his direction, but 'twas a heartbeat and then she laughed gaily in the bear of a man's embrace.

Collin returned, picked up his mazer and sighed. "Truly an angel, but one with a touch of sin, methinks."

"How could you know?"

"Trust me, brother. I know women. This one"—he pointed her out with the finger around his cup—"is spirited, and I'm not talking about heavenly spirits now."

"Hush!" Violet said. "I'll hear none of this!"

Devlynn finished his wine and while the tapers burned low and a jester tried to regale him with a bawdy joke, his attention never strayed from the bewitching woman as she danced. His eyebrows drew together and he wondered yet again who she was, why he'd never met her, how she'd come to be invited here.

As if he read his brother's mind, Collin said, "I did not catch her name. But mayhap I will the next time." The music faded and he started to climb to his feet, but Devlynn laid a hand upon his shoulder.

"Nay, 'tis my turn," he said, surprising even himself.

"Ah . . . So brother, you not be made of stone after all." Collin chuckled gruffly as Devlynn waded through the crowd, nodding to well-wishers as he passed, walking to the knot of guests near the fire where the woman swept a lock of hair from her cheek. He was not alone in his quest. More than one man was following her with appreciative and lust-filled eyes.

"Excuse me," he said as he approached.

"Lord Devlynn." She dipped her head.

"Could I have this dance?" he asked as a musician began to play a harp.

She smiled, her lips parting to show just the hint of white teeth. Gold eyes sparkled at him, yet there was something deeper in her gaze, something hovering beneath the surface. One honey-colored eyebrow raised haughtily. "Aye, m'lord, 'twould be my pleasure, to be sure," she said, then tossed back her head to stare directly at him. "As it was, I thought I would have to ask you."

"You would be so bold?" He was surprised.

"As to approach the lord of the castle?" she asked, some of her gaiety fading. "Aye. I assure you I would."

Who was she to flirt so wantonly with him? "And had I denied you?"

"Then I would have asked your brother." He swung

her easily into his arms and she moved flawlessly. "*He* would not have said nay."

Devlynn didn't doubt it for a second. Even now he felt the weight of Collin's gaze boring into his back. "Who are you?"

"You know not?" she teased, moving easily as the tempo of the music quickened. Other couples stepped lively and swirled around them. Fragrant smoke spiraled to the ceiling and conversation buzzed beneath the lilting music.

It had been years since he'd danced, forever since he'd wanted to hold a woman and spin her across the floor, but this one molded tightly against his body and followed his steps easily when they were together, held his gaze when they danced apart, her feet moving quickly over the rushes, her snowy dress smooth and shimmering. She smelled of lavender and roses and the sheen of sweat that covered her skin glistened in the candle glow. She cocked her head as if silently defying him, as if beneath a false layer of civility there was a wild, rebellious spirit lurking within the deepest part of her soul.

For the first time since his wife's death, the Lord of Black Thorn experienced a heat in his blood, a lust running through his veins, a throb in that part of him he'd thought long dead.

She angled her head and he saw the curve of her neck, long and slim, and fought the urge to press his lips against it. 'Twas foolishness. Nothing more. Too much wine and Collin's cursed suggestion that he bed a woman this night. 'Twas all. And yet as he caught sight of the tops of her breasts, plump white pillows pushed seductively above the squared neckline of the dress, blood thundered in his ears, and his manhood, so long dormant, began to come to life.

She was innocent beauty and wicked seduction in one instant. Glancing up at him from beneath the sweep of honey-colored lashes, she met his gaze and didn't back down for a second. As if she could read his thoughts, her smile diminished and her eyes darkened.

By the gods, he wanted her.

Deep in the most vital part of him, he yearned to sweep her from her feet, carry her up the curved staircase, strip the glittering white dress from her body, drop her onto his bed and press his hot, insistent flesh against hers.

Oh, for the love of Jesus!

Silently he condemned his soul to hell for his wayward, wicked thoughts. 'Twas reckless desire brought on by too much wine, the spirit of the revels, the rapture of the night and the absence of a woman for too long in his life. Nothing more.

"We've never met before," he said. "I would have remembered."

"So would have I," she said, her voice without any trace of teasing. "Apryll of Serennog." She said her name as if it should mean something to him, yet it only conjured up vague thoughts of a castle some believed to be in ruin, a keep that was rumored to be haunted, a once-prosperous barony that had, under this woman's dominion, shriveled into poverty.

And yet she was here, in jewels and finery, boldly flirting with him.

Deep inside he knew he should tread warily here, that something was amiss, but the seduction of her smile caused him to cast caution to the winds. Tonight he would not be so suspicious. Tonight he would enjoy the festivities. Tonight he would let the tight reins on his desires slip through his fingers.

Tonight, mayhap, he would bed the lady.

Chapter Two

Payton crouched low in the cold turret. From his hiding spot he heard the sounds of merriment rising up from the great hall. Conversation buzzed softly. Music lilted. Laughter rolled ever upward from the windows, through the crisp, clear night air in this, Devlynn of Black Thorn's keep. While the sentries dozed, or rolled the dice, or sipped ale and wine, Payton had infiltrated the thick stone walls of Black Thorn. Like a shadow in the night, he'd spied upon the stables and pens of the castle. Aye, there were swift steeds, long-fleeced sheep and fatted pigs aplenty.

A cloud passed over the moon and he straightened, surveying the dark, wintry landscape with a practiced eye. 'Twould be so much easier to slay Devlynn outright, to kill him while he was hunting in the forest, but nay, then he would become a martyr, a saint to those who remained.

And his death would be far too swift and painless.

There would be no reveling in vengeance for Payton, and revenge was what he craved. The sweet trappings of a prosperous keep—fine clothing, jewels and

wine—were second to what he wanted most. Besting
the baron of Black Thorn, watching him suffer and become the object of shame—that was Payton's objec-
tive.

And it had already begun.

Payton savored every second of it, enjoying stealing
into the high, guarded walls of Black Thorn with his
small, deadly band, meeting with the traitors who, like
he, wanted to see Devlynn's downfall, waiting for the
precise moment to strike. He glanced down at the
guard at his feet, so quickly dispensed. Easy prey. All
the sentries had been sipping far too much mead in
celebration of the revels. It had been easy to secure the
positions they needed.

He heard the hoot of an owl and a wicked grin slid
across his beard-darkened jaw. 'Twas the signal. All
was ready. The traitors within the keep had ensured
that tonight he would succeed. He had but to steal
down a few steps and wreak his vengeance.

He thought of the empty stores at Serennog, the
few remaining animals in once-flourishing herds, and
his anger burned hot. Devlynn of Black Thorn would
pay, Payton thought bitterly as he stepped over the
dead, slumped body of the guard. And he would pay
dearly.

"My sister invited you?" Devlynn asked, scouring
his mind for some snippet of conversation concerning
Serennog or the castle's mistress. "Forgive me, but I
don't remember Miranda speaking of you."

"Should I be offended?" Apryll shook her head.
"'Tis of no matter. She knows me not." He noticed the
pulse beating wildly at the base of her throat. "I came
without invitation tonight."

"And without escort?" he asked, sensing something was amiss, then chiding himself for all his cynicism.

"I needed one not." She placed her hand in his and spun away for a few seconds, only to return. "I heard the gates of Black Thorn were thrown open to all during the revels and I decided to see for myself."

"'Tis true. All are welcome."

"Even strange women?" Her eyes twinkled with mischief so bright it pulsed. He couldn't help staring at her lips and wondering what it would feel like to kiss her.

"You are not strange."

"Am I not?"

"You did not just appear from the mist on the river or the clouds in the sky."

"Oh? Did I not? How disappointing." She laughed and the sound was a trill that sent shivers up his spine, that touched the coldest, darkest chambers of his black heart.

Her gaze swept the grand hall from the far balcony where the musicians played to the raised table at which most of his family gathered around the yule candle and mazers of half-drunk wine. Servants scurried, the castle dogs watched the festivities with suspicious gold eyes and a singer began a ballad in a warbling voice.

Devlynn felt a shaft of happiness enter his soul and he found himself drowning in this woman's charms. The music was soft, the night inviting, the—

Bam! Bam! Bam!

Devlynn stiffened.

The music died.

Conversation stilled.

In his arms, Apryll tensed. All eyes turned toward the main door.

"Who goes there?" Devlynn thundered.

"'Tis only I. Father Christmas," a deep voice bellowed back.

"Enter." Devlynn nodded to the guard who yanked hard on the handle. Along with a rush of snow-kissed wind and a trumpeter's blast, a troupe of mummurs, poor townspeople and farmers disguised in costumes, arrived.

Children squealed in delight and the guests gathered around the spectacle, at the center of which was a brilliantly colored dragon composed of eight men covered in blankets, the first and tallest of whom supported the beast's great head. The masked peasants as well as those hidden within the dragon bowed at Devlynn's feet.

From the corner of his eye, Devlynn noticed Lady Apryll catch her breath and pale a bit, though mayhap it was because one of the mummers tipped his disguised head in her direction, as if he mistakenly thought she was the lady of the castle.

"'Tis . . . 'tis a glorious keep you have, Lord Devlynn," Lady Apryll said quietly, her eyes following the troupe as it snaked through the great hall. Father Christmas was in the lead, the dragon wending ungainly behind him, children laughing and trailing behind the troupe.

"And what of Serennog?" he asked.

A shadow chased across her eyes. "'Tis much smaller than this. Not nearly as grand."

"Are you not the baroness?" he asked.

"Aye, once my father passed on a few years ago." She offered him another smile, one not quite as bright as before, and sent a nervous glance toward the mummers. "I suppose you might call me the lord."

"I think not." He laughed at her joke, for she was clever and witty, a woman who tested and tempted him. Bold and spirited. And mysterious. "So what of the revels at your own keep?"

Was it his imagination or did she tense a bit? "My brother . . . he attends to them."

"You have a brother yet he be not lord?"

"He's not of my father's blood," she replied, her voice taking on a serious edge.

"A bastard."

She ignored the comment and waved a hand toward the festivities. "And our celebration . . . 'tis not as grand as this . . . not nearly so."

The mummers and Father Christmas were soon off and the music began again, the balladeer plucking his lute. Deftly Devlynn drew the Lady of Serennog against him, holding her firmly as they danced together, bodies fitting close, spinning apart, only to press intimately together again.

When the song ended, the lady tried to release his hand, but Devlynn refused to let go. "Join me at my table," he offered.

"Oh, nay, 'tis not my place . . ."

"It is if I say so," Devlynn insisted, though he told himself he was being foolish, that he'd drunk too much wine, that this woman, ethereal though she might seem, was flesh and blood, a creature so bold and sassy as to warrant his interest, aye, but not his trust. "Come."

"But—"

"Now."

Flush-faced, ribbons streaming from her hair, she

followed after him as they wended their way through the crowd of revelers, many of whom were staring pointedly at him. Not since Glynda's death had the Lord of Black Thorn been in the company of a woman; never had one been asked to sit at his table. Though he didn't understand why, he linked his fingers through hers and held tight, almost as if he expected her to run off.

At the raised table, he drew her forward. "Lady Miranda, Sir Collin," he said, pointing to each in turn. "My sister and brother." Motioning with one hand, he added, "May I introduced Lady Apryll of Serennog?"

Collin, resting lazily upon his spine and cradling a mazer of wine, appraised the woman with cool blue eyes and the lift of one eyebrow. Forcing himself to his feet, he said, "We met earlier, though I wasn't lucky enough to catch your name. Welcome to Black Thorn." He leaned forward, took her hand and brushed a kiss across her knuckles while looking up at her. Again Devlynn thought he caught a deeper reaction in her eyes, as if Collin's familiarity was somehow distasteful.

"Mayhap you would save me another dance?" Collin asked.

"Of course," she said and Devlynn felt the cords at the back of his neck tighten as they did when he readied for battle.

Miranda, for once gracious, stood slowly and smiled as she appraised the woman. Nearly as tall as her brothers, Miranda was a large, rawboned woman, regal and stately, with wide features and a wicked tongue. Her eyebrows elevated a fraction. "May I echo my brother's welcome?"

"I am pleased to meet you," Apryll said, inclining her head slightly as Devlynn carried on with the introductions.

"And this is my Aunt Violet."

Violet twisted to view the newcomer with curious opaque eyes. "A pleasure, to be sure, but . . . did you say you are the Lady of Serennog?"

"Aye." Apryll shifted a bit.

"But I thought that castle was long abandoned . . . the lord having been disgraced . . . or . . . was it elsewhere . . . are there not ghosts of Serennog . . . or . . ." She let her words drift away and frowned. "Oh, I may be mistaken. These days I remember not well." She waved off her muddled thoughts. "Welcome, child. My, but aren't you lovely?"

"A pleasure to meet all of you," Apryll said, blushing and bowing her head slightly as the piper started another tune and Devlynn offered her a chair. "You have a lovely family," she whispered to him.

"And you've not yet met my boy." He couldn't keep the pride from his voice and then spied Bronwyn as she dashed behind the table. With one long arm, he grabbed his niece and she squealed in delight. "This is the castle imp," he explained as, giggling, the little girl squirmed and tossed her curls from her mischievous eyes.

"I be *not* an imp."

"Nay? Then a sorceress, mayhap? A witch?" With a wink at Apryll, he let Bronwyn slide to the floor.

"Aye. And I'll cast a spell upon you, Uncle," she cried, flitting off.

Apryll watched the girl dance between the benches and land with a plop in her mother's arms.

"A spirited one, Bronwyn is," he said, chuckling.

"Aye," she said softly, then bit her lower lip before forcing a smile. He offered her wine and she accepted, sipping slowly, eyeing the festivities, making conversation with those around her. She was as enchanting as any woman Devlynn had ever met, as engaging and well-spoken as any lord as she matched wits with him. She laughed at his jokes, the sound touching an icy, banished place in his heart that somehow began to thaw. She spoke of tournaments and hunts and travels far within Wales as she sipped wine and nibbled at the jellied eggs.

He found it impossible to resist her charms. Her face glowed in the mellow warmth of the yule candle and when they took the dance floor again, she was light and airy in his arms.

As the candles burned low, the wine took hold and she pressed against him, Devlynn gave in to the magic of the night. Though sanity and reason told him he was being foolish, he ignored their warnings. Somehow, because of this woman, the lost luster of Christmas began to shine in Devlynn's battered soul again and the guilt he'd been bearing eased.

"Why have I not known of you before?" he asked as the hours slipped past ever more quickly. Holding her close, he dropped his gaze to the curve of her mouth.

"Mayhap I was hiding."

"At Serennog?"

"Or in the very forests surrounding your keep. It could be that I am not who I seem."

"No doubt you are a sorceress and you have bewitched me."

"Oh, that I could bewitch you, Lord Devlynn," she said with a naughty smile and the lift of one contrary eyebrow. "Oh, but that I could."

"I fear you have, vixen."

She laughed throatily. "I doubt I have that power."

"You would be surprised."

"Pleasantly so?" Again that saucy twist of her lips. Aye, she was a tease. An enchantress.

"What else?" She laughed lightly then and he could no longer resist her. His blood was streaming through his veins, his heart pumping with newfound life that pounded in his head and caused a swelling between his legs. He thought of kissing her and oh, so much more, of joining his body to hers in lusty pleasure and wicked seduction. She was innocence and sin wrapped together.

Tossing back his wine, erotic images playing through his mind, he knew he had to have her. No matter what the cost. Regardless of any consequence. And why not? Was he not the baron—Lord of Black Thorn?

He caught a knowing glance from his brother and felt only but a moment's shame that Collin could so easily read the desire sizzling through his mind. Swiftly, disregarding any raised eyebrow cast in their direction, he grabbed her wrist and pulled her away from the crowd and into a dark alcove beneath the stairs. She laughed nervously, but he didn't stop. Wrapping his arms firmly around her slim waist, he leaned forward and pressed his eager lips to hers.

She gasped but didn't push away.

His fingers splayed over her back and the heat in his loins burned hot and hard.

She sighed as if in longing. She trembled beneath his touch, her eyelids fluttering closed as his mouth moved gently over hers and her breath mingled with his. Blood thundered through his veins, desire ran dark through his soul, and he knew in an instant that he would have this woman, one way or another.

His pulse pounded in his ears, the noise of the castle drifted away. She smelled of roses and violets and all things feminine. In the darkness of the alcove they were alone in the universe. His fingers twined in the thick curls of her hair. His mouth molded over hers. His tongue pressed hard against her teeth. Slowly her lips parted, giving him access to the moist haven of her mouth.

'Twas hours or an instant. He knew not which.

But he wanted her.

Burned for her.

Pushing her back against the wall, he pressed his body closer to hers, thigh to thigh, chest to breasts, lips to lips. Beneath the downy folds of her dress he felt her mound.

One hand lowered to cup her breast.

"Nay," she whispered breathlessly, though her words quivered and he felt her heat, sensed her own blood running hot. In his mind's eye he saw them lying naked upon his bed, the fire casting golden shadows on her naked flesh.

Now, in the alcove, with the sounds of the celebration drifting through the curtain, she forced her mouth from his. Her breathing was as ragged as his own. "Please . . . do . . . do not . . . ." Swallowing hard, licking her lips, she stared at him as if suddenly afraid. "Oh, dear God in heaven," she said, blowing out a breath as she drew away. "I cannot . . . we . . . we cannot." She shook her head as if to convince herself. She placed one hand over her breasts and she bit her lower lip. "Lord Devlynn," she whispered, her voice deeper than he remembered, "I . . . I am not what you think. . . ."

"And what do I think you are?"

She glanced into his eyes, hesitated, then looked away as if uncertain. "'Tis of no matter," she said. "Oh, curse it all!" To his surprise, she placed her soft palms on either side of his face and dragged his mouth down to her upturned lips. She kissed him soundly, as if she would never stop. As if she couldn't. Her lips were warm and trembled slightly.

Ah, she was a tease and a tart and looked the part of an innocent. Every muscle in his body screamed with the want of her and he could think of nothing save laying atop her, joining with her. . . .

"Nay!" she whispered as if at herself and pulled back to stare at him in dismay, as if she were ashamed. "Nay . . . I cannot—"

"Stay with me. Here." He said the words before he'd thought them.

"What? Oh . . . nay."

"Apryll, I—"

"Shh." She placed a finger over his lips and before he could suck it into his mouth, she jerked her hand away and pulled away from him. "This is madness! Oh, for the love of St. Jude, I be such a fool!" Flushing crimson, avoiding his gaze, she pushed hard against his shoulders and shook her head. "Forgive me." His arms dropped to his sides. "I'm sorry . . . I mean . . . I . . . need . . . if you could tell me where I might find the latrine. . . ."

"'Tis on the second floor, around the first corner, up a short flight of stairs to the tower."

"I—I will be back," she vowed, nearly stumbling as she approached the stairs. Cheeks burning, she turned on her heel swiftly. Lifting the skirts of her glittery dress, she flew up the stone steps and disappeared around the corner.

"I'll wait," he called after her, not knowing that she lied.

Chapter Three

Apryll bolted up the stairs. Oh, this was madness, sheer, horrifying madness! Why had she ever agreed to Payton's bold, vengeful plan? She dashed around the corners of the upper hallway without error, meeting no one, her heart pounding as she found a small alcove, where she found, as Payton had promised, a change of clothes, huntsman's garb.

Her fingers flew over the buttons holding her gown together and she stepped out of the frothy white dress that had been the bridal gown of her mother, Rowelda. With a fleeting thought of the woman who bore her, Apryll threw on the rough-sewn tunic that chaffed her skin after the finery of the wedding dress. *Oh, mother, I'm sorry.* She yanked on leggings and heavy boots, then tucked her hair into the cap that had been left, but nowhere did she find her dagger, the weapon she'd entrusted to Payton. Her fingers scrabbled over the few shelves but encountered no blade.

And time was hurrying past. Soon the baron would become impatient with waiting for her and come looking.

She ducked out of the alcove and made her way along a hallway where sconces burned low. Payton was inside a bed chamber and he was holding a boy who was slumped over his shoulders. "What is this?" she asked, stepping around a nursemaid snoring softly on a pallet in the corner. But she knew. The boy was the baron's son.

"Are you daft?" she asked, striding across the fresh rushes. The boy was sleeping soundly, his head propped upon Payton's shoulder. "What are you thinking? You cannot take the child."

Another man entered the room—a huntsman from Serennog. "'Tis time," he said. "All is as planned."

Apryll tossed her mother's wedding dress onto the floor. "Come, let us go. Leave the boy."

Payton's face grew hard. "We need more to bargain with." His eyes flashed in defiance.

From the corner there was a moan. The plump nursemaid was rousing. "Ooh," she groaned, her eyes opening a slit only to close again.

"We must be off," Payton insisted.

"Not with the boy!" Apryll thought of Devlynn, how proud he'd been of his family, how he'd teased his niece.

"There is no time to argue. She"—he hitched his chin toward the groggy nurse—"will come 'round soon, and the baron will come searching for you, m'lady. We must be off."

"Nay, Payton, I will not allow it. Leave the child."

"We must be off," the huntsman insisted.

Apryll took a step closer to her brother. "Do not defy me, brother, I still be the ruler of Serennog and—"

"And we're not in Serennog any longer," Payton

snapped, fury flushing his face. "We leave now with the boy, or you stay and face the baron alone. However, if that be your choice, I swear to you that Devlynn will never see his son again and you, dear sister, will be held accountable for this lad's disappearance."

"You would not harm him."

"Not unless he gives me trouble."

"He is but a child," she argued and reached forward, intent on snagging the boy.

Payton pushed her back. "I have no time for this."

"You will leave him!"

"We must be off." The guard at the door was nervous.

"Not with the child—"

"Hush, woman!"

"I will not—" Smack! Payton backhanded her, the sharp metal on his glove slicing her skin. Pain exploded in her cheek. Blood spurted.

She flung herself at him, determined to wrest the boy away. "How dare you. I am the ruler of—"

"What you are is a pain in the backside. Nothing more." Payton pushed her backward and her feet, tangling in her soiled dress, tripped her. She landed on the gown her mother wore to marry her father.

"Foolish woman. I will wait no longer," Payton sneered, looking at her with contempt.

"Please, Payton, listen to reason," she pleaded, pushing herself to her feet. "If you do this all the wrath of Black Thorn will strike our keep. You can't take the boy."

"But I can. And I will. That is the trouble with you, sister, you are never willing to do what must be done. You are a dreamer. A silly woman who cannot admit that she has let her castle fall to ruin and let those she rules starve because she has not sought vengeance, and she has not the will nor the balls to go to war. Now, hear me and hear me well. Stay if you will or come, but do it now. I'll not wait."

The boy moaned groggily. Payton dashed into the hall. The huntsman was at his heels. Apryll took off after him.

She could not fight Payton, not with bone and muscle, but surely she could outwit him. Stealing along the back stairs, she vowed to right this hideous wrong—a wrong of her own foolish making. If she could escape before the baron caught up with her.

Devlynn paced by the stairs. His pulse raced and his thoughts chased after the sassy woman who claimed to be the ruler of Serennog. 'Twas foolish to feel so smitten. So eager to lay with her. For three years he had been chaste, refused to look at a woman, wallowed in his guilt and mourned his wife. But now, from the moment he'd caught Lady Apryll's gaze, he'd thought of little but ending his self-imposed celibacy. For the first time since Glynda's death, his wife's image faded from his mind.

From the archway he listened as the singer finished a morose ballad. He glanced toward the upper landing. Still she did not appear. But, in truth, she had not been gone long and mayhap needed some time to compose herself. A maid carrying an empty tray scurried past him, pausing to nod quickly in his direction before hurrying on.

Straightening his tunic, Devlynn leaned against the pillar at the base of the steps. Servants filed up and down, a few guests wandered up stairs and sentries changed posts, but there was no sign of the lady.

Be patient, he told himself, though patience had rarely been his companion.

A second song ended and he looked up the stairs for the dozenth time. Still she didn't appear. Anxious, feeling the first niggling of doubt that she might have abandoned him somehow, he waited longer, nervously tapping his fingers on the pillar as the candles were dimmed and a bowl of raisins splashed with brandy was carried into the room.

Devlynn tried vainly to push his edginess aside as the bowl was lit. Several of the braver souls tried to pick a raisin from the flaming pot, wincing and hollering, their fingers singed as they played snap dragon.

"Ouch!"

"Damn!"

"Cursed things."

Laughter rippled through the castle. Bronwyn was half asleep in her mother's lap. Aunt Violet had begun to doze, but Collin was still laughing, swilling wine and looking toward the hallway, his eyes meeting Devlynn's before the lord glanced up the now dark stairs.

"Get one!" Collin yelled at a be-ringed guest trying to snag a flaming raisin.

Smoke collected near the ceiling and conversation hummed around the fire as the lighted bowl, illuminating the guests' exhilarated faces, was passed from one to the other.

Footsteps sounded behind him. Devlynn whirled, expecting Apryll and finding a balding Sir Henry instead. "My lord, would you like to partake of the game?"

"Another time," Devlynn snapped. What if she

were lost? Black Thorn was a vast keep, with winding corridors and hidden doorways. If she made a wrong turn on the way to the latrine tower . . .

The game ended, the candles were relit and Devlynn's elation ebbed, replaced by a slow-growing anger. Had she intentionally left him standing here like a besotted page? Walking to the archway leading to the great hall, he swept the vast chamber with his gaze, wondering if she'd eluded him. Had she somehow returned from another staircase and stolen quietly into the crowd? Impatience gnawed at him. He clenched his fists in frustration, searching the room, but as his gaze scoured his guests, there was no sign of her, no glimpse of a shimmering white gown in the midst of scarlet, jade and royal blue.

"Lose the woman?" Collin asked in amusement as he, a pouty-lipped maid attached to his arm, breezed past.

"Nay."

"So where is the 'angel,' as Aunt Violet so aptly named her?"

"Upstairs. She'll be down anon—"

AAAWWWWHHHH! A blood-chilling scream ripped down the stairs from an upper story.

Devlynn's heart froze.

Apryll was upstairs.

The music stopped.

Laughter died.

All the guests hushed.

"What the devil—?" Collin asked as the woman on his arm paled.

Without a word Devlynn unsheathed his sword. He ran up the stairs, taking the steps two at a time. Boot heels rang behind him. Collin was at his back. As were guards. Swords rattled. Boots thundered.

Apryll, Devlynn thought wildly. Something's happened to her. His heart leapt to his throat.

"What the bloody hell happened?" Collin demanded as they reached the second floor.

"I know not."

"The woman—?"

Devlynn's heart was a drum. Weapon held high, he rounded a corner, nearly running over the nursemaid, a round ninny of a girl with a face as white as curdled cream, her eyes wide with fear.

"M'lord . . . oh, by the saints, he's missing," she cried, her hands wringing in her skirts, fright evidenced in the trembling of her lips. "I don't know how or—"

"Who?" he demanded, but he knew in a heartbeat. His son. The woman's charge. "Who's missing?" His blood turned to ice and he pushed past the stricken girl. God forbid it be Yale.

"'Tis your boy," the maid mumbled, stumbling after him, tears streaming down her cheeks. "I . . . I closed me eyes but a second, honest I did . . . and . . . and . . . oh, for the love of Jesus," she crossed herself and slumped down the wall as the pound of boots reverberated through the corridor.

Soldiers shouted, an alarm bell pealed.

Heart in his throat, Devlynn barreled through the open door of his son's chamber. Red embers glowed in the grate. Yale's bed was mussed but mockingly empty.

The Lord of Black Thorn's son had been kidnapped, stolen from beneath his very nose.

"No!" Devlynn yelled, damning the fates. Disbelief

and anger surged through his soul as he spied evidence of a hideous betrayal.

In a crumpled pool beneath the window, stained with smears of fresh blood, lay the shimmering white dress that had so recently been worn by Apryll of Serennog.

Chapter Four

"Where is my son?" Devlynn demanded, looming over the woman who was supposed to have been guarding the boy. His fists balled in rage and it was all he could do not to grab the feebleminded woman and shake her to loosen her silly tongue. "Where the devil is Yale?"

"I know not," the nursemaid admitted, her lower lip quivering in fear, her eyes round in the flickering light from the fire. She seemed dull and disoriented, blinking and crying piteously.

"You were here. Yale was your charge."

She threw herself onto the rushes, bowing low at his feet. "Oh, m'lord, please forgive me," she said, her voice breaking on a sob. "I am so confused, 'tis not like me to fall asleep and yet I could not keep my eyes open . . . I . . . I only dozed for a moment. . . ."

"One moment too long."

Her shoulders shook. "Oh, I know, I know," she said, sniffing loudly.

The woman was no help. Devlynn kicked the bloodstained dress and wished to heaven that he had not been so trusting, opening the castle gates, allowing strangers into the keep. And Apryll . . . if he ever got his hands on her he'd wring her beautiful, traitorous neck.

The splotches of red on the white fabric sent fear into the depths of his heart. Was the blood Yale's? Apryll's? That thought should have appeased him. It did not. Nothing did. Not the gawking looks from the soldiers who had rushed into the room, not the pathetic nursemaid's hiccuped apologies and not his brother's stern, reproachful look.

"'Twas Apryll of Serennog who stole my child," he admitted, glancing at the small crowd that filled the doorway and corridor. Soldiers, servants and a few curious guests were clustered under the sconces. Snagging the damning dress from the floor, he clutched it in fingers made of steel. "And she shall return him." His nostrils flared at the thoughts of her deceit, her audacity and how easily she'd duped him. His gaze narrowed on Collin. "Order the castle gates be closed! No one shall leave. And send sentries and guards around the perimeter of the castle, they could not have been gone long nor gotten far." He pushed past the priest and stormed out of the room, his head pounding with anger, his heart hollow with fear. What if harm had already come to Yale? What if even now he was dead or dying?

Christ Jesus, it could not be. But a dark pain cut through Devlynn's soul and he suddenly knew a fear deeper than any he'd met before. "Fetch the captain of the guard. Now!" He stormed down the hallway and the crowd parted. The baron of Black Thorn's temper was legendary—no one dared cross him.

"You cannot hold your guests prisoner," Collin warned, catching up to his brother.

"Like hell."

"But—"

Devlynn whirled and, ready for a fight, advanced upon Collin. Every muscle in his body tensed. "Am I not the baron?"

Collin's lips tightened. "Aye, but—"

"Then do it. And do it the hell now!"

"Brother," Collin said in that ingratiating, irritating tone that scraped on Devlynn's already raw nerves. "Listen, you cannot treat the baron of Wybren as you would a common thief or pickpocket and you cannot delay Lady Monteith."

"You listen to me," Devlynn ordered, grabbing Collin's mantle by its laces. "My son has been stolen. Kidnapped. Mayhap injured. Or . . . or worse." The vision of Yale's limp body burned through his mind. "We will find him and the culprits who did this atrocity. And we will find them tonight." His lips barely moved as he added, "Tell the sheriff to interrogate every man, woman and child within the castle walls and get me the captain of the guard. Now." Spittle sprayed upon his brother's face. Devlynn released Collin's tunic as if it burned in his hands. "I want the names of everyone, every blasted person who entered the gates tonight, and I want to know why that woman"—he shook the dress in his fist—"why Apryll of Serennog, if that be who she really is, was allowed into the castle."

"We've searched the castle from the turrets to the dungeons and there is no sign of the lad." Rudyard, captain of the guard, stood rigidly in Devlynn's chamber. Collin was seated at a small table and Devlynn glowered out the window to the bailey. His chest was tight, his heart drumming with fear, and anger surged through his blood. His fists clenched and he imagined his hands around Apryll's slim, white throat. "But there is more bad news."

The cords in the back of Devlynn's neck tightened.

"A sentry is dead. His throat slit. It appears as if several of the invaders infiltrated."

"Bloody hell," Collin growled. "And no one saw this?"

"And the treasury . . . the guard there, too, is dead. I've posted another." Within seconds Devlynn was through the antechambers and a side door to the small room where most of the castle's valuables were locked in a heavy chest. Collin and Rudyard were on his heels. As he'd said, the guard lay dead, slumped in a corner, blood spilling from the dark purple gash on his neck to a pool on the floor. "Saunders," Devlynn said and stopped to check the man who was still warm but surely dead. He had no pulse. "Call the priest."

Murderers. Butchers.

Fear congealed deep inside him.

The monsters had Yale.

By the gods, he couldn't, wouldn't lose his son, not his boy. Not after Glynda and the baby. His hands curled into fists and he forced himself to his feet to stare at the empty chest. The lock had been broken, the contents emptied.

"Search the castle again."

Rudyard hesitated and Devlynn seized the man by his throat. "I said, 'Search it again.' Turn this castle upside down. Scour the huts, the stores, the kennels, the stables, the gristmill, the chapel, the garrison, everywhere. Look under the rafters and in the dungeon. Leave no stone unturned, do you hear me?" He pushed his nose into the taller man's face and added through lips that barely moved, "'Tis your responsibility to find my son."

The captain's Adam's apple bobbed. His pointy little tongue flicked around crooked teeth. Christ Jesus, the man was scared. The damned captain of the guard was frightened. No wonder they were in such a mess!

"Devlynn." Collin's voice was reproachful, his expression grim. "We will search again. Aye. But do you not think we should take after the thieves? There is little doubt that they have Yale and they have had hours to flee the castle and hide. We should waste no more time but try to track down the wretches. And the woman. She is surely a part of this deception."

Devlynn's fingers slowly uncoiled. His lips flattened over his teeth. "Aye," he agreed solemnly. "Dispense a dozen men to search the castle again and ready twenty to ride with me."

"Surely you should stay," Collin suggested. "You are the lord and you are holding your guests here, some against their will. You needs speak with them. I will hunt down the bastards who did this and I'll take the dogs, the best huntsmen and the strongest soldiers with me. Believe me, they will pay."

The thought of staying in the castle, pacing his chambers, waiting for news of his son, was too much to bear. He couldn't remain here by the fire, listening to the complaints, his mind running in circles about Yale's safety, and do nothing. "I will speak to my guests briefly. Afterwards each will talk with the sheriff. On the morrow they will be allowed to leave."

"They will be angry."

"Not near as angry as I."

"They may turn on you. Become enemies where once they were allies."

"I care not about their allegiance. Only about my son," Devlynn growled.

Collin looked perturbed. "Brother, please. 'Twould be best if you stay at the castle. You are the lord."

"Aye, and 'tis my son who is missing. I will go." He pointed a long finger at his brother's nose. "Call the sheriff."

"He's on his way."

"Then you"—he pointed a commanding finger at the captain of the guard—"prepare the search party. We will need men, weapons, horses and provisions. I want the best to go with me." Pacing angrily, he ordered, "Collin, you are to find the traitor. Someone within these walls allowed the enemy in. Find out who."

"The enemy was the woman," Collin said as he glanced at the stained dress.

Devlynn's gut twisted. "But she was not alone. Someone within these walls betrayed us all. He allowed the woman in. He plotted my son's disappearance, mayhap even gave him something to make him drowsy earlier. If so, he is someone I trust." Devlynn's eyes bored into his brother and in a low, determined voice he said, "Make no mistake, I will find the Judas and expose him. When I discover who he is, he will pay and pay with his life."

Collin's smile was as cold as death. "And I will help you."

"Good. Everyone, I mean every man, woman and child within Black Thorn, is under suspicion." A dozen faces flashed before his eyes. His guts twisted. What trusted servant had betrayed him and why? For gold?

For vengeance? On the promise of a better freedom? Why?

Or had it been a family member? His sister or brother?

What of his guests? Neighboring lords who would gladly betray him for a chance to win Black Thorn?

Or was it someone else? He considered Father Christmas and the mummers who had followed him inside. Masked. Costumed. Faces hidden. Strangers.

"Except for the family," Collin clarified.

"Including the family," Devlynn growled as he reached for his sword. "I trust no one."

As the words flew from his mouth, Miranda strode into the room. Her face was red with fury, her eyes sparking with anger. "This is an outrage!" Holding Bronwyn close to her breast, she impaled her brother in her furious green gaze. Music rose from the great hall again and conversation buzzed, but the revelry of a few hours before had diminished. Suspicious glances, indignant expressions and gossip replaced the merriment that had rung from the castle walls. "You cannot keep the Lord of Derwynn as a hostage. And what about Lady Camille of—"

"They will stay until the morrow," Devlynn insisted. "Most of the guests planned to stay the night, so it is of no inconvenience."

"Because they *wished* to, not because they were forced."

In Miranda's strong arms, Bronwyn sighed dreamily, her little lips parting. Devlynn's heart wrenched. Where was his son? Was he injured? Alive or . . . nay, Devlynn cut his dark thoughts short. He would not think the worst. Could not.

"You suspect your guests? Your friends? And your own family? *Me? Aunt Violet?*"

"Everyone." His voice was as cold as all of winter as he hurried down the rest of the stairs. Ignoring his guests, he cut through a long corridor and headed for the stables. He would find his son.

If Yale was alive.

Payton was gone. One minute, he'd been ahead of her, carrying the boy and stealing through the shadows, the next, as they'd rounded a hayrick, he'd disappeared. Along with the soldiers who had been with them.

She glanced around the inner bailey, her gaze scraping quickly over the huts therein. The smith's forge glowed red and there were candles in a few other outbuildings, but she saw no sign of her brother.

Originally, the plan was to meet the rest of their small band at the stables, where they intended to steal the horses. Now, as she crept through the dark grass, silently praying that the kennel dogs wouldn't put up a ruckus or that she might run into a sentry, she realized that this plan was fated to fail. And it had been changed. Perhaps Payton had intended to leave her all along, she thought, for he had always been an ambitious sort, a man who'd walked through life burdened by the knowledge that he was a bastard, the son of a man who had raped their mother, a constant reminder of the shame their mother had borne.

At the hands of Morgan of Black Thorn, Devlynn's father.

The stakes were high for Payton this night and yet she didn't believe that he would abandon her to the dungeons of Black Thorn. But then what did she know of Payton and his motives? He stole the boy and the sting on her cheek was a reminder of his ruthlessness.

She started for the stables when she heard the first alarm—a bell clanging wildly, accompanied by the sharp shouts of soldiers. Oh, for the love of St. Jude, they'd been found out already! With little thought to the consequences she ran across the bailey to the stables. Horses neighed nervously, their hooves shuffling in the straw.

She slipped through the doorway and stumbled over a man lying just over the threshold. He was gasping for breath and one hand reached upward. "Help me," he said, his lungs rattling horridly. "Please, lad . . ." He struggled and she saw the dark stain on his shirt, the hilt of a dagger—her dagger—rising from his chest.

"Lie back," she ordered and pulled the weapon from his flesh. It slid out with a horrid sucking sound and the blood flowed fast. "We have to bind the wound," she said and knew she could not let this man die. "Help! There's a man injured!" she cried, yelling through the doorway. "Help me—"

A soldier appeared. "For the love of God, what happened?" Some of the horses started squealing, as if the stench of blood had them panicked.

"Take this man to the physician. He needs his wound bound."

The sentry didn't so much as cast her a second glance when he spied the bleeding man. "Who did this to you?" he demanded as he bent on one knee and touched the stableman's shoulder. "Seth, who?"

"I know not. A stranger—two strangers. They met up with some others and they . . . they had the lad, Yale, with them . . . they took the lord's stallion . . .

they . . . ooooohhh. Tell my wife . . . tell her . . ." His voice faded and his eyes grew glassy in the growing light.

"He needs help, not questions," Apryll insisted, pocketing the bloody knife as the smell of smoke reached her nostrils and she heard the menacing crackles of flames. Horses were screaming in terror now and she saw a small fire racing through the straw. "Oh, God."

"Fire!" the soldier called, hauling Seth out of the stables. Apryll flew into the stalls, tearing at the tethers, setting the crazed animals free. Hooves slashed, wild, white-rimmed eyes rolled and horses bolted into the bailey.

"Fire!"

"My God, it's a fire! Get the buckets . . ."

Horses and men ran through the bailey as the stables filled with smoke and hellish flames crawled over the beams and straw, crackling and spitting and smoking. Apryll ran to the well where men were already drawing buckets and women were running with wet sacks. She grabbed one of the sacks and ran into the stables, attacking the flames, praying that, once the fire was under control, she could make good her escape.

This is Payton's doing. He's killed men. Horses. Stolen from the baron and kidnapped his son. As she flayed at the flames, coughing and breathing in smoke, she realized her brother would stop at nothing to get what he wanted. Even if it meant killing the baron's son.

Chapter Five

"Fire!"

"Fire in the stables!"

"Curse it all!" Devlynn was already on his way out of the keep. Now he bolted, shoving open the door and racing into the night. Outside the wind was high, the night clear aside from the smell of smoke. Moonlight washed against the castle walls and glistened in the dry winter grass where servants, soldiers and guests had taken up wet sacks and pails. Horses ran throughout the bailey and the dogs barked wildly. Men and women shouted, children cried and pandemonium reigned.

He rushed down a well-trodden path where, beneath sweeps of the windmill, ice sparkled in puddles. Ancient gears creaked and men carried buckets of water from the stream and the well. Devlynn grabbed two pails and carried them toward the stables where the fire was smoldering.

"What happened?" he demanded of one of the soldiers whose face was blackened with soot.

"I know not. The stable master, Seth, was stabbed when the fire broke out."

"Stabbed?" Devlynn growled, dousing a few remaining flames. The fire sizzled and hissed but slowly died.

"Aye, when the horses were taken."

"'Twas not an accident?"

"Nay. Before he died, Seth said that the men who had taken Yale stabbed him."

"Men?" He repeated. "No woman?"

"Nay, not that he said."

"But they had my boy with them and he was alive?" Devlynn demanded.

"I . . . I know not." The guard lifted a brawny shoulder. "'Twas Henry who spoke to Seth."

Devlynn eyed the warm, sizzling ashes. Most of the stables had been saved, it seemed, though the beams were charred, the walls blackened, the smell of water-soaked, burned wood dispersing into the cold winter air. Some of the guards were rounding up the horses.

So where was Apryll of Serennog? If she had not escaped with the men who had taken his boy, was she still trapped within the keep? Or had she escaped alone? He searched the eyes of the men and women in the bailey. Could she still be hiding within these very walls? Two men, maybe more, had taken his son, but what of the woman?

His jaw grew tight as he thought of how easily she'd deceived him, how he'd been drawn to her beauty and wit, how warm and supple her body had felt against his, how boldly she'd kissed him. "An angel," Aunt Violet had called her, but the old lady had been sadly mistaken, for Apryll of Serennog was far from holy. If anything, she was Lucifer's mistress.

Jaw tight, he strode to the stables which smoldered from the fire damage. Lanterns glowed. Men barked orders. Horses shifted nervously as saddles were strapped to their broad backs.

Two soldiers were carrying the body of the dead stable master outside. The man's young widow, Grace, clutching her three-year-old son, followed after them, shivering and wailing and trying to cling to a body that would never move again. "Nooo," she cried, over and over again, though Father Luke, a short, squat man, was following after her, offering a weary shoulder and hollow words of consolation.

From the kennels the dogs began to bay.

Soldiers amassed. Nervous horses reared and snorted as they were harnessed to heavy carts laden with supplies and weapons.

Two men dead. Mayhap more.

The treasury robbed.

The stables burned and the best horses taken.

And Yale missing.

Because he was foolish enough to be enraptured by a woman.

A Jezebel.

He strode into the long, low building and stopped at the empty, burned stall where his steed had been stabled. The gray. Gone. Phantom's box empty.

"God's teeth, there will be vengeance," he growled under his breath.

One person knew the truth and that one person was a woman, a beauty, an "angel," Aunt Violet had called her. Aye, the angel of death and deception. Apryll of Serennog.

He yanked a pitchfork from a smoldering haystack and hurled it like a spear into the wall. A horse tethered nearby started and snorted. Devlynn barely no-

ticed. His thoughts were centered on the traitorous, seductive, bold woman.

By the gods, he wouldn't rest. He'd hunt her to the
ground. When he caught up with her, he'd take great
and slow satisfaction in wringing her pretty, lying
neck.

Right after he bedded her.

Apryll watched the lord's fury from the safety of
the chapel window. As soon as she'd seen that the fire
would die, she'd slipped through the garden and hurried along a well-trodden path to the first place of
refuge she'd found and this was it, a wide room lit by
a few dying candles. She'd crossed herself, then stared
through the window, spying the lord easily. He was
not what she had expected, given his dark reputation.

Aye, he was tall, but there were others who were
taller, and he was broad-shouldered, yet lean, but it
was his commanding attitude that caught her attention. Others, though larger than he, seemed to shrink
in his presence. He spoke to several of the men, strode
into the stables, returned to the outer bailey and was
giving orders that she could not hear, could only imagine. But even in his fury she could not imagine him
capable of the cold-blooded murder the rumors accused him of. Especially of his own child. Not after she
had seen how much his son meant to the lord. But
killing someone who caused his child harm? Aye, perhaps he could. She would not stay to find out first-
hand.

How could she escape? The portcullis had rattled
shut, the gates to the keep closed, and Apryll would be
an idiot to think that the baron would not search every
nook and cranny within the walls. There were escape

routes within the castle, she was certain of it; every fortress had them, secret passages and sally ports, back doors mounted high on the exterior walls where soldiers could sneak out unobserved, but she knew not where they were. She could tempt the fates and face Devlynn, approach him and beg his forgiveness, offer to help him find his son, but she knew her efforts would only be met with cold, cruel disgust. Damn Payton, why had he left her here? Had it been intentional?

"God help me," she whispered, glancing at the crucifix mounted over the altar. She could not hide here forever, for certainly she would be discovered, and she knew so little of Black Thorn, she knew not where a good hiding spot might be. One way or another she had to escape, chase down her brother and somehow free the boy. Only then would she be able to face Lord Devlynn again.

She spied a heavyset man, the priest, leading a woman to the chapel and her heart sank. Quickly she looked for a place to hide. Certainly not at the altar. Stealthily, she crept into an adjoining chamber wherein she spied a single pallet and small table. There was a curtain covering an alcove. Quickly, Apryll swept the drape aside and found herself in a small passageway only a few feet square with another door on the other side. That door was locked. Though she pressed her shoulder against the thick panels and tugged on the handle, it didn't budge. She was trapped.

Her only hope was to hide within this closet of sorts, wait for the priest to fall asleep and sneak past him.

She heard him enter and, over a woman's sobbing, listened to him chant a prayer, offer condolences, speak of the husband being now in heaven and a son who would not know his father. The woman's sobs softened but reverberated through Apryll's heart. This was only one widow, one child left fatherless. How many other lives had Payton taken?

Apryll had known there were risks, of course, that some lives might be sacrificed, but Payton had assured her that there was little chance of death, that unless something went terribly wrong with his plan, no one would be seriously injured. He'd been certain that most of the inhabitants of Black Thorn would be a part of the celebration and those left to guard the keep would be drunk or listless and that he would easily subdue them. "'Twill be easy to take their weapons and bind and gag them," he'd said when she'd asked how he intended to get past the guards. "I have people within the keep, yes, sister, spies who know where the sentries will be, and they are certain that they will be able to offer the guards ale and mead and wine, enough that our small party will pass by unnoticed."

What a ninny she'd been to believe him. Now, sitting in this cobweb-infested closet, listening to a grieving widow's moans and a child's innocent, troubled questions she felt a horrid sense of guilt. She would never be able to make things right. Not since lives had been lost. She ventured a peek through the crack between curtain and doorjamb and her heart twisted when she saw, in the flickering candlelight, the portly priest softly praying, one fleshy hand upon a woman's dark crown, a child of two or three hanging onto his mother's skirts. His eyes were smudged from lack of sleep and he sucked his thumb anxiously.

You caused this woman to become a widow.

'Twas your doing that this boy will never know his father.

*Somehow, someway, you must repay these people—
return the boy to begin with and then face Lord Devlynn.*

*If you get the chance. Mayhap Payton has already
usurped your power. Even now, he could be on his way back
to Serennog, proclaiming himself lord.*

Soon she heard the woman and child leave, the
shuffling of feet, then the quiet . . . as if the chamber
were empty. She'd been certain the priest would enter
his bedchamber, but she heard nothing save for the
scratch of claws, mice scurrying behind the walls of
her self-imposed prison.

Should she brave it?

Tentatively, she edged the drape aside, carefully
peering past the edge of the curtain. She stepped into
the priest's bedchamber, her ears straining. The chapel
was empty. She made two steps toward the door when
she heard footsteps on the path. Quickly she withdrew, through the bedchamber and into the cursed
closet again. She swiped the curtain closed and
stepped back, to rest against the door, but when she
placed her hand behind her to feel for the hard oaken
planks, her wrist was caught by a hand with fingers
like steel.

"Oh!" she whirled, but the manacle only tightened.

"Who the devil are you—?" Lord Devlynn demanded in the darkness and her knees nearly crumpled. He dragged her through the open doorway and
up a flight of curved stairs, yanking on her arm, forcing her to follow him ever upward until at last he
pushed open another door and yanked her into a wide
chamber where a fire glowed and candles burned
bright. Tapestries and weapons decorated the walls
and a huge bed sat squarely before the grate. Her heart

sank, for she knew she was in the baron's private chamber.

This was it.

There was no escape.

Her destiny, was that not what the sorceress, Geneva, had proclaimed?

Gritting her teeth and squaring her shoulders she inched her chin upward to stare into the furious gray eyes of the beast of Black Thorn. The fingers around her wrist nearly crushed her bones.

"Lady Apryll," he whispered harshly, his lips thinning in dangerous recognition. "Well, well, well, as luck would have it I've been looking for you." He kicked the door shut with a resonant thud. His lips barely moved and his jaw was set in pure hatred when he said, "Tell me and tell me quickly, where the devil is my boy?"

Chapter Six

It was all he could do not to shake the life from her. Devlynn's hands clenched and released as he paced in front of the fire. He thought of the lies, the deception, the way she'd played him for a fool in front of all his guests, and beneath all that was the deep, underlying fear that harm had come to his boy.

"Your son is with my brother," she said, pushing herself up from the bed and lifting a haughty brow. Oh, she was a prideful one, and her tongue rolled easily over the lie. "They are on the way to Serennog. It was not part of the plan to steal him, at least I thought not, but apparently my brother had other plans."

"Your brother?"

"Payton."

The name was familiar and distasteful, but he didn't know why, nor did he care.

"It matters not who has taken him, nor why, only that he is returned."

"That I vow."

"*You* vow?" he scoffed, surprised at her nerve.

"You cannot vow anything, *lady*. You cannot *do* anything. You are a prisoner of Black Thorn."

"Oh, no." She shook her head as if she had some say in the matter and her cap fell off, letting that flaxen hair tumble free to her shoulders. "'Tis true that I cannot do anything from here, but if you would allow me to ride this night, I swear I'll catch up with Payton. I will persuade him to release the boy." She said the words with such conviction he was tempted to believe her, liar that she was. Her gold eyes were round with promise, her hands reaching outward.

"You think I would ever trust you?" 'Twould have been laughable if the situation were not so dire. "Lest you've forgotten, two men are dead, mayhap more, my son is missing, my horses and treasury stolen, the stable nearly burned to the ground, all because of you." He glowered down at that upturned face with its smudges of soot and dirt and something else . . . a welt upon her cheek.

"How did you get that?" he asked and touched the tip of a finger to her cheek.

She winced but didn't draw back. "'Tis of no matter."

"Tell me."

"An argument."

"With?"

"My brother. About the boy. When I discovered that he intended to take him as a hostage we quarreled."

"And he struck you?" Devlynn demanded, wanting at that moment to tear Payton of Serennog limb from miserable limb. *And now the bastard had Yale.*

"You are a very convincing liar," he said, eyeing her and well aware that time was ticking fast away. Each second the men who had taken his son were gaining greater distance from Black Thorn. "You could have received the welt when you were attempting escape."

"But I did not," she said, her spine stiff, her expression hard with conviction as if she meant every word she spoke. "I promise you if you let me go, I will hunt down your son and bring him back."

"And I think I will have better luck if I hold you prisoner." He stepped nearer to her and grabbed her upper arm, drawing her so close that he caught the faint scent of lavender, the fragrance she'd worn when she'd bewitched him but a few hours earlier. Even in his anger, he remembered kissing her and the feel of her body molding close to his, the view of soft breasts that now were covered with coarse russet.

"But I can help."

"I think you 'helped' enough already." He glanced over his shoulder to the open doorway. "Guard!"

"Nay, please, Lord Devlynn, you must trust me, I can help."

"Trust you?" he repeated. "Never."

Jamison appeared in the doorway to the great hall and Devlynn cast the woman at him. "This is Lady Apryll of Serennog. She is an enemy to Black Thorn and my prisoner. She is to be kept in the dungeon—"

"Nay, I can do naught if I am locked away."

Devlynn glanced down at the innocence in her eyes. For the love of God, why did he still find her attractive? He thought of her in the dungeons with the rats, filth and other prisoners, where no light reached and the guards were randy and crude. It would be but hours before they would make sport of her, each of them mounting her in turn; though he loathed the situation and had tried to curb it, punishing those he caught, he was certain Apryll wouldn't last an hour before she was ravished for sport—rutted upon on a dare. Not that he should care, he reminded himself, but he said to the guard, "Take her to the empty hermit's cell in the north tower. And guard her yourself. No one is to see her but me."

"Aye, m'lord."

She wrested her way free of the guard to stand in front of him and beg. "Please, let me go. I will return with your son, I vow it! I can do nothing here."

Devlynn felt himself weaken as he stared into those intriguing gold eyes. 'Twas madness. She was the bane of his current existence, the reason his son was in danger. Angry with himself, Devlynn broke the spell and glanced over her shoulder to the sentry. "Take her away and guard her with your life!" Then he turned on his heel and strode down the back stairs where he'd just happened to discover her on his way to the stables, where his soldiers were preparing a search party. He pushed the woman from his mind. He had to. Right now he had to find his son.

Then he'd deal with her.

Alone, Geneva sat before the dying fire in her hut at Serennog. The flames burned low and the wind whistled through the thin thatches of the roof and cracks in the old walls. She shivered but not from the cold that seeped into her bones. Nay, she had withstood a much colder brace of the wind, had survived in winters much more dire than this, but this day she was chilled in her heart.

Her cat, usually a wild thing, curled beside her on the straw mat that covered the bare earth of the floor.

From the pen in the corner the goat bleated forlornly, as if the skinny beast, too, felt the tremble in the air, the ill winds, the desperate fear that created ice in Geneva's heart.

"What have I done?" she whispered and rubbed her flat belly, wherein, she knew, her babe was growing. "Oh, Morrigu, mother spirit, forgive me, for I have lied." Closing her eyes she took a small dagger from her pocket and with the blade scratched an image like a cock's talon, a rune for protection, in the earth near the coals. "Look after Lady Apryll and Payton." She cleaned her blade upon her dress, then laid it upon her palm and curled her fingers around it. Sharp steel cut into her skin and a few drops of blood dripped from her fist onto the rune. "Protect them. And the child. Let no harm come to them."

She dropped her knife and stared into the fire. Black smoke rose through the hole in the roof and she saw another vision, one darker than most, one that could not be denied. One that brought tears to her eyes.

Already blood had been shed for Serennog and more would be spilled before long. "Nay," she whispered as she tugged a tattered cloak around her shoulders. In the flames she saw death rising to claim those she loved.

The hermit's chamber was a bare room with a cot and blankets. Fresh air flowed into the tiny cell through a slit in the mortar, little more than an arrow loop. The guard provided a pail of drinking water and an empty bucket for her to relieve herself. When he closed the door behind him, Apryll was left in total darkness.

She kicked at the cot, then sat down on the stupid thing. Planting her elbows on her knees, she rested her chin on her palms and plotted escape. But how? By calling the guard and stabbing him with the knife concealed in her pocket? By trying to overpower the brute and lock him in this room when he brought in food? Oh, 'twas hopeless. She felt around the wall, hoping for an opening that she might not have seen in the torch's glare when she'd been brought here, but she felt nothing but stone and mortar.

The airhole was too small and, even if she could squeeze through it, she would be dozens of feet above the ground. No, she would have to use her wits. . . . Pacing the small area, she thought of Payton's betrayal. Damn his need for revenge. Damn his ambition and damn, damn, double damn his lying tongue. Why had he not confided in her? Why had he disobeyed her and stolen the boy? What, exactly, had he planned?

The questions circled fast and furious through her mind. But a few moments had passed when she heard footsteps on the stairs, a quick, light tread.

Keys rattled in the door.

Apryll stood and clenched the handle of her knife.

In the darkness, the door creaked open.

"Lady Apryll?" a voice whispered.

"Aye. Who are you?"

"I be your salvation," was the raspy reply.

A man? Woman? She could not tell. Old? Young? Again, she could not judge from the harsh whisper. "The less you know, the less danger there is. Now, hurry. We have not much time. There is a horse waiting for you outside the gates. Follow me."

The figure, clad in heavy robes with a cowl covering a shadowed head and sheltering a hidden face, locked the door behind them. Then, grabbing a near-dead torch from the wall, her savior led her quickly down the spiraling stairs and outside, where the smell of smoke and wet ashes lingered in the crisp night air. Apryll could barely believe this twist in her fate. Was the stranger leading her to freedom or certain death? Was her companion a friend or foe? She knew not but followed closely behind.

The traitor to Black Thorn walked swiftly, stealing through the shadows, face always averted from the pale light of the moon. There were men still milling about the stables and lights glowed from the windows of the castle where but a few hours before she'd danced and flirted with the baron. Dear God, it seemed an eternity.

Behind the windmill and along a pebble-strewn path they hurried to the rear gatehouse. Apryll braced herself. Surely some of the soldiers were within these barracks, but she followed the darkly cloaked figure through a doorway and up two flights of stairs, encountering no one.

"They all be at the fire," her companion, as if reading her mind, said, then opened the door to a small chamber where metal blades glinted in the light of the torch. "Now, hurry." Across the room to a thick oaken door her cohort glided. "'Tis an old sally port," the Judas explained and tossed a coil of rope out the opening. "Slide down, drop to the ground and run to the woods. A horse is waiting near the old bridge."

"Who are you?" she asked. "Why are you doing this?"

"Consider me a friend of Serennog. Make haste. The

baron leaves within the hour and then there will be no hope."

Apryll did as she was bid but glanced over her shoulder and saw a pale face deep within the cloak. White skin and dark eyes that reflected red in the dying light of the torch.

She took the rope in her hands, sent up a prayer that it was long enough to reach the ground and let the rough coil slide through her fingers as she dropped into the yawning darkness.

Chapter Seven

"Run, you beast, run!" Apryll dug her heels into the sides of her laboring mount. The mare had been tied to a leafless apple tree and Apryll had wasted no time vaulting into the saddle, burying her knees into the bay's sides and taking off after her brother and his small band of soldiers.

Unerringly she headed across the fields, knowing that she could cut some distance by avoiding the road and realizing that within minutes the Lord of Black Thorn's army would thunder through the gates. Would he know that she'd escaped? Or would he think she was still held prisoner to be used as something to bargain with her brother?

Leaning low over the jennet's neck, she rode hard, over the frozen fields, riding north toward Serennog. If Payton had remained true to their plan, there was a chance she might catch him. Alone, she could take a shortcut while her brother was carrying the boy, pulling extra horses and dragging a small army with him.

If she was lucky, she could catch them at the crossroads. If she was not, then all was lost, for the specter of death would be chasing them.

Devlynn of Black Thorn, when he realized how she'd duped him, would be flying after her with all the vengeance of Satan.

God help us all, she silently prayed, leaning lower over the mare's sweating shoulders. Her teeth chattered in her head and the reins were brittle in her frozen fingers. Her cheeks stung from the bite of the wind.

But inside she seethed. Burned with rage.

What a fool Payton was! And to leave her!

Oh, if she could, she would wring his arrogant neck. How dare he alter the plan? Go against her orders? Risk the lives of all who resided at Serennog? Again she kicked her mare, hoping to catch up to the other horses and their thieving riders, men she had known all her life, men who were not her partners in the raid on Black Thorn.

Curse and rot Payton's sorry hide!

Her brother was addled, that was it, Apryll thought, as her horse made up lost ground. She shuddered to think what would happen to them when Devlynn caught up with this mad band of thieves and kidnappers. No torture would be too cruel to satisfy him, no pain too great.

Geneva's grim words reverberated through her mind. *'Tis about destiny, m'lady.* Right now that destiny seemed as bleak as the winter night.

"Hiya!" she urged the mare as she rode into a copse of trees where moonlight filtered through the skeletal branches. In her mind's eye, Apryll envisioned Devlynn—his face hard, his eyes cold, his big hands curling into fists of silent fury at the audacity and pain of having his child kidnapped from right under his nose.

Aye, there was sure to be hell to pay.

Damn Geneva with her pale eyes and dire predictions. Damn Payton for the vengeance that burned bright in his heart. And damn her for being a dreamer, the ruler who always hoped the fortunes at Serennog would someday turn. She'd been a fool.

And what about tonight, with Devlynn of Black Thorn? Her teeth gritted as she remembered how she'd flirted outrageously with the baron and even gone so far as to kiss him wantonly on his lips. Her body quivered beneath his touch and she'd wanted so much more. Dear Lord, what had she been thinking? 'Twas to have been part of a well-planned act. But she'd allowed herself to get caught in the spirit of the revels, of the warmth and joviality within the castle, of the merriment.

And you didn't expect Lord Devlynn to be so attractive. 'Twas not his square jaw and broad shoulders, though, as much as the glint you saw in his gray eyes, the hint of passion in their flinty depths. And the feel of his lips, the promise of more. Never in her life had she felt such heat in her blood, experienced the pleasure of pure seduction. Oh, bittersweet temptation.

And now his son is in danger, because of you.

"You've been a fool," Apryll admonished now, her teeth chattering as she caught her first glimpse of Payton's band riding in the moonlight. Her brother was astride a huge gray animal, surely the baron of Black Thorn's destrier, and holding fast to his prize. Though the distance was too great to see clearly, Apryll knew it was the boy, the baron's son. "Idiot," she muttered, kicking her mare hard, closing the distance as the band reached a streambed.

With Payton's charger in the lead, the horses swarmed through the creek, spraying icy water and scrambling up the far bank.

How could she have trusted her brother? As her game little mare galloped after the faster horses and the wind streamed through Apryll's hair, Payton's words mocked her.

That is the trouble with you, sister, you are never willing to do what must be done. Payton's accusation stung far more painfully than the cut on her face, for his words rang true. Now the devil of Black Thorn was after these men, the tattered band of Serennog's finest and bravest soldiers turned thieves and kidnappers. Most of them had wives, two had young daughters, and yet they had risked their lives on this fool's mission. For Serennog.

If they were caught they would surely all be hanged or drawn and quartered.

Through the forest they careened, hoofs pounding as they raced away from Black Thorn. Apryll's stomach clenched. Oh, it was a foolish, foolish plan and they would all surely be killed. Everyone at Serennog would be taken prisoner. Mayhap tortured. Forced into servitude.

Because of you, Apryll, and you are their sworn protector.

Rose, the seamstress with her sparkling eyes and bawdy jokes, the skinny cook, Wynne, who could stretch one goose to serve twenty, little Millie, the laundress, and oh, so many others would face the gallows or bondage to a baron who detested them. Some of the women would be turned into whores to service the soldiers . . . all because Apryll had been weak and trusting.

"Lord help me. Help us all," she whispered as they crested a knoll and the rutted road split. As planned three groups of riders followed differing courses. Payton headed due west upon his gray destrier—again just as planned, though Apryll lagged behind. She and he had agreed to take the longer route to Serennog while Bernard and Samuel, dragging extra horses, turned east and the others, Roger, Issac and Melvynn, kept to the northbound path, the direct route over the mountains to Serennog. When they reached the ridge, they were to light torches to lure Devlynn's soldiers away from their true meeting spot, an abandoned inn, west of Serennog.

Oh, this was madness! Heart drumming at counterpoint to the thunder of her mount's hoofbeats, she chased after the gray on the rutted cart path. Would the beast of Black Thorn be duped so easily?

She remembered staring into his eyes, recognizing a deep, guarded intelligence in those gray orbs.

Far in the distance, she heard the baying of dogs. Trained hunters upon the scent. Closing the distance. By the gods, they were doomed.

Devlynn rode as if Satan were chasing him. With dogs in the lead, his band of soldiers following, he drove the poor horse beneath him mercilessly. The hounds were on the scent. He'd let them sniff Yale's clothes and the curs had circled and yipped until they had been unleashed, then they'd taken off, on the road leading north.

To Serennog.

Through the fields and into the woods, faster and faster. Time was his enemy. The longer he was separated from Yale, the more likely the boy would suffer. He thought of how easily he'd been seduced by the woman and how quickly she'd betrayed him. Teeth gnashing, he spurred his mount as the beast stumbled through a creek, sliding on the slippery rocks before scrambling up the far bank and shooting into the woods.

Down the road, faster and faster, until he came upon the dogs barking and shifting at a junction where the road splintered into three directions. He pulled up, his horse sweating and lathered, the breath from his hot lungs fogging the air. The lead dog headed north toward Serennog, but that seemed too easy. The smart bitch chose the western bend, and a few others were sniffing and barking toward the east.

Devlynn hopped lithely to the ground and, with only moonlight for illumination, studied the tracks as the rest of his small army reached him.

"Which way?" Rudyard asked.

"North," Devlynn said with more certainty than he felt. Could he be leading his men into a trap? Would the enemy have gathered, joining forces with more of their own, hiding and ready to strike when Devlynn and his troops reached a certain point on this lonely stretch of road? Should he send a spy ahead to report back? Nay, he had not the time.

Angrily, he kicked at a pebble in the path and sent it reeling into the bole of a nearby oak. Thunk. "We'll split up," he decided.

"Is this not what the enemy expects, m'lord?" Rudyard dismounted to join him. "Divide and conquer?"

"To what end?"

"Mayhap they have stolen the boy only as a means to lure you from the castle. Whoever is behind this might not be after your son but has used him to capture or kill you."

"So be it," Devlynn said furiously as the wind rustled through the few dead leaves hanging on brittle branches. "Better me than my son."

"Better yet neither."

Other huntsmen and soldiers dismounted to study the roadway in the pale moonlight. "The horses' tracks, they go north," Kirby, the rotund archer, insisted, his eyes reading the frozen roadway.

"Aye, there are others leading to the east." Spencer frowned and tugged on his short beard. "And west, as well. 'Tis too dark to be certain. With all the travel for the revels, all the carts, wagons and horses, 'tis hard to tell."

"We'll split up," Devlynn decided.

He knew in his gut that whatever cur was loyal to Apryll of Serennog would ride straight to Serennog, to seek cover behind the grate of the portcullis and thick walls of the castle. So be it.

"M'lord!" One of the soldiers had reined his mount and was looking westward along the ridge. "I see firelight, nay . . . moving fires . . . torches."

"Aye, I see them as well," another soldier called.

Devlynn squinted and saw, far in the distance, the lights winking through the bare branches.

"'Tis the army." Rudyard was certain. "Leading north. The shortest route to Serennog, over the mountains."

"Why would they risk torches?" Devlynn thought aloud, the gears in his mind grinding. "'Tis a lure—a trap."

"Unless the traitors thought there was enough distance, that we would not ride until morn because of the fire. Mayhap they think they are safe and cannot be seen yet cannot risk resting. It could be that they must use the torches to illuminate their path," a soldier suggested.

"Aye," Rudyard agreed. "The cliffs upon the ridge are treacherous and they cannot see the path to travel safely. Yet they dare not rest. Mayhap they would rather risk being noticed than take a chance on being caught."

"Or tumbling down the mountainside," another soldier said.

Devlynn wasn't convinced. He looked at the dogs circling anxiously. The lead dog had never failed him, though usually the bitch was a tracker as well. She was whining, half running down the fork leading west, then returning to whine and bark loudly. Aye, she had the scent of something. Yale? Or was she as confused as these men—his best soldiers? Leaning down, he touched the earth with his gloved fingers as if in touching the soil he could divine which direction to follow.

"We split up," he said, watching the bitch whine and circle, then head off to the west yet again. Standing, he dusted his hands. "I'll head west. Six men will travel with me. You, Rudyard, and six others, follow the torches north." Straightening, he motioned to Sir Benson. "You take the rest of the men and head east. We ride all night and through the morrow." His eyes narrowed against the cold wind. "If we've not found Yale by that time, we shall all meet at the gates of Serennog. Each party will send a messenger back to Collin at Black Thorn with a report and requesting more troops, supplies, the battering ram and catapults to be sent to Serennog."

"Would we not be stronger as one force?" Rudyard asked.

"Stronger, aye, and slower. Now, be off with you and find my boy!" Devlynn swung onto the back of the horse he'd claimed. His fingers wrapped around the reins. There was no wall high enough that he would not scale it to save his son; there was no gate strong enough to keep him from rescuing Yale.

It mattered not who got in his way. He kicked his mount and rode west. He should have brought Lady Apryll with him, he thought now. He might have been able to read her expression and learn which route her band of thieves and cutthroats had taken.

Wrapping the reins around his gloved hands, he kicked his mount as the cold night wind shrieked through the canyons. The horse bolted and he leaned forward, setting his jaw and silently damning himself for his fascination with the woman. Oh, she'd been lovely and coy and sweetly seductive in her jewels and white gown, and he'd been addled by her beauty, her charm, her wicked wit.

Had he not learned about women from his wife? She, too, had been a beauty, a seductress, and she'd never given him a moment's peace. The horse flew down the road and Devlynn tried to force his thoughts away from Apryll. 'Twas a stroke of luck that he had found her hiding in the priest's chamber.

His horse valiantly struggled up the final rise of a hill and the empty road stretched out before him. He pulled up, allowing his mount to breathe, waiting for the soldiers lagging behind.

Could they not hurry? Yale's fate was at stake.

Mayhap it was already too late. His heart shredded at the thought. Something vital within him died—that spark of humanity that separated him from a cruel, savage fiend intent only on blood-lust. There was a chance that it wasn't ransom the kidnappers were after, but pure vengeance.

Christ Jesus. No!

He wheeled the horse. He would find his boy. And soon.

Then he would dispense with the kidnappers.

Those who held Yale would pay dearly.

Even the woman.

Chapter Eight

"Halt!" Apryll yelled once she had closed in on her brother. "Payton! Stop!" For the moment there was enough distance between herself and Black Thorn keep that she could spare a few minutes.

Payton turned and, spying her, drew back on the reins. He was holding fast to the boy, who slumped over the pommel of the saddle. "Where the devil have you been?" Payton charged, riding back to her. "I turned around and you were gone!" Fury etched his features. "What happened?"

"You disappeared." She pulled her laboring mare to a stop and the two horses milled around each other, walking, blowing, bridles jangling.

"You knew we were meeting up with . . ."

He didn't finish and she wanted to reach over and slap him. "I knew nothing. This entire plan has been changed."

"I thought mayhap you decided to stay with the beast of Black Thorn."

"And why is that?" she demanded, then waved in the air, pushing aside the argument as if it were a bothersome fly. "It matters not. We don't have time to argue."

Her poor mare was breathing so hard Apryll thought the beast might collapse beneath her, and she was tired to the bones. Devlynn's son did not look better. As Payton turned in the saddle to skewer his sister with a disgusted glare, the boy was limp as a wet rag in his arms.

"The plan has changed," she insisted. "If we are to survive tonight we have to ride to the next town and release the boy to the local priest. He will see that the child is safely returned to Black Thorn and then, may-hap, we can prevent a war—"

"I took the boy for a reason." Payton glowered down at her from his taller, more regal destrier.

"And we will all suffer for it."

"I think not."

"Devlynn of Black Thorn will never rest until not only you and me, brother, but all of Serennog pays. There will be devastation the likes of which you can't imagine."

"Not if he is worried for the boy's safety." Payton's eyes glowed in the moonlight, his teeth, set in a cruel smile, flashing white. The boy groaned and Apryll's heart went out to him. "Now we have Black Thorn where we want him. He will do nothing to risk harm-ing the child; he will give us everything we want and more."

"He will give us vengeance and death."

"Nay, I have seen to it."

"You disobeyed me."

"I did what I had to."

"You promised no bloodshed."

Payton lifted a shoulder as the boy moaned. "I lied."

Somewhere in a nearby tree an owl hooted and the wind rustled eerily through the brambles.

"You betrayed me."

"I did what had to be done, sister, to bring Devlynn of Black Thorn to his knees. Now, there is no time to waste and I'll not listen to your complaints. Either you ride with me, or you face the enemy and you face him alone." He slapped his reins against the stallion's sides and the big horse bolted. The child, still drugged, muttered something thickly.

Gritting her teeth, Apryll kicked her mare and followed after him. She had no choice for the moment, but as the moon rose higher in the sky, she knew that she would have to right this wrong herself—find a way to get the boy back to his father, yet save her castle in the bargain.

Aye, Payton was right on one score. She had been a foolish woman, a dreamer, but no longer. Despite what Payton might think, she could be as ruthless as he. And she would start tonight.

'Twas too late, Geneva thought as she glanced at the crumpled bed within the small hut where Mary, a large sweating woman, was trying to deliver twins. She'd been at it for hours and the withered old midwife, Britt, had hurried off to fetch a pail of water and summon the priest.

The laboring woman moaned piteously from her stained cot. "Help me. Help my babes," she whispered, her fingers clutching Geneva's sleeve, her face contorted in pain in the dim light from the embers in the grate.

"'Tis not my place."

"Please," Mary begged, her face bloated and distorted in pain, her hair molded to her head in wet ringlets. "Before the midwife returns. Britt, she cares not for the babes she brings into this world . . . her eyes are weak, her hands clumsy. You know this yourself."

"She is old." Geneva glanced at the door, still slightly ajar. Oh, 'twas a night of the full moon and shrill wind. A night filled with foreboding. Geneva had felt the chill of forewarning deep within her soul, as if the forces of nature, the spirits in the forests, fields and oceans, were restless.

Because of Payton.

She bit her lip and felt her heart tear a little when she thought of the man she dared not love though she had willingly allowed him into her bed. He'd stolen her virginity and, worse yet, her heart. Absently she smoothed her tunic over her flat abdomen, where deep in her womb Payton's seed had been planted.

"Aye, Britt is too old," Mary agreed. "She's lost her touch . . . please, for the love of whatever god it is you pray to, help me. The twins, they be comin', but I fear . . . I fear I've already lost them." Mary was desperate, her thick, calloused fingers clutching the fabric of Geneva's ragged sleeve. "I beg of you, help me. Help my babes."

How could she not?

Knowing she would incur the wrath of Father Hadrian as well as the miserable midwife, Geneva stole quickly to the door and shut it soundly. Steadfastly she pushed all her thoughts of Payton aside. Aye, she would help this woman who spent her days plucking feathers and singeing hairs off the fowl for the lady's table, though deep in her heart Geneva suspected it was too late.

Reaching into her basket, she found bits of dried thistle, catmint and raspberry. She sprinkled the herbs over the tapers burning near on a table, then placed clumps of mistletoe on the bed for protection and tossed a handful of silver fir into the fire to bless and protect both mother and children. Chanting softly, invoking the Great Mother to help and protect this woman and her unborn babes, she sprinkled oil upon her hands and placed them on Mary's bare belly— touching gently—but she felt no vitality within the woman, no signs of life from the twins.

Mary let out another agonized cry and bucked upon the stained cot. Outside the wind keened and a lone dog barked from the castle kennel.

Using the dagger hidden in her basket, Geneva scratched a rune in the dirt beneath Mary's bed, a triangle within a square, intersected to create the family, hoping this symbol of protection would save the babes. Again she laid a hand upon Mary's protruding belly. She felt only cold, empty despair.

"They—they are strong?" Mary asked as Father Hadrian swept into the room, his vestments billowing, the candles flickering with the cold draft of air that chased after him.

"What is going on here?" he said, his deep voice gruff. "Geneva, if you've been practicing the old ways, 'twill be your downfall. Now, Mary, lass," he said as his gaze fell upon the sweating woman, "mayhap we should pray." He shot a knowing look at Geneva. "To the one true God." As if by instinct he slid one shoe under the cot and rubbed out the rune.

Britt, toting a pail of water, hurried into the room and sniffed loudly at the scents of burning herbs. "What be ye doin', Geneva?" she demanded. "I'll be having none of that pagan talk and"—she pointed to the candles as she adjusted the blankets—"what is that ye've sprinkled? Don't ye be callin' on Lucifer, woman. This 'ere's a Christian castle, I'll be remindin' ye, if the good Father is too kind to tell ye himself. There now, Mary, ye just breathe deep, and I'll see to them babes fer ye."

"Ye would not be invoking' the devil now, would ye, Geneva?" Father Hadrian asked, seeing the greenery on the bed.

"'Tis but holly, mistletoe and ivy, for the yule time." Geneva lied easily to this man of God.

He snorted, disbelieving. "I'll have to tell Lady Apryll upon her return."

If she returns, Geneva thought, feeling a chill deep in the marrow of her bones as she cast a final glance toward Mary and slipped through the door of the hut. Outside the wind was bitter cold, the night clear but for a few clouds that ringed the moon, yet something was wrong, terribly wrong. Geneva sensed a shifting in the fates this night and in her mind's eye she saw Apryll of Serennog's ruin.

All because the sorceress had lied.

Chapter Nine

Apryll's mount was no match for the gray. Within seconds Payton was out of sight and the jennet began to lag, her strides uneven. "Hurry, hurry," Apryll urged, but she heard the beast's ragged breathing, knew the feisty little mare was spent. "Oh, for the love of St. Jude," Apryll muttered, reining to a stop and sliding to the ground. Holding the reins in one hand she began to walk to let the animal cool down, only to realize the mare was favoring a foreleg. *Now what?* Apryll wondered as she continued to walk through the forest. They were far from the old inn where the soldiers from Serennog were to meet, farther yet from the castle. And there was a fairly good chance that Payton had ordered the men to gather elsewhere, at a hidden spot unbeknownst to Apryll.

Payton's plan was more treacherous than Apryll had imagined. To what lengths would he go? He'd already lied, betrayed her, stolen from Black Thorn and kidnapped the boy. He'd killed to make good his escape.

Lost in her thoughts, she heard a rumble. Low. Far away. But getting closer. Horses. Damn. The ruse didn't work. The beast of Black Thorn was approaching. Quickly, she pulled the unwilling mare into a thicket, a small copse of saplings and briars. 'Twas little cover but the night was dark.

Then she heard the hound.

With a bloodcurdling bay that echoed through the forest.

"Cursed beasts," she growled. She tied the mare to a sapling, then flung her hat down a ravine, hoping the damned dog would follow it down the steep cliff, allowing her more time. But where to hide? There was no cave, no hut, nothing.

The dog's soulful cry drew nearer. Hoofbeats thudded louder. Closer. Apryll's heart was pounding so hard she could barely hear herself think. She could run, but wouldn't get far . . . nay, her best chance was to hide and, as the army passed, double back upon her own trail, her own scent mingling with those of the soldiers and horses . . . if she could outwit the dog. She pulled off her mantle and threw it down the ravine, farther along the path, hoping to fool the bloody curs. Then, running headlong toward the coming search party, she plunged through the forest, feeling twigs and briars pull at her sleeves and tangle in her hair.

Men were shouting. Oh, Lord, they were close. Over the roar of blood rushing through her head she heard deep voices, excited yips and the crash of hooves on the hard, icy road.

Lord help me, she silently prayed, diving behind a burned stump and pressing her back to the charred bark as the army sped by. Dogs barking, horses galloping, men shouting, bridles and swords rattling.

Heart in her throat she waited, certain that at any moment the small band would turn and hunt her down.

Yale opened a groggy eye. 'Twas dark except for moonlight and he was being held by strong arms as the horse beneath them seemed to fly through the night. His head spun and he wondered why his father had taken him from his bed to ride like the wind on horseback. Yale's head pounded with every jarring hoofbeat and he was so tired, so sluggish, and something was wrong, very, very wrong. Yet Phantom's strides were long, his gait sure.

"Father?" Yale muttered, his tongue thick as the ghostly forest flashed by in a blur.

"I be not your father."

The voice was unfamiliar and Yale twisted his neck to look at the man who was hauling him off by horseback. 'Twas that of a stranger, a bold, angry man from the looks of him, but Yale wasn't certain, his head felt about to explode and his stomach weak, and the darkness from which he'd emerged threatened to take him over.

"Who . . . who are you . . . ?" he managed to get out and he heard the rider laugh.

"You want not to know."

Yale blinked once and then, as the ground swept by at a dizzying speed, he lost consciousness again.

Apryll waited, forcing her breathing to slow, straining to listen, daring to peek from behind the stump to search the darkness. She slipped away from the stump, dashed onto the main road and ran as fast as she could, heading toward Black Thorn. She remembered crossing a creek a few miles back. With enough of a lead, she could make it to the frigid stream and, using the water to hide her scent, follow the creek for a mile or so, to the next road, then circle back to Serennog or the inn where Payton's men were to meet him. Behind her brother's lying back, she would steal the boy and ascertain his safe passage to Black Thorn . . . or, better still, she would bargain with the devil, promise Devlynn the safe return of his son along with his horses and stolen valuables from the treasury in exchange for peace.

Even if he agreed, it would not be the end of it, of course. Devlynn would still want to mete out his vengeance, but mayhap it would be tempered.

And what of Serennog? Would it not be in worse shape than before? What kind of a leader are you?

Mayhap Payton had been right all along. She would have to marry a wealthy baron, one she could barely stomach. She considered wealthy Baron William of Balchdar and shuddered. He was a cruel one, no doubt, but no worse than her other suitors, and Balchdar was a rich barony.

Her legs ached and her lungs burned and the sounds of the soldiers had faded, if only for a few minutes. She slowed to a fast walk, hoping that the cover of darkness would last until she reached the creek. She'd take off her clothes and carry them so that they wouldn't become wet, then don them again . . . she hurried faster until she reached the banks of the stream, and, confident that she'd lost her pursuers, she stripped out of the huntsman's garb, carefully tying the breeches and boots in the arms of the tunic's sleeves.

The wind was cold against her bare skin, the water icy as she stepped onto the slippery rocks and made her way downstream. Dawn was beginning to break, gray slats of light creeping over the eastern hills and piercing through the brittle, empty branches of the trees. Shivering, biting her lower lip and thinking of a dozen ways to kill her brother, she picked her way along the creek. Fish slipped by her ankles and calves, but she didn't feel them as soon as her lower extremities were numb. The bite of the wind, however, brought goose bumps to her flesh and her teeth chattered so hard as to cause a headache.

She was hungry and tired and when she thought of those few moments when she was in the great hall of Black Thorn, held tightly in Baron Devlynn's arms as they danced, her mother's wedding dress glittering in the glow of a thousand candles, it seemed centuries past rather than a few, short life-altering hours.

As the winter morning dawned, she heard a rooster crowing in a nearby village and spied an arch-shaped bridge spanning the creek bed. She crawled up a mossy, root-strewn bank and hid in the sparse foliage as she stepped into the trousers and reached for the tunic.

The blade of a sword pricked the back of her neck.

"Don't move," a man ordered and she froze.

Her heart sank.

She recognized the voice.

It belonged to Devlynn of Black Thorn.

"Turn around. Slowly." His voice was low as the wind and just as cold.

Cursing her luck, Apryll held her tunic to her chest, covering her nakedness as she faced the lord. How long had he been standing in this shadowy part of the forest where the morning light shifted over the frozen ground and nary a winter bird sang? Had he seen her naked, watched as she slogged through the icy water? Flushing at the thought, she rotated to face the Lord of Black Thorn.

His face was a mask of anger and contempt, his flinty eyes slitted, his lips curled back over his teeth. The blade of his weapon didn't move and as she faced him, its deadly point settled into the hollow of her throat. Despite the goose bumps she felt upon her flesh and the menace of the blade, she inched her chin upward and tossed her hair over her shoulder to stare up at him.

"You escaped."

She didn't respond.

"Who helped you?" he demanded, pushing his face closer to hers. When again she didn't say a word his visage became deadly. "You escaped to join the others, but this is not the way to your keep." Fury flared in his eyes and she felt the bite of the sword against her skin. "I'll ask you again. Where is my son?" he demanded, furious eyes raking down her body. "What have you done with him?"

"He is with my brother."

"And where is that?"

"Farther ahead on the road."

A muscle worked in the baron's jaw. "Then he's alive."

"Oh, yes!" *Dear Lord, did he really believe she would kill his son? Harm any child?*

"Then why are you not with them?" Beneath the steely calm of his voice she sensed a dark worry and a deeper rage.

"I was. I did catch Payton, but . . . but . . . my horse became lame and I could not keep up. I heard you behind me . . . and . . . and I knew I had to flee, to find help."

"To save your sorry skin," he muttered, disgusted.

"To get help to wrest Yale from Payton."

Devlynn glowered down at her, weighing her words, judging their worth, as he stood beneath the moss-laden branches of a sturdy oak.

"You wanted help to free the child that you stole and yet you did not come to me?"

"Because you would not have believed me. And . . . and I knew not where you were nor what you would do to me if you found I had escaped." She swallowed hard but didn't move, felt the pinch of the sword but let her throat lay open. Exposed. She felt her pulse pounding in the circle of bones beneath the sword's deadly edge, saw his eyes take in the movement, then drop to the rise and fall of her chest, hidden by her wretched, wrinkled tunic. Something chased across his eyes—a memory—something lustful. Whatever it was, it scurried away, a dangerous, passionate thought quickly banished.

Could this be the man she'd so brazenly kissed, the man with whom she'd shared a mazer of wine and danced so lightheartedly? He looked like a demon. Black hair curled and fell over his forehead, his jaw was dark with the start of a beard and every visible muscle in his face and neck was taut. Nostrils flared, he breathed pure loathing.

"As I said, my horse turned lame—"

"My horse," he corrected, and she bit her lip. The sword slid lower, down her breastbone, not breaking the skin but scraping.

"Please, Lord Devlynn, you must believe me that I . . . I did not intend for the boy to be taken."

"But he was."

"Aye." Lower still the wicked blade sank, pushing aside the rough folds of her disguise, exposing the tops of her breasts. She resisted, saw a flare in his eyes and let the tunic fall to the frigid ground.

"So . . . your intent was only to rob me blind, steal my horses and kill some of my men."

"There was to be no bloodshed," she said, feeling herself turn crimson despite the cold wind.

His jaw slid to one side as the tip of his sword slid over her abdomen to the thatch of curls at the juncture of her legs. "Oh, but there was. Two men dead, others dying and my boy taken out from under my nose, drugged by someone, a traitor, within my keep." Anger burned through his words. "Enough crimes have been committed to send you to the gallows several times over but none of that matters. Only my boy." Devlynn's fury was palpable, seeming to shimmer through the bare trees and across the silvery stream rushing by.

"Would I could change things," Apryll said.

"Oh, lady, you can, and trust me, if you want to save your neck, you will."

"Not unless you sheath that damned sword and we make haste. There is no time to waste with . . . with . . . idle threats."

She stepped back and reached beneath her to gather up her clothes. "What is it you think I can do for you?" she said, turning her back to him.

"'Tis simple. Either your brother returns my son safely to me, or you suffer the consequences."

"Oh, so you will hack me to pieces, is that what you are suggesting?" she said boldly, angry at being subservient. 'Twas not her nature.

"I can think of punishments that are not quite so brutal, but may still cause you to tell me the truth. There are ways, lady, to loosen a woman's tongue."

"Without threatening to butcher her?" she threw over her bare shoulder as she struggled into her leggings and realized that her buttocks and the cleft between them were more than visible to him. Well, so be it. Let him stare. 'Twould harm nothing but her pride and that had been battered black-and-blue already.

She slid her arms through the sleeves of the tunic, yanked it over her head and slithered into the scratchy fabric. Feeling those hot eyes upon her she turned to face him again, her shoulders straightening. He'd lowered his weapon, but the cords in the back of his neck tightened and his eyes lingered a little too long on the slit of her tunic that was not yet tied.

"How did you find me?"

"'Twas not difficult."

"Then tell me." She laced her tunic tightly, unwilling for him to see even the slightest hint of her flesh.

"I came upon your horse, knew that we'd nearly caught you and that the hounds were confused. 'Twas simple enough. I put myself in your boots, considered what I would do when I knew I was about to be captured." He flashed his sword at the sorry leather boots she was about to don. "There was but one sensible option, to double back, find a creek, try to confuse the dogs, then find a horse to steal."

Her hastily made plan exactly.

His knowing, cold smile irritated her. His demeanor, that of a prideful lord looking upon a captive, made her want to put a blade to his throat when he was naked and see how he would like it. Oh, she would love to reverse the spin of the wheel of fate, to hold him prisoner while she found a way to wrest Yale from Payton without further bloodshed. But she had not the time for such idle dreams, not if she wanted to catch her brother.

Was it possible to reclaim Devlynn's son and barter to save Serennog? She yanked on one boot, then the other.

Payton would never give up his prize. Not without a fight. Or compensation.

As she straightened, he held out a hand. "Your weapon."

"I have no—"

"Do not take me for a fool," he said through lips that barely moved. He saw the defiance in her eyes, the tilt of her chin. She reached into her pocket and withdrew the small dagger with a bone handle. He grabbed the knife with his free hand, then hitched his chin toward his horse. "You will do as I say," he asserted. "From this moment forward."

Apryll didn't argue. 'Twas of no use. For the moment she would abide by his wishes. But only for the moment.

Devlynn saw the defiance in her eyes, the way she clamped her jaw down hard as if she were controlling her wicked tongue. She was used to giving commands, not taking them, and the flare of her nostrils when he ordered her about would have been amusing if the situation were not so dire.

And her body. By the saints, 'twas perfect. Even now as she walked to the horse and tossed that mane of gold hair over her shoulder, he imagined the curve of her spine, the split of her buttocks, her long, bare thighs. Aye, she was covered now by her huntsman's tunic and breeches but as long as he lived he would not forget the tilt of her breasts with their button-hard pink nipples, nor the inviting V of honey-colored curls hiding her woman-mound.

Sword drawn, he watched as she reached the horse and, thinking he didn't see the sideways glance, looked longingly down a path to escape. She was a spirited one, he'd give her that.

And she stole your son. Forget it not!

Dawn had erupted in a bright, wintry fury, offering a few shafts of light to the gloomy forest and dappling the frozen ground but bringing little warmth to the Lord of Black Thorn's frigid heart. Yet this woman, Jezebel that she was, caused his blood to heat. With fury? Or desire? Perhaps a little of both.

Long ago, with his wife, he'd learned there was a fine line between love and hate, that passion could be fueled by anger as well as lust. Apryll of Serennog, with her stiff pride, sharp tongue and beguiling body, inspired both.

"We ride now. To my son." He swung onto the bay's broad back and warned her, "Do not think of escape. 'Tis of no use." He sheathed his sword, reached down and offered his hand. Indecision darkened her gold eyes. For a second he thought she would spit into his open glove, or try to run through the brambles and vines of the forest. Her back was ramrod stiff, her shoulders square, defiance radiating off her in palpable waves. "If you disobey me," he said evenly, "not only will you be punished, but those you love will be as well."

No fear showed in those intelligent eyes. Only quiet, determined rage. Lips pursed, she placed her hand in his and he lifted her easily into the saddle in front of him, wedging her between the pommel and his crotch. His longer legs were pressed against the back of her thighs and the pressure of her sweet, round rump was impossible to ignore.

Reaching around her, he grabbed the reins and cursed the fates for the hardness in his groin. That he would want her bespoke his foolish masculinity, but the pressure of the split of her buttocks against his shaft was undeniable. As he nudged the bay into a gallop, he felt her rub against him and knew that he was in for hours of torment. It would be so much easier to drop her to the ground, to leave her to her own fate, but she was a bargaining chip and she alone knew where his son was.

Much as he detested the thought, she was valuable to him.

And you want her. More than you have ever wanted a woman. You want to feel her beneath you, writhing and calling out your name, screaming with pleasure as you claim her.

In his mind's eye he envisioned her beneath him, soaked in sweat, her pert nipples rising upward, begging for his tongue and lips. He saw himself twining his fingers in the shimmer of gold that was her hair as he entered her.

The back of his throat turned to dust.

Oh, 'twould be heaven as well as hell to bed her.

He felt the heat of her body as he leaned against her back and whispered into her ear, "Tell me where I can find my boy."

When she didn't reply, he reached upward and cupped a breast in one hand, felt the bud of her nipple between his thumb and finger.

"There are ways of getting the truth from you, Lady

Apryll," he said. "And I vow I will use every one of them on you."

She swallowed hard but tried to show no reaction. His gloved hand was warm and she despised herself for not feeling revulsion at his touch. The man held her life in his hands, had imprisoned her, had sworn to seek retribution against her and yet she couldn't keep thoughts of kissing him, of touching him, of laying with him from her mind.

What had gotten into her? Now, wedged between the pommel and his crotch, she shouldn't be aware of the stiffness pressed hard against her buttocks, of the shaft of his manhood rubbing erotically against that sensitive cleft, but of the danger that surrounded her.

She had to get away from him, to elude him again and to reach Payton first, try to reason with her brother and to return Yale to his keep.

Mayhap then she could get away from the devil of Black Thorn.

Then again, mayhap not.

Chapter Ten

A t last the torturous ride was over, Apryll thought as Devlynn reined in his sweating mount near the campground, little more than a fire pit with a spit, one tent and a tethering line for five or six horses. Nearby a creek gurgled as it cut through frozen banks. A few men milled around the fire and they all looked up as horse and riders approached.

Shame burned her cheeks as the soldiers watched the Lord of Black Thorn help her off her mount and onto the hard ground.

"So you found the woman, did ye?" a fat one asked, his slitted, feral gaze running up and down her body. "And dressed like a huntsman. I thought she was locked away at Black Thorn."

"You were mistaken," she snapped.

"Mayhap that's not such a bad thing." The soldier's voice was lusty and Apryll inwardly cringed. "We could use ourselves a woman here, to cook and clean and keep a bed warm at night, eh?" he said, winking broadly at the others gathered around the single tent in a small clearing where the fire smoldered in a ring of mossy stones.

"Aye, she's a pretty one, she is, and feisty, too, I'm willing to bet," the man added, his thick lips rising into a hideous grin.

"Touch me and you'll wish you never had," she said angrily, stepping closer to the pig-eyed man. She didn't bother to toss her tangled hair from her face or stiffen her spine. Nor would she cower. It was enough that she held him in her steady glare. "If you value your hands, you'll keep them to yourself."

He laughed. "What will you do to them, bite off my fingers, eh . . . ooh, that you would try." He wiggled the dirty digits in front of her face.

If she expected Devlynn to come to her rescue, she was disappointed.

"Ow . . . I like a woman with a bit o' spirit to her." The soldier wheezed at his little joke and she wished she had her little knife to keep him at bay. As it was, she would have to use her wits.

"'Tis not spirit, it's a simple fact."

She lifted a haughty brow, then, as she'd seen Geneva do so many times before, dug the toe of her boot into the dirt and drew two runes, a pentagram and, next to the five-pointed star, the symbol of a male. "Since you are so fond of your hands, I'll curse another part of your body," she said and, using the heel of her boot, dug deep in the earth, cutting off the arrow part of the circle, the point that indicated it was male.

> "Holy Mother, heed my prayer,
> All your secrets here unlock,
> Touch the sinner who disbelieves,
> Wither and rot his pathetic cock."

"Wha—?" the man exclaimed.

Others laughed.

"Know you not that the women of Serennog are known for the spells they cast? That there is a curse about the keep? That all within have magical powers?"

"'Tis . . . 'tis a lie. A joke."

She glanced down at the juncture of his legs and lifted a shoulder. "You should know soon. Within the fortnight. But if you want me to reverse the spell, if you would not take a chance, then stay away from me. And that goes for the rest of you." She glanced around the small circle of men who had pledged their fealty to the Lord of Black Thorn and were now his most trusted soldiers.

"If you be a witch," one of the men ventured, "then why have you not escaped?"

"I have once," she reminded him. "I can again."

"Yeah, yeah, then just snap yer fingers and disappear."

She clucked her tongue as if they were schoolboys who were so stupid she could not believe it. "'Tis not how it works. But you will see . . . all of you . . ." Again she slid a knowing look at the bulgeless crotch of the pig-eyed soldier's breeches. "Such a pity this one here will never sire a son."

"Enough," Devlynn growled, though, in truth, he was amused at her handling of Sir Lloyd, for the man was a pain in the backside with his bawdy jokes and constant complaining. Were he not sure with a bow and arrow and loyal to Black Thorn, Devlynn would have left him at the castle.

Hitching his chin toward the fat soldier, Devlynn ordered, "You, Lloyd, take two men on a hunting party. Don't return without a stag or boar." He turned to a tall, dark-eyed, surly looking man. "Bennett will scout ahead on the trail and you . . . Dennis, ride back to Black Thorn and explain that we have Lady Apryll prisoner. Tell my brother that there are traitors within the keep and I'll not rest until every last one of them is exposed."

"And you, m'lord?" Dennis asked, his gaze sliding to Apryll. Her response was chilly indifference.

"I shall interrogate the prisoner." With that he nudged Apryll forward, indicating the single tent. She hesitated and all her boldness of a few minutes before faltered. He felt a moment's satisfaction. "Inside."

"Why not here?"

"Where you can run away? I think not."

Her spine visibly stiffened as she preceded him into his tent. He glanced over his shoulder to see that his men were doing his bidding and saddling their mounts. Good. He wanted a few hours alone with Lady Apryll of Serennog, the angel Aunt Violet spoke of, the woman whom Collin found intriguing, a self-proclaimed witch and Devlynn's own personal nemesis.

This day he would find out all there was to know about her and then decide her fate.

This was a poor excuse for a camp, but it would damned well have to do, Payton decided as he eyed the dilapidated building surrounded by brush and brambles. He hauled his hostage, the baron of Black Thorn's groggy son, over one shoulder and the boy moaned incoherently. He'd be waking up soon and Payton wanted him firmly imprisoned.

As the boy groaned more audibly, Payton strode quickly, hurrying along an overgrown path toward what had once, in more thriving times, been an inn.

That was long ago, before the bridge spanning the river had washed away in a flood and the road had been diverted to a more prosperous village. For half a century the building had been left to fall into disrepair and few remembered that it existed.

Payton's mother had told him of it long ago and he found it fitting somehow that the very site where she'd been ravished and impregnated by the beast of Black Thorn's father was now a prison for his son.

His back teeth ground together. He'd grown up knowing he was unwanted, the product of a rape, ignored by the lord who had sired him, tolerated by the baron who had raised him, Lord Regis, a man who had never been able to sire a son of his own. Apryll's father.

Even now the taunts of childhood rang in his ears. *Payton the Bastard, Payton the Unwanted, Payton the Devil's Spawn.* He'd heard the taunts, borne them, broken his hand on more than one boy's face, but it was the whispers that were the worst, quiet gossip that followed him and his mother about.

"Poor thing," some of the old hens of Serennog had clucked, looking upon his mother with pity in their eyes. "Ever reminded of that horrid time."

"She should never have borne him. 'Twould have been better if she would have drank something . . . you know, to get rid of it."

"Or ended her own life. I would have. Never would I have borne such ill seed."

The tops of Payton's ears had burned bright red, for he'd heard the comments over and over again, suffered the pitying glances cast his mother's way and realized that many in the keep believed that because of his mother's rape and pregnancy there was a curse cast upon Serennog; that it was *his fault* for the troubles that had beleaguered the castle for close to two decades.

And now he would finally return the favor.

The boy moaned in his arms as Payton ducked through the sagging doorway where the door itself, a few rotting boards, hung drunkenly from rusting hinges. The walls were a drab gray color, weathered by the years that had stripped the shutters from the windows and allowed the brambles to claw upward. The building reminded Payton of a dying beast, broken spine exposed where the thatching from the roof had given way, ribs made of cross beams evident.

Inside, faint sunlight filtered through the holes in the siding as Payton dropped the boy into a musty pile of straw.

"Oooh," the urchin cried, opening one eye a crack and rubbing his head. Black, tousled hair fell over his forehead, freckles dappled the bridge of his nose and his curious gaze bored into his captor. "Who the bloody hell are you?" he asked, showing not a smidgen of fear. "Where am I?"

"You can call me sire," Payton said, enjoying the moment.

Blinking rapidly, as if to clear the cobwebs from his mind, Yale scowled. "You're not Longshanks."

"Hardly."

"Then why should I call you sire? Be you a king?"

"Not yet," Payton said and smiled inwardly.

Propping himself onto one elbow, the boy glanced around the shabby old inn. The floor was packed earth, a chimney crumbled at one end of what had once been a large, open room and supplies, carried in by the mule and cart a few days earlier, were piled near the blackened grate. A broken bench had collapsed against the back wall and spiderwebs and abandoned wasps' nests hung in the darkest corners. Owl droppings and scattered bones littered one corner beneath a high, sheltered beam.

"Where's Father?"

Good question, lad. Payton shrugged. "Lost, I presume."

"Nay, not Father. He is never lost." Yale pushed himself into a sitting position and winced. "Aye, my head. It feels as if a thousand horses are racing through it."

"It'll pass." Payton strode to the supplies packed into a corner.

"When?"

"Soon."

"Why am I here?"

Payton had expected this question. "All you needs know is that you are now our prisoner and you shall not attempt to escape."

"This is a game? Because of the revels?" Yale's young eyes brightened at the prospect of a challenge. A smile of anticipation pulled at the corners of his lips. "Aye, he was much like the man who had sired him. "Aunt Miranda told Bronwyn there was to be a surprise game at the revels!" An excited grin stretched from one side of his mouth to the other, showing teeth too large for his face, as he quickly surveyed the dilapidated interior of the old inn.

"'Tis no game, I assure you," Payton growled.

Yale ignored the answer. "Am I to escape? Is that it?"

"That would be a grave mistake," Payton warned as the boy clambered to his feet and, still dizzy, leaned a shoulder against the wall. He winced and blinked and

Payton watched the boy think as his gaze swept the walls and what was left of the ceiling, searching for ways out of the building other than the broken door.

But he was in no shape to escape yet. He still seemed woozy from the drug that had been added to his mazer and he winced at the dull rays of sunlight streaming through the rotting slats.

"Have you drink?" Yale asked. "I'm thirsty."

"There is water at the creek."

"I'm hungry as well."

"Soon—when the others join us."

"What others?"

"'Tis none of your concern."

"But I'm hungry now."

Payton hadn't realized what trouble a boy could be. "You'll just have to be patient."

"My aunt says I'm like my father, that patience eludes me."

Smart woman. "Hush now. I have work to do."

"What?" The lad was struggling unsteadily to his feet. "What work?"

"Again, 'tis none of your concern, so just sit there and be quiet. When the others arrive we will eat. Until then you wait."

The lad's eyes narrowed suspiciously. "Are you robbers, then? Cutthroats and the like?"

"Aye, cutthroats," Payton growled.

"Is there a bloody band, then? Am I part of it?" Yale perked up, his hunger and thirst quickly forgotten at the thought of adventure.

"You're the captive," Payton warned.

"Am I really?" Yale was impressed. "How must I act?"

"As I said. Quietly. You are to sit here and wait," Payton snapped, obviously tired of the questions.

"For what?"

"To be rescued, of course."

"Bloody hell, then it is a game, and a grand one!" Before Payton's eyes Yale transformed from a dull-witted and drugged prisoner to an active, excited boy ready to set upon a great adventure. "And my father, is he to rescue me? And Uncle Collin and Aunt Miranda, are they playing, too? Though she be a woman, she is a marksman with a bow and arrow and I've seen her swing a mace. Is she on our side?"

Payton's color rose. "Aye," he said. "They are all part of our band."

"But what of Bronwyn? She's a girl and . . ." His nose wrinkled. "A crybaby, methinks. Can't hardly ride or hold a weapon. She's not like her mum but—"

"Enough!" Payton rubbed the back of his neck and wanted to cuff Devlynn's son to shut the boy up. 'Twas better when he was drugged and slumped in the saddle. Quieter. And Payton needed time to think. To figure out what he was going to do with his sister, for surely she would appear any second. He'd known he'd left her behind and hadn't worried about it; her mare was not nearly as fleet as the gray destrier he'd claimed as his own—Baron Devlynn's steed.

"When is the game over?" the boy asked as Payton's head began to ache.

"All you need to know is that you are my captive and you are to stay here. Quietly."

"Until my father saves me, is that it?"

Payton's lips thinned. "Aye. Until he tries to save you."

"Then am I to not try and get away?" he asked, crestfallen, an edge of suspicion to his voice.

Payton latched onto this idea. "Aye. That would be best. You must do everything I tell you to do. Elsewise the game will be ruined."

"Am I to stay prisoner?"

"A quiet, obedient prisoner."

The freckled nose wrinkled. "'Tis no fun."

"In the next go-round, you can be the kidnapper," Payton offered, throwing the brat a bone.

Yale visibly brightened. "Can I? Yes. I would like that." He narrowed his eyes and curled his lip. "I'd be a nasty one, too, I would."

Payton believed him.

He glanced out the window to the clouds thickening in the sky and wondered what had happened to his sister. Even accounting for the difference in speed of the horses, she should be appearing soon.

At the very least within the hour.

Unless something happened to her.

Unless . . . He considered the man who was his enemy. Surely there was no way he could have caught up with Apryll. Not after her escape from the tower.

And yet . . .

Worry pricked at Payton's conscience.

What if she'd been captured? What if, even now, she was prisoner to the beast of Black Thorn? Would he torture her? Find a way to loosen her tongue? Even now the soldiers loyal to him could be riding to this old inn, blades drawn, blood-lust running through their veins.

He glanced back at the boy who was now silent and staring hard at him with the same intensity Payton had witnessed in the Lord of Black Thorn's eyes.

It crossed his mind that this boy, so like his father, was his nephew, for Devlynn, by the black blood of a rapist, was his half brother. Though, it seemed, few at Black Thorn knew. Probably because Morgan of Black Thorn had pillaged and raped many times, and his seed was scattered widely over Wales with bastards such as he too many to count.

Except that he was the son of a lady, not some country wench or tavern whore.

He looked at the boy. Devlynn of Black Thorn's son. His only heir. Payton felt no kinship with the lad.

Yale was but a means to an end. Of no more value than the horse Payton had stolen . . . and in many ways worth much, much less.

Chapter Eleven

Apryll shuddered as she entered the lord's tent. On the floor, squarely in the middle of the makeshift room, was a pallet that had been covered with furs.

Lord Devlynn's bed.

Her throat turned to sand. She heard the sound of hoofbeats, knew the other soldiers had ridden off and that she was now alone with the beast of Black Thorn.

Alone with him in his bedchamber, for that's what this tent is, Apryll.

"Sit," he commanded and nudged her toward the bed.

"I would rather stand as I've been riding and—"

"Sit."

She did as she was bid. 'Twould do no good to make him angry. Nay, she had to lure him into a feeling of security; she needed him to think that all thoughts of escape had left her head. Dropping onto the soft pallet she wondered how many women he'd bedded on this very mattress and if she'd be the next.

Would it be so bad? To lay with this man? Aye, he is your

enemy, Apryll, but have you not felt the fever of his kiss, known your skin to quiver for his touch, sensed the hardness of his manhood pressed against you as you rode? How much longer will you remain a virgin when no man pleases you and you think you will never marry?

Would it be a sin to join with a man you do not love? It happens often for others and might just be the means of your escape.

She'd heard gossip in the corridors of Serennog often enough. Once, when Apryll had been on the staircase, she'd paused to lace her boot and heard the silly, gap-toothed laundress, Daisy, complaining that her man fell asleep after laying with her.

"He be not the only man afflicted with the ailment," Frannie, the head seamstress, had assured her. Cackling loudly, Frannie had confided in the younger woman, "'Tis a woman's curse, you know, to want more, to hope that your husband is man enough to take care of yer needs as well as his. But it don't happen much, Daisy, not at all. Most men make quick business of it, then just when you be ready to enjoy yerself, they roll off of ye and start snorin'. That's the way it is, I tell ye," Frannie said as they started down the stairs again. "Ye'd be wise to pleasure yourself afterwards."

"But if I have a man—"

"You'll not be satisfied." Their voices were fading and Apryll had stolen after them, listening to the conversation as Frannie's voluminous skirts had swept the floor.

"Oh, they talk a lot, about rutting and rutting until long in the night," she was saying. "My man, he swears to his friends that he can make me howl all night long, when the truth of the matter is he barely rolls off me before he sleeps the sleep of the dead. What a man says he does in bed and what he does, well, they be not the same. Not at all. Me husband, Tim, he brags to me, tells me he'll love me until I be spent, when we both know it's a lie. The trouble is, Tim believes the lie hisself."

Now a plan was hatching in Apryll's head. Could she go through with it? Lie with this man and hope that he fell asleep? He had to be as weary as she, for he'd spent as many hours awake. She looked up at him, a big man, too tall to stand in the tent, hunched over a bit, arms folded over his broad chest, piercing gray eyes staring at her so hard she was certain he was reading her thoughts.

"Lie down."

She stiffened. Her heart thundered as he took a step closer.

"Lie down."

"I need not . . ."

"Oh, yes, you do. We both do. We will sleep and when my men return we will awaken. You will tell me then why you attacked my castle and took my boy and if I think you have not lied to me, I will let you eat, for you must be hungry."

As if on cue her stomach rumbled.

"Lie down."

"I be not tired," she lied. Oh, it was one thing to consider lying with the man, feeling his body around hers, but now, when it was time, she had doubts that it would be wise.

"You do not take orders well."

"Nor, I think, would you."

"But I be not the captive. Now . . . lie back or I shall have to force you. Is that what you want?" There was a spark of fire in his eyes, a bright pinpoint of sexual light that caused a quiver deep inside.

She licked her lips and heard his swift intake of breath.

"You be a vixen woman," he growled, the fire flaring and hissing.

She laid back upon his bed and could barely breathe as he slid into the pallet next to her. Grabbing both her wrists in one big hand, he stretched her arms over her head, then, with his free hand pulled up the furs so that they covered her body as well as his. Tense, every sense aware, she dared not breathe as he settled beneath the soft furs and, wrapping his free arm around her waist, snuggled up to her in much the same position as when they were riding. The front of his body folded tightly—possessively?—around the slope of her spine and buttocks.

She tried to pull her hands free, but the fingers surrounding her wrists were strong as steel—a flesh, bone and sinew manacle. "You cannot get away," he said, stirring the hair at the back of her neck. "Do not even consider it."

"But I cannot sleep with my hands above my head."

"I can. And you'll not escape. 'Tis all that matters."

"You are a beast."

"Aye."

"Everything that has ever been said about you is true."

"And more. Remember it."

"But—"

"Shh." His breath was hot against the back of her neck, the hand around her waist pulled her tight against him, his long fingers splayed across her abdomen creating heat through her itchy tunic. She felt every pad of his fingertips in hot pressure points upon her skin, the smallest of which skimmed the nest of curls where her legs met. Her breeches separated skin from skin but the coarse cloth was a thin barrier and Apryll wondered what it would be like to feel flesh upon flesh.

Don't think about it. Be glad he needs sleep. Once he is snoring you might be able to wriggle away. No guards are about and there is a horse or two to steal. Pretend sleep and then, quietly, gently, ease out of his embrace.

'Twas a simple plan. All she had to do was be patient and wait.

"The prisoner has escaped." The soldier was nearly shivering in his boots as he faced Collin, who was seated in the lord's chair warming the bottom of his boots at the fire in the great hall. The dogs were restless, their dark eyes never moving from the master's chair.

"The prisoner?"

"Aye, the woman. She's . . . she's not in the tower."

Slowly Collin rose to his full height. "Are you meaning to tell me that Apryll of Serennog is missing?"

"Aye, m'lord," the guard said, nodding quickly, his brown eyes filled with shame.

"Were you not at your post?"

"I was. From the moment I heard that I was to be the guard I stood at the door. It never opened."

Collin glared at the smaller man. "She could not have disappeared. Show me." He didn't wait for the soldier but threw on his mantel, grabbed his sword and shouldered open the door. Crossing the bailey he heard the sounds of hammers, as already the stables were under repair and the smell of smoldering, wet timbers laced the air. With the guard on his heels he made his way to the tower and climbed up the steep, curved steps to the small chamber, now unlocked, with the door flung wide.

Indeed, it was empty.

"Where is she?"

"I—I know not."

"She is not a witch, could not have disappeared into thin air."

The soldier swallowed nervously. "I think . . . I think mayhap she escaped before I came on duty."

Collin threw the man a blistering look. "That would be convenient in saving your miserable neck, now wouldn't it?"

"There be no other explanation."

Snorting his disgust, Collin kicked the empty pail that had been left for her to relieve herself in. It banged against the wall, sending a rat hiding in the corner scurrying through a crack near the door.

"Call the guards, or what's left of them," he ordered, his gaze sweeping the small interior one last time. "Search the castle. *Again*. Christ Jesus, none of the guests are to leave yet. Look through every cart, every wagon and turn this place upside down." He was on the stairs again, his boots ringing loudly. "And when Lord Devlynn returns, you will be the one to give him the message that his prize prisoner has escaped!"

"Where do you think you're going?" Father Hadrian asked as Geneva tried to slip through the main gate.

She froze, turned and faced the repugnant man of

God in his fine alb that shimmered like pure silk in the sunlight. Oh, that he was more like Father Benjamin.

"To the forest to gather herbs," she said, managing a frozen smile that she knew wouldn't placate his suspicious mind.

"For what purpose—to chant your heathen spells and make your deals with the devil? Oh, I know who you are, witch, and though others may be charmed by you or blind as Father Benjamin to your charms, I can see through your sham."

"Cook needs herbs as her garden is depleted." 'Twas not really a lie. Geneva had spoken with the cook herself, suggesting she go out to replenish the sparse larder with spices that grew wild in the hills.

"'Tis winter," Hadrian pointed out. "Little grows."

"But roots can be dug, dried herbs still found if one knows where to look and winter apples can be gathered."

His lips thinned, for there was no argument unless he called her a liar. "Would you not take someone with you? 'Tis not safe beyond the castle walls."

Safer than within, she thought but held back the words. "'Tis daylight, Father, and I'll be back anon. There is no reason to worry."

Frowning, he glanced past the gatehouse where the portcullis with its sharp bars was suspended above. "Fine, fine," he muttered, "but be quick about it. I promised Lord Payton that I would look after everyone while he was away."

"You mean Lady Apryll," Geneva said, wondering at Hadrian's slip of the tongue.

His nostrils flared smugly. "Aye, I mean the lady."

"And is not Sir Brennan in charge while Lady Apryll is away?"

"Of course he is," the self-centered man of God said with a nod. "I but do Brennan's bidding. He asked me to tend to the servants and peasants while he is busy with more important matters."

"Such as?" she asked, smelling a lie.

"Running the keep, of course. He has much to do with the garrison, legal arguments and dealing with that miserable steward, Andrew. Why the lady keeps him is something only God the Father can divine."

She heard a shuffling and saw Father Benjamin walking with a young yellow-haired boy of six or seven who was his guide for the day. "What goes here?" he asked, his sightless eyes looking the wrong direction, toward the carter's hut where a wheelwright was mending a broken cart wheel.

"Geneva wants to wander around the forest gathering nuts and roots and herbs," Hadrian snorted, and the blind priest turned his head to face his younger cohort.

"And you disapprove?"

"'Tis not safe."

"Ah, this is where you and I disagree," the older man said with a kind smile as he patted his young guide's head with gentle fingers. "The Lord will protect her as He protects all His children. Go, Geneva, be off, and if you find any of that root that tastes of anise, bring a little back to me."

"I shall," she promised and hurried through the gate before Hadrian came up with any more excuses to keep her within Serennog's crumbling walls.

She had to right the wrong that she'd committed,

the sin of a lie. Oh, she'd been a fool. Because she was in love. With a man who could never give her his heart.

Mayhap because he had no heart to give.

Chapter Twelve

Now! Try to break free now!

Devlynn's breathing was even and slow as if he'd fallen asleep, though Apryll could not see his eyes. If the hard length of him was to be believed he was still aroused, for she felt his member pressed into the cleft of her buttocks. Every time she moved, or he shifted slightly, the pressure moved and created unholy feelings deep within her.

She had tried to pull away several times but each time she attempted to ease out of his grasp, he responded by holding her even more tightly.

She'd dozed on and off and the bright day had darkened as clouds had blocked the sun.

She was warm on the bed and, ridiculously, felt more secure and safe than she had ever since she'd agreed to the idiocy of raiding Black Thorn. Ah, to relax and sleep, to find some peace in slumber.

But not here. Not with Devlynn. Not when she needed to escape.

She eased her body from his, slowly, putting inches of air between them, trying to slip her hands free of his hard grasp. His fingers seemed to slacken and her heart leapt. Mayhap she could get away, take whatever horses were left and leave him here alone.

She smiled for she wanted to escape for reasons other than her freedom. She wanted to prove to him that she was sly and able to best him. That she was a worthy adversary. And yet . . . a rebellious womanly part of her wanted to stay here in this bed, to nestle up against him and pretend that he cared for her, that they were lovers, that he would protect her.

She scowled at the thought. How could she be such a goose? She was his worst enemy, a woman who had dared lead a band of thieves and kidnappers over the threshold of Black Thorn. He would never trust her again. Not even if she returned his son. Nay, the baron of Black Thorn would be here and evermore her sworn enemy. She had to break free.

She edged farther still, sliding her hands slowly, ever so painstakingly out of his grip. One foot was free and she inched it to the edge of the bed. Yes, yes . . . now her legs and buttocks as her fingers were slipping steadily from his fingers.

She began to sweat with the effort of being so quiet.

Outside the wind raced and a few drops of rain began to fall, plunking against the tent and sliding down its sides. *Lord help me*, Apryll silently prayed and, just to make certain that she was heard, put up a mental prayer to the Great Mother as well.

The other foot had caught its mate, but still her arms were stretched. Until . . . oh, by the gods, his fingers opened and she moved across the bed to—

Thump!

He was on her quick as a tiger pouncing, pinning her flat against the mattress with his body, his chest pushed hard against her breasts. "Think you it would be so easy to fool me again, lady?" he asked, his eyes dark silver in the shadowy tent.

"I—I needs to relieve myself," she said, ready with the lie.

"Then why not wake me?"

"'Tis a private matter," she said as if miffed.

"I would walk you outside."

"I can do it myself."

"Oh, nay, little one. Not after you have twice eluded me and my men. So?"

"I'll wait," she replied, not relishing the thought of him following after her through the naked brush to a somewhat private spot where she could untie her breeches. "Until dark."

"Whatever you wish." But he didn't move. His chest was crushing hers, his breath warm and enticing upon her neck, and he was staring at her with a look that she could only describe as hunger.

Inside she melted, her blood heating despite the cold winter day. "What I wish is for you to get off of me," she said breathlessly.

He lifted a skeptical dark brow. "So that you can run away?"

"So that I can breathe!"

His smile twisted in sardonic disrespect as he eyed the rapid rise and fall of her chest. "You seem to be breathing easily enough."

She tried to wriggle away, but his weight kept her flat on her back and as she moved he placed one arm through her legs, the other plucking at the laces of her tunic.

She gasped. "What are you doing?"

"Perhaps I should see for myself if, indeed, you cannot get air," he said.

"Nay! You have no right."

"No, you have no right. None. Not one. You gave them all up when you breached my keep and stole from me." Slowly he slid one of the laces through the eyelets holding the tunic together. The thin strand of leather scraped against her skin. She squirmed. The arm hooked between her legs pushed upward so that the bulge of his muscle was pressed to that intimate juncture as the flat of his hand slid beneath the hem of her tunic to brush against the bare flesh of her back.

"This is monstrous," she breathed but felt a throb of desire deep within, a wanton lust that she denied.

He pulled the leather lace from the tunic. "Monstrous? My touch? Compared with taking my child, murdering my guards, stealing my horses and breaking into my treasury? This—touching you—is monstrous?"

"A gentleman would never treat a lady so."

"A lady would never commit the sins and deception you have." He stared at the open V of the tunic and the wild beating of her pulse. There was hunger in his gaze and lust, a quicksilver shadow of indecision against features chiseled as if in stone.

Oh, he was a handsome devil and capable of dark, dangerous seduction. Had she not been thinking of laying with him in order to get him to sleep so that she might elude him? Could she do it? Give up her body to save her keep?

Now, staring into those flinty-hot eyes, she knew that should she lay with him, 'twould be only the start. His gaze promised a taste of delicious and decadent delights that, she knew, would leave her craving more.

Slowly, he leaned forward and with his tongue

pushed the slit over her breasts further open. Her skin tingled at the wet, strong touch.

"Nay—do not—ooh—"

He laved at the circle of bones at her throat, then whispered across them, "Mayhap now you will talk to me, Lady Apryll."

"Talk?"

"Tell me what you planned when entering my castle, why you stole from me, where you took my boy."

"I—I—told you."

His lips nipped at the soft flesh under her chin. She trembled. Oh, what would it feel like to have those hot lips upon her own?

"You told me your brother betrayed you because he wants to wreak vengeance against me."

"'Tis true."

His mouth scraped down her neck, concentrating again on the gap in her tunic. Hot air slipped beneath the coarse fabric and her nipples hardened in anticipation. Dear God, she *wanted* him to kiss her there.

The fingers on her back began to knead her flesh. "Tell me, Apryll," he said, nudging the fabric of her tunic with his nose as his fingers massaged the small of her back, drawing her closer, his arm pressed oh, so torturously close to the center of her womanhood.

Blood rushed through her veins as his teeth nipped, his lips caressed and his tongue washed her skin, searching lower, touching the tops of her breasts, making them full while far below she felt a great yawning, a dusky want that swirled deep within.

"Tell me what I want to know."

"I told you. We were to meet at Serennog, though I knew not about . . . about the boy."

He nipped at her again. "Liar."

"'Tis the truth. We split up at the fork in the road, north of Black Thorn, near . . . near the old mill . . . oooh . . ." There was a dampness between her legs now, warm and oozing, a slickness she knew was to welcome a man . . . this man . . . oh, God, what was she thinking? She could not lay with him.

"Why did you divide your forces?"

"To confuse your soldiers. We knew . . . we knew you would give chase and . . . oh, please . . ."

"Please what?" he asked.

"Please . . ." She wanted to beg for him to strip her bare and take her virginity, do anything to end this sweet torment tearing her up inside. Instead, she said, "Please stop."

"That is what you want?"

"Yes."

He slid his hand inside her tunic and rubbed a thumb over her nipple. "'Tis not what your body says, *m'lady*. It cries out for me."

"Nay—"

"Oh, yes, and . . ." He shifted, removing the arm wedged between her legs so that he could position himself there, his body atop hers, his legs long against hers, his manhood hard and stiff upon her abdomen. ". . . and I want you, as you can tell. 'Twould be easy enough, methinks, but not until you confide in me, give me Yale's location."

"Payton told me not, but I would think he would take the boy to Serennog and hold him prisoner until he bargained with you." She was fighting to speak coherently, for she could barely concentrate with his cock so close to the center of her femininity. The back of her throat tightened and an aching want throbbed for the feel of him.

He sighed. Shook his head and, in one swift motion, rolled off of her. Before she could move, he peeled the tunic from her and lifted her hands above her head to bind them with the leather laces he'd taken from her neckline.

"Nay, you cannot. What are you thinking?" she threw out at him, horrified that he could see her nakedness. She struggled to her feet and he pushed her gently back onto the mattress.

"Where is my boy?"

"With my brother."

"Where?"

"Mayhap at the keep by now. Why do you not believe me?"

"Because you lie, lady. You lie through those beautiful teeth of yours and I need the truth."

"Which is all I have given you," she argued as he stared at her bare breasts.

"God, you be a beauty," he said, and the bulge in his beeches appeared larger. "A treacherous, lying beauty." Raindrops peppered the tent now, running down the sides, and Devlynn, as if appalled by his purely male response to her, strode out of the tent.

"You cannot leave me like this," she cried. "I'll freeze."

He felt a prick of conscience. What possessed him to act so? Aye, he'd wanted to pry information from her, to be sure, but he'd be lying to himself if he didn't admit that a part of him wanted to see her naked, to hear her beg for him to bed her, to listen to her moan as he stroked her. It had been years since he'd wanted a woman, lusted after one so. And now his thoughts were filled with touching her in the most intimate places, kissing her lips, her throat and breasts. He would spread those long, alluring legs and probe her with hand, tongue and . . . stop! His member was so hard it ached, throbbed against his breeches.

Christ Jesus, he was a fool. Beguiled by the wench, half mad with desire for her. 'Twas idiocy.

Striding around the campsite, he pushed all thoughts of her aside as he added wood to the fire and felt the icy drops of rain slither down his neck and beneath his collar to cool his blood. Being this close to her was madness.

He could not forget that all he wanted from her was to find his son.

But the thought of punishing her in the most erotic and carnal of ways still blistered through his brain and he knew that if they didn't find Yale and soon, he would bed the bitch and, he feared, never be the same.

"Still no word from our brother?" Miranda asked as she found Collin half in his cups, brooding by the fire.

"Nay."

Bronwyn scampered up the stairs and whistled for the dogs, laughing gaily as they bounded after her.

"Nor did you find the woman?"

"Nay again, sister," Collin growled, gulping from his mazer and snapping his fingers for the page. "Another," he ordered, then, thinking better of it, kept his cup. "Bring the jug."

"You have duties," Miranda reminded him.

"To hell with them. The woman is nowhere to be found. The guards have found her not. Bloody hell." He straightened from Devlynn's chair and his back popped in a loud series.

"All of the guests have gone."

"And good riddance." He glanced around the

room, where ivy, holly and mistletoe still draped the
mantle and walls, and most of the candles had burned
down. The rushes were dirty from the revels and he
was weary. Being lord, even for a day, was exhausting.
All the petty squabbles that he was expected to smooth
over, all the worries and responsibilities. Aye, 'twas
too much trouble.

The page returned with the jug of wine and Collin's
mood improved. "Mayhap the woman drowned in the
moat while trying to escape." He sighed as he thought
of her comeliness. "A pity," he thought aloud, for he
had envisioned himself bedding her . . . once Devlynn
had his fill of her, of course.

At that thought his nostrils flared, for it bothered
him to be second born and therefore second best. He'd
thought he would enjoy playing the part of baron but
found it really, dreadfully tiresome.

"What have you done to the guard who let Lady
Apryll escape?"

"Locked him away," Collin said with a lift of his
shoulder. He poured himself another cup of wine and
held it up, silently offering a drink to his sister. She
shook her head. "Yes, I left the sentry in the very cell
where Lady Apryll was to be held captive, with the
bucket in which she was to relieve herself. Devlynn
can deal with him when he returns."

"I see." Miranda's eyes clouded. Her thoughts
seemed far away as she walked to a window and
stared at the sleet falling from the leaden sky. "Let us
pray it is soon that Yale is found and our brother
brings him back to us."

"Ah, yes, the family together again." Collin took a
long swallow of wine.

"'Twould be a blessing," Violet said as she entered

the room, her head tilted regally, her tiny mouth a knot. "You know 'tis what your mother wants."

"Our mother is dead," Collin reminded her, irritated at the old woman's addled state. One never knew if Violet was coherent or not.

"I know she is dead! But 'tis what she would have asked."

Collin stuffed his nose in his mazer. He did not need to hear the old woman's prattlings for the dozenth time in a week.

"Morgan, your sire, he was a bad seed, you know. I hate to speak so of your father, but 'tis true. He was powerful and used that power against other baronies, some of which were our allies. And the women . . . his conquests of which he bragged so often, broke your mother's heart, you know. Broke it."

"So she died of a broken heart, is that what you're trying to tell us?" Collin asked, ignoring the dark look his sister was sending him.

"She died in childbirth, of course. But aye, Morgan trampled all over her heart. She loved him and that was her curse."

"Is it not a woman's lot?" Collin mocked.

"Hush!" Miranda took the older woman's velvet-draped arm. "Come, Aunt Vi, let's leave Collin to his drink. He's in a foul mood."

"Well, of course he is, dear, he's just found out that he's not cut out to be a baron." Violet hoisted her pert little nose toward the ceiling and huffed out of the room. Miranda, escorting her, sent a scathing look over her shoulder to her brother.

"And a nice day to you, too, Auntie," Collin muttered, lifting his cup in mock salute to the two headstrong women. He wondered why he bothered with his family.

"I heard that," Aunt Violet called over her shoulder. "Trust me, neither I nor your mother, if she were alive would approve. You should curtail your affinity for old wine and young women, Collin. 'Twould serve you better!"

The old lady was daft. Completely addled, though he heard her tittering seep down the hallway and wondered if she had more of her mind than he thought.

So where the hell was Devlynn?

Collin strode to the window, looked out at the bleak day and slammed the shutters closed. Devlynn should have returned or sent a messenger by this time. Then again, it was so like the bastard not to keep him informed.

Scowling darkly, Collin tossed back the rest of his drink and settled into Devlynn's chair again. He rested one booted ankle on the other knee. Unfortunately there was nothing to do but wait.

Chapter Thirteen

Hoofbeats shattered the stillness and Devlynn, who had spent the last quarter hour stirring the fire and standing in the sleet until his manhood had softened, flipped open the flap and stepped into the tent again.

Apryll was lying on the pallet, her eyes closed, her breathing even, the furs pulled haphazardly over her breasts. He felt instant remorse. What had he been doing? Goading her sexually? Threatening her and promising her and torturing her in an effort to find out Yale's whereabouts?

Or to satisfy some baser need in yourself?

She appeared to sleep and her mouth was slightly open, a perfect rosebud, the glint of white teeth visible, a tangle of blond hair falling all about her head upon the pallet. Aye, she was lovely. A temptress. And yet, despite all she'd done, the pain she'd caused, there was the hint of innocence in her eyes, a curiosity and intelligence that touched him on a deeper, more disturbing level.

He would not allow himself to be attracted to her; 'twas impossible. Not until Yale was found. And even then, once the boy was safe, Devlynn could never trust the lying, murdering wench.

He gazed down at her, at the arms bound uncomfortably above her head, and he bent down on a knee to untie the leather straps. There was nowhere she could run where he could not catch her; he'd only restrained her to make a point, to ensure her subservience, though, from the toss of her hair and the defiance she'd shown as he'd bared her breasts and tied her hands over her head, she'd never conceded to him. He hadn't broken her spirit.

Is that what you want? To break this proud, bold woman? To strip her bare and see her shivering and crying in a corner?

His jaw tightened and he discarded the image. Apryll would never break . . . but oh, she would bend and how he would love to be the one who was bending her. Just at the thought of it, his manhood twitched.

She sighed and rolled over upon the bed, curled in a small ball and continued sleeping peacefully.

Over the sound of the sleet, he heard horses approaching. Finally. He flipped open the flap to step back into the wind and rain.

The hunting party had returned with a small stag, a boar and several doves.

"A feast tonight, eh?" Lloyd said, proud of his skills.

"Good work."

"The lady . . . she's still in the tent?" Lloyd stole a glance at the tent and licked his thick lips as he eyed the flap. "She's a wild one in bed, I'm guessin', one who could go all night long. Ah, I'd like me a piece of her, I would, but those spells and chants and—say wha—? Ouch, fer Chrissakes, m'lord, yer tearin' at me chest hairs!"

Devlynn's fingers fisted in the fat man's mantel and he dragged him off his feet so that their noses were nearly touching, Lloyd's flat, oft-broken beak so near Devlynn's straighter nose that he could smell the man. "You are not to refer to our captive as anything but Lady Apryll. You are not to make jokes at her expense. And you are not to inquire about her person. Understand?"

"A murderin' bitch! That's what she is. Seth's dead. Saunders! Others, too."

"Do I have to remind you of your station, Sir Lloyd?" Devlynn demanded, his lips barely moving, sleet washing down his face as the other men, wide-eyed, looked on.

"Nay, m'lord, nay."

"Then get about skinning the stag and boar." Slowly Devlynn released his grip and Lloyd's boots sank into the mud. "You, James, help Lloyd, and the rest of you set up a lean-to. This blasted weather isn't going away and we'll need shelter until we ride out."

"So there's been no word from Bennett then?" Lloyd dared ask, sniffing loudly and wiping his nose on his sleeve.

"Nay."

The scout had not returned and Devlynn glowered at the empty trail. He was eager to ride ahead and find his son. His muscles were edgy and taut, his entire body restless. Being near the woman only made him more so and he ached for some kind of respite. He could lose himself in her, spread her legs and bury his shaft deep in her deliciously moist warmth . . . but 'twould only lead to more trouble.

If only the damned scout would return.

He helped the men build the lean-to by stretching hides over a brace made of sticks they gathered and whittled into shape. When the lean-to was finished it was only shoulder high, large enough for the men to sit near the fire while watching the stag and boar sizzle over the coals, but not tall enough to allow anyone to stand.

'Twas good enough for one night, Devlynn thought as he looked into the fire and watched smoke curl into the darkening heavens. James turned the spit. Fat slid onto the coals, hissing and sizzling as it burned, and the scent of roasting meat made Devlynn's stomach growl. He stretched an arm over his head and yearned for slumber. Tired to his bones, he dared not try to sleep next to Apryll.

He couldn't trust himself around her. She was forbidden fruit and he a starving man.

Settling onto his haunches, he stared at the fire, watching the golden flames crackle and spark, his ears straining as he listened for the sound of hoofbeats. Where the devil was Bennett? Surely he would return by nightfall.

Thinking of the scout and what harm might have happened to him, Devlynn picked up a wet stick, tore it apart and threw the bits of wood into the fire.

Was his hostage telling the truth? Had Payton stolen the boy away to Serennog? It seemed the logical thing to do and yet Devlynn wasn't convinced. Why not then straight to the castle? Why take the time to try and confuse the trackers by splitting up at the junction in the road? Why not keep the band together, for surely there was safety in numbers?

He glanced toward the tent where Apryll slept and

wondered of the dreams running through her pretty head. Dreams of lovemaking? Or of Yale? Plans for escape? She knew more than she was saying, he could see it in her eyes.

And, God help him, what beautiful eyes they were. Eyes that had somehow reached deep into his soul and cursed him forever.

Apryll awoke in the darkness and for several seconds she didn't know where she was. A warm reddish glow was faintly visible through some kind of screen and she was lying on a hard bed with furs tucked to her chin. The smell of roasting venison and smoke touched her nostrils and her stomach cramped in anticipation of food.

Somewhere nearby a dog let out a soft woof.

Her heart sank as she remembered. She was a captive. To Devlynn of Black Thorn, the man who had dared bare her body and bind her wrists. But her hands were free . . . and her tunic nearby. Hastily she flung the hated shirt over her head, slipping her arms through its scratchy sleeves, but she could not lace the slit in front as the ties were missing.

Damn the beast of Black Thorn! Embarrassment burned the back of her neck and her cheeks when she remembered him stripping her and tying her hands over her head. If she ever got the chance, she'd gladly return the favor. But for now . . . she slunk from the bed and, using her hands, searched for a sag in the hem of the tent, a spot where there would be enough room to wiggle beneath the folds, squeeze her body through the opening and . . . what? Scurry through the forest in the darkness? Steal a horse? Try to outwit the dog? For the love of Mary, she needed a plan. She heard footsteps and flung herself onto the pallet, as if she'd just been awakening.

The tent flap opened and the Lord of Black Thorn, carrying a candle, appeared.

"I was about to wake you," he said, as if they were fast friends . . . or lovers. His eyes scanned her quickly donned tunic, but he didn't comment. "'Tis time to eat."

Apryll's stomach growled, reminding her how long it had been since she'd had a meal. Though she loathed facing the men who had captured her, especially the gruff, heavy one called Lloyd, she complied, pushing herself to her feet and pausing to draw on her boots.

As she slipped through the tent's opening, she surveyed the campfire where the pig-eyed soldier and another man were slicing up thick pieces of charred meat. There were puddles on the ground but the sleet had stopped and the night was icy cold, the wind singing through barren branches overhead.

Devlynn cut off a slice of venison for her and they ate seated on mossy rocks, warmed somewhat by the fire that flickered and snapped, tiny embers rising to the sky in the thick, curling smoke.

The soldiers sat in a shelter that faced the fire and the fat one's eyes glowed evilly, red embers reflected in their slitted depths. Lord, he was a hateful creature.

"Where are the others?" she asked, licking her fingers, for the meat was the best she'd ever eaten. She licked the grease covering her lips, then wiped her cheek with her sleeve. "The scout. Has he not returned?"

"Not yet," Devlynn admitted, glancing toward the path as if willing the man to appear. He tossed the dog a bone and the cur grabbed her morsel and slunk to a spot between two trees where she began gnawing on the fleshy rib.

Devlynn stood and dusted his hands.

"What if he doesn't return?" Apryll asked.

Devlynn's visage hardened. "You'd best hope that he appears and soon, for if he doesn't I will assume that he came upon foul play at your brother's hand."

"He may have left on his own."

Thin lips flattened. "Nay, Bennett is loyal." But she'd planted a seed of doubt in Devlynn's mind. Someone was a spy; more than one man. Someone had allowed Apryll and her band of thugs into Black Thorn and someone had helped her escape from the hermit's cell in the tower. He considered the men with whom he rode—these who had followed him along this fork and the others: Kirby, Spencer, and even Rudyard, captain of the guard. Were they loyal? Or traitors? Would they serve him, or willingly slit his throat in the middle of the night? Staring across the fire to the men who had sworn their fealty to him, Devlynn realized he knew little about them—their lives, their ambitions, their dreams.

Mayhap their loyalties weren't so steadfast.

Wondering about their allegiance, he took a long pull from the jug of wine, then wiped the back of his hand over his lips. What cur who'd sworn to serve Black Thorn had turned traitor and helped with the abduction of his son? Had one man within his trusted army killed Seth or Saunders . . . who? Who would rob him of his horses, money and jewels? Who hated him so and had such ambition, such daring?

A dozen faces flashed through Devlynn's mind. His

hand curled into a fist as he realized, not for the first time, that he could trust no one.

Especially this Jezebel claiming to be a lady.

The men had finished eating, tossing bones toward the fire, taking a long drought of wine and wrapping their cloaks about them as they settled in for the night beneath the lean-to.

"I'll take the first watch," Devlynn announced as he glanced at the darkness beyond the shifting circle of light cast by the fire. "We ride at dawn."

"And what of Bennett, m'lord? What if he doesn't return?" Lloyd asked.

"We ride without him."

"Humph. Mayhap the witch there, she can conjure him fer us." Emboldened by too much wine, he sent Apryll a look of lusty loathing.

"'Tis not my specialty," she said tartly. "I'm best at turning fat, lazy soldiers into toads."

Lloyd snorted a laugh.

"Toads with warts upon their bodies and skin that itches as if it's on fire," she added calmly, then frowned as if suddenly remembering something important. "But . . . I must admit, sometimes the spell goes awry and the change isn't complete, so I'm left with a fat, lazy soldier with warts and pimples upon his skin and a hunger for flies." She leaned back on her heels and glared at Lloyd through serious gold eyes. "Do not doubt me, Sir Lloyd," she said and casually slid a finger into the mud, where she began drawing runes. "Because once the spell has been cast it can never, never be broken and 'twould be a pity to think that you would spend the rest of your days at the dung heap, hoping your next meal would land and you could snap it up with your slimy tongue."

"You lie," he charged.

"Mmmm." She continued drawing and Lloyd squirmed, jabbed his elbows at James and pretended not to notice, but his eyes continually flickered back to the lady in a huntsman's garb, a woman who concentrated on the complex figure she sketched in the mud.

The little golden-haired vixen. She knew exactly what she was doing to Lloyd, though the soldier deserved it. 'Twas time to end this nonsense. Devlynn leaned over and whispered in her ear, "You've had your fun, now, 'tis time for you to return to the tent."

Her brows pulled into a single, unhappy line. "May I first be allowed to wash and . . ." She cleared her throat. ". . . I needs relieve myself."

Of course she did. He took her arm and without any word dragged her through the brush to a spot where the stream pooled and eddied beneath the roots of ancient trees upon the banks. "Here." He let go of her. And waited.

"You can go now."

"I think not."

"But—"

"*You* can go now," he said meaningfully and she gasped at his insolence.

"M'lord, I needs privacy."

"I think not. Did you not use this same ploy on the night Yale was taken?" he asked. "Now . . . wash and do whatever else you have to. I will remain here."

She sucked in her breath, then, in the gathering moonlight, muttered something about bullheaded beasts with ill manners and added more loudly, "At least turn your back, *m'lord*. 'Tis the gentlemanly thing to do."

"I thought we already discussed my lack of gentlemanly skills. Now, take care of your needs and be quick about it. I have not all night."

"Bastard," he thought she muttered as she sidled to a spot behind a tree, where all he could glimpse through a fork in the trunk was her flaxen hair, shining silver in the moonlight. While she was half hidden, he relieved himself as well, forcing his cock to soften so that he could create a stream that he arced at a flat rock. The woman was more trouble than she was worth, he decided, shaking himself before stuffing his member into his breeches and lacing up. 'Twould be best to send her back to Black Thorn and lock her in a dungeon.

As if that would keep her. She's as slippery as one of the eels in the pond at the castle! You'd best keep a close eye on that one.

He glanced over his shoulder, didn't see her silhouette, and fury tore through his veins. In less than a minute she'd slipped away. Again! He was about to call out when he caught a glimpse of silver-gold hair and realized she hadn't escaped but was indeed leaning over the rocky bank of the creek and washing her face.

Mayhap he'd been too hard on her, he thought suddenly, his fury turning to fascination as she held her hair up and cleaned the smooth contour of her face with her free hand. Was it possible that she was telling him the truth? That her brother had double-crossed her? There was a part of him that wanted to believe she wasn't a part of so vile a deception as to kidnap his boy, but he couldn't forget that she was the bait, the lure that kept his guard down in the plot to rob him blind and steal his son. Nay, he couldn't trust her and it would serve him well to remember it.

"Hurry," he yelled, his voice echoing through the icy, brittle forest. "As I said, we've not got 'til dawn."

"Coming," she shot back, and he saw her straighten, pull up the hem of her tunic and dry her face with the rough cloth. He caught a glimpse of her flat, white abdomen and his crotch tightened. Never had a woman affected him so. Not even Glynda, his wife, and for that betrayal he felt a jab of guilt.

Suddenly Apryll appeared before him and walked stiffly along the path to the firelight flickering through a copse of pines. Most of the men were already wrapped in their cloaks, lying upon the ground, though James was scraping the stag's hide clean with his knife, and another man watered and fed the horses while Lloyd sharpened his sword, frowning as he tested the sharp blade between his thick, calloused fingers.

Obediently Apryll ducked into the tent and, as he'd promised, Devlynn stood watch.

"We only have feed enough for three more days," Rearden, the man who'd tended to the small herd, advised him.

Devlynn nodded. "We'll buy grain at the next village."

"Aye."

"So we ride tomorrow whether Bennett returns or nay?" Lloyd observed, running the whetting stone over his blade again.

"Aye."

"And what of the woman?"

"She rides with us."

Lloyd stopped stroking his sword long enough to look up at Devlynn. "A tracking party be no place for a woman." He glanced meaningfully at the tent.

"They're useless creatures, you know, good for only one thing."

"And what would that be?" Devlynn asked in a low whisper, the muscles at the back of his neck bunching.

"Warming a man's bed. 'Tis all."

"What about motherhood?"

"'Tis overrated. Me own mum, she died givin' me birth, she did, and it hurt me not." His smile was all knowing. "Your own son, he has no mother and he seems a fine lad."

"He has Miranda and Aunt Violet to guide him."

"And he'd do just as well without 'em."

The man was a fool.

"Lady Apryll rides with us," Devlynn said, tired of the argument. "And I'll hear no disrespect."

"She's a prisoner, ain't she?" Lloyd said.

"Aye, and a lady."

Lloyd snorted but held his tongue and Devlynn, jaw tight, resisted the urge to throw a fist in his fleshy face.

Apryll listened to the argument and with the light from the fire as her guide searched the tent. If only she could find a knife of some kind, something sharp enough to make a slit in the tent wall, she could make her escape now, while the men were talking between themselves, while the dog was happily chewing on her bone, before Devlynn returned to the tent.

She could cut through the forest on foot, again use the stream to confuse that miserable dog and find a horse to steal or beg a ride from a farmer's wagon once she found the main road.

And you'll be caught. The men have horses and that damned dog. They'll track you within hours . . . no, you need a better scheme. You have to sneak past Devlynn's small army, steal the horses, make sure that you have time on your side.

Oh, fuss and bother, what to do? She found no knife, not even the one that Devlynn had removed from her when he'd taken her captive again. 'Twas an impossible situation and yet one she had to rectify.

She lay back on the pallet, feigning sleep should Devlynn step inside, and tried to come up with some scheme, a means of escape. But as the hours ticked by, the voices of Black Thorn's soldiers stilled, and the campfire glowed dim, she found no way to save herself.

All too soon she heard a shuffling of feet, Devlynn's deep voice ordering another man to stand watch.

She didn't move. Didn't want to think about what would happen next. She had only to remember the last time they'd lain on the pallet together—how his hands and mouth had teased her, tempted her and caused a deep, shameful want within her.

Even when he'd bound her hands and bared her breasts there had been disgrace, yes, but also a bit of desire . . . an awakening of a dark, hungry lust within her, an emotion more disturbing than the man himself.

The flap fell away and the Lord of Black Thorn entered.

Chapter Fourteen

Devlynn slipped onto the pallet beside her, his large frame cuddling up to hers. Apryll forced her breathing to sound regular though her heart was beating wildly, her lungs constricted. She let her mouth go slack though every muscle in her body was stretched taut, every nerve fiber jangled. How could she bear the next hour or so next to him, feeling his body curve over hers?

Be calm. Pretend. Relax. Do not *let him know that you are awake.*

She felt him shift, sensed that he levered up on one elbow to look down upon her. What could he see in the darkness? His breath was warm as it whispered against her face and ruffled her hair. She let out a soft sigh, then nearly flinched when she felt his finger trace the welt upon her cheek.

"I'll kill the bastard," he vowed. "For Yale and for this pain to Apryll . . . oh Christ Jesus, what am I saying?" There was a tortured edge to his voice, a hint that he felt the same confusion as did she.

He flung an arm around her waist and burrowed under the blankets, drawing her close, fitting her body next to his. She knew he had to be tired, that by now exhaustion should bring deep sleep within minutes, so she didn't stir, listened to the sound of his breathing and saw the shadow of the sentry playing upon the tent as the man paced in front of the fire.

Sleep, she thought, hoping all the men, the horses and especially the bloody hound would drift into a deep impenetrable slumber and she could make good her escape.

Devlynn burrowed further under the furs and the arm around her reached beneath her tunic, his hand scaling her ribs until his fingers found her breast.

Her stomach tightened. Her blood heated and despite her intentions of feigning sleep her nipples puckered. He rubbed a calloused thumb over the tip of one. Dear God, what sweet, sweet torment. Her breasts seemed to fill, as if they were engorged with milk, and Devlynn groaned.

Was he asleep?

Or very awake?

She knew not. His fingers were warm and he breathed against her shoulder onto a spot on her neck that tingled in anticipation. *Stay distant. Do not let your body betray you. You must escape! Remember that above all else, Apryll.*

With a groan, he tugged, rolling her over so that she lay on top of him, her spine against his chest. Both his arms surrounded her, both hands reached beneath her tunic. Oh, Lord, this was madness! Two sets of fingers massaged her breasts and it was all she could do not to move her buttocks rhythmically against his abdomen and the tip of his manhood, that hidden head she felt pronging upward against his breeches.

Oh, so little separated their bodies. She wanted to

arch and writhe against him, to twist about, face him and cover his mouth with hers, yet she dared not. His lips brushed against her shoulder and she shuddered, wanting, longing, aching for the dark void deep within her to be filled.

In her mind's eye she saw herself naked, turning upon him, running her fingers through the stiff hairs of his chest, feeling his scarred, strident warrior muscles, searching out the flat nubs that were his nipples. She imagined her naked body sliding downward, mounting his thick, smooth shaft, feeling him fill her, experiencing the wonder of her maidenhead shattering, knowing what it was finally like to be a woman . . . to take a lover. To join with the Lord of Black Thorn.

Oh, God, what was she thinking?

As his fingers kneaded her flesh, 'twas all she could do to remain immobile, pliant as if in sleep, and unresponsive. His hands tightened and he moved beneath her, his stiff manhood prodding, poking, rubbing against the rough fabric of her breeches, teasing the cleft of her buttocks, making her wet.

She could stand it no longer and moaned softly, curving her spine, wondering what would be the loss to allow him entrance into a body that was quivering inside, hot with want, anxious to feel all of him.

One of his hands lowered, dipped beneath the tie of the uncomfortable breeches, skimmed her flesh with expert fingers that caressed her skin and invaded the thatch of curls below her navel.

She trembled.

No! She couldn't allow this!

But she didn't move, just closed her eyes and

sucked in her breath as his fingers explored further, touching the edges of her most secret places, parting her, sliding inside.

"Aye, little one, you want me," he whispered. "Even in slumber, you want me."

He thought she was sleeping. Oh, Lord, could she keep up the deception? Would her body allow it?

"You're wet for me, Apryll of Serennog, and I'm hard for you . . . so hard. I could take you in one thrust, lady."

Sweat prickled her crown. 'Twould be so easy to turn in his arms and kiss him, aye, and beg him to do just as he suggested.

His finger delved deeper, touching a spot she didn't know existed. She let out a soft groan.

"Oh, you like that, do you?" His finger teased, moving against her, creating heat in a body already aflame. She thought she would go mad with this new anxious wanting. "And would you like my tongue as well? Or just my cock?"

His *tongue?* She'd heard of this before but had no idea he could cause such an ache with a mere suggestion of something she'd heretofore thought repellent. Now the thought of his mouth upon her, touching, tasting, caressing any part of her body sounded like heaven . . . nay, hell . . . nay . . . oh, God, he was parting her again, inserting another finger. She wiggled involuntarily, taking more of him, wanting everything.

"Be you awake, Lady Apryll . . . can you not feel my lust for you? How much I want you? You're so hot and wet . . . and I bet you taste of woman and wine together." He whispered his lusty words against her bare shoulder while exploring the cleft between her legs with one set of fingers and massaging one breast with his other hand.

"I'm going to bed you, little one. But not now," he said, slowly withdrawing his hand and leaving her yearning for more of his touch.

Nay! He couldn't stop now, not when there was so much she wanted to know, so much he could teach her, when she was so close to . . . to . . . what?

"Oh, no, not now . . . not when you sleep, but when you're awake, then, lady, when you can look into my eyes and watch me touch you, witness the length of me claiming you, then . . . then I'll show you what it means to be bedded and bedded well."

Was he mocking her as he extracted his fingers? Had he known all along that she was awake? He lowered her onto the pallet beside him. In the darkness, without a word, he adjusted her breeches and tunic, smoothing her clothes over her as if he'd never disturbed her, never so much as traced a finger along her skin. Her body cried silently for more of his touch.

With one arm securing her to the mattress, he pulled the covers to her neck and whispered, "Pleasant dreams, little one." And then he chuckled softly as if everything that had gone before was a game—a game for his amusement and her humiliation.

Her cheeks burned in shame and yet . . . despite her embarrassment, she couldn't wait until the next time he touched her. At that thought she nearly cried out. There would be no next time.

She would see to it.

Tonight she would escape. Somehow, someway, she'd put as much distance as possible between herself and this horrid, intriguing, mystifying man.

*   *   *

"So where are the others?" the boy asked, eyeing Payton from the other side of the fire. "Your band of cutthroats and thieves, where be they?"

"They shall come. On the morrow," Payton replied, though, in truth, he wondered as he searched the darkness through the window. He'd paced all day. Waiting. Checking the supplies, keeping the damned fire lit, every second aware that Devlynn and his army could appear. The plan was that they would meet here by nightfall of this day. And yet there had been no sign of Bernard or Samuel, who had angled east. They were to have cut back on the far side of the river and arrived here no later than nightfall. As for Roger, Isaac and Melvynn, those who had traveled along the ridge with the torches, they were to have led Devlynn's army on a great chase, splitting up further and riding here. At least one of them should have appeared.

Then there were those he'd left at Black Thorn, the spies who had helped him, those disloyal to Devlynn. He'd expected a report from one of them . . . and yet, nothing.

And what about Apryll? Where was she?

Had they all fallen? Had every one of his men and his headstrong sister been captured? Had Payton so vastly underestimated his enemy?

"This be a boring game," the boy said. He'd been whittling all day, fashioning a sword with a dull knife Payton had allowed him. "Where is my father?"

A fine question. "He's searching for you, to be sure."

"Then he will find me." Yale nodded to himself. He was so confident, so certain of his father's strengths. What would it be like to have a son, one who had abject faith in you? "And when he does, you will lose your game."

"I think not."

"My father is the best swordsman in all of Wales!"

"If you say so." Payton was tired of hearing about his enemy, a god in his son's eyes.

"Aye, he'll make short work of you and of a dozen of your men should they appear!" Payton's nerves were stretched thin and he was irritated by the lad with his incessant questions and buoyant spirit. By the gods, if he would only sleep . . . there was more of the drug and the thought of doctoring Yale's mazer was tempting. Give the boy some wine and the potion and finally get some peace.

But he had to save the sleeping potion he'd brought for the next segment of the ride. Better to have the boy dull when they were moving him so that he would give them no trouble.

Yale stood suddenly and began slashing and parrying with his sword, moving quickly around the fire, slaying imaginary enemies. For a young one he was quick on his feet, lunged and jabbed with sure strokes, twirled and feinted effortlessly. He twirled closer to Payton, slicing his "sword" in quick strokes. Involuntarily Payton reached for his own weapon only to see the boy's smile at the thought of a real challenge.

"Ha!" Yale said, thrusting and retreating. "Should we duel, then?"

"I think not." Was the boy daft? "Your sword is wood. Mine is steel. 'Twould be no match."

"I could make you one," he offered and, swinging his "blade," watched his shadow as it danced across one of the sagging walls. Payton gritted his teeth. He needed more than a vial of the sleeping potion, he could use a vat of the stuff with this boy as his prisoner. Mayhap he should dispense with the act of this "game," tie and gag the boy and be done with it.

Suddenly Yale stopped fencing with his imaginary foe. "From now on my name shall be Death."

"Death?" Payton repeated. "Why?"

"Because all dastardly types have fiendish names. As I am part of your band"—he looked around the cavernous, dilapidated room and lifted an eyebrow to point out that there was no one else within the walls— "I shall have a dangerous name. From now on you are to call me Death. 'Tis all I will answer to."

Praise be, Payton thought, rubbing his temple, perhaps now the boy would be quiet. "Get in your blanket," Payton barked. "'Tis time for bed."

Yale didn't appear to hear.

"I said, drop the sword and go to sleep."

The boy sent him a chastising glance.

"Now!"

Not so much as a cringe.

Payton took a step forward and to his astonishment the boy, rather than cower, did the same. Payton blew out his breath and the damned kid mocked him, sighing loudly. Payton shoved his hands though his hair. The boy could not be intimidated. Would he have to actually hurt the dolt? Yale ran his own fingers through his hair and rolled his eyes in parody of his keeper.

"What's this?" Payton demanded.

"What's this?" was the reply.

"Listen, boy, if you know what's good for you you'll not—"

"Listen, boy, if you—"

Payton lunged, grabbed the kid by the front of his tunic. "Do not mock me."

"Do not mock me."

"Are you daft, boy? I could snap your neck with one hand."

"I'm not daft and my father could snap your stupid spine, bone by bone, with one finger. Now, remember, you are to call me by my new name. Death."

So be it, Payton thought. "Then, *Death*, it would serve you well to wrap yourself in one of the furs I was kind enough to give you and go to sleep." Slowly he uncurled his fingers and to his surprise the boy did as he was bid, taking his wooden sword, tucking it close to his body and using one of the furs for his blanket. He nestled into a clean spot on the floor, away from the owl droppings but close enough to the fire for warmth, and offered Payton a boyish grin.

"Good night," he said.

"Good night to you, too."

The boy just stared a him with those damnable gray eyes so like those of his father. In a gesture far older than his years, he arched one black eyebrow.

Payton understood. "Good night, *Death*."

Apparently finally satisfied, the boy closed his eyes and rolled over, facing away from the fire's shifting flames. A few seconds later he was asleep, softly snoring and thankfully not jabbering on and on.

The tense muscles of Payton's shoulders relaxed a bit and he decided to open a jug of wine.

After the last two days and nights, he deserved a drink.

Mayhap two.

Death. 'Twas a foolish name. Stupid. Proof of the boy's innocence and brainlessness. *Death*. Payton strode to the corner where the supplies were kept and glanced up at the owl's roost. The big bird had abandoned his nest to avoid the humans and fire and to hunt. *Death.*

Payton grabbed the wine jug by its handle, pulled out the cork and took a long swallow. The soothing liquid eased down his throat and he closed his mind to the thought that the boy's self-proclaimed new name might just be a premonition of what was to come.

Apryll eased her way to the side of the pallet and to her surprise, after only a bit of resistance, she eased away from her captor. Her heart thudded in her chest, beating as wildly as the wings of a suddenly caged bird, but she, ever so slowly, made her way to the flap of the tent.

She'd watched and waited, witnessed the guard's shadow stop its pacing as he sat in front of the fire. From the slump of his shoulders, she thought he might be dozing and now, as she peeked through the slit of the flap, she had the ready excuse that she had to again relieve herself, that she was certain her monthly time was upon her. The way men shied away from such talk by women, she was certain she could convince him to let her have some privacy.

As it was, she didn't need to resort to the lie, for the guard was, as she had hoped, leaning against the bole of a sturdy oak. His eyes were shut, his mouth slightly agape.

So the dog . . . where was the dog? Quickly, she scanned the camp and saw the bitch curled into a ball, only a piece of bone beside her, ears down. Fortunately the wind had kicked up again and rustled though the branches overhead. Along with the gurgle of the stream and crackle and hiss of the fire, the rush of the breeze gave her more cover than a still, quiet night. Carefully she slunk around the perimeter of the tent, ducking through the shadows to the tether line where the horses were dozing.

She searched for the fleetest, did not recognize the stallion in the dark of the night and, with freezing fingers, took the first animal she could untie, a dark mount with splashes of white upon his legs and chest.

Her ears straining for any sound from the camp, she held her breath as she wrapped the reins of her horse's bridle around her already freezing fingers. The night was bitter cold, though she was sweating from sheer nerves, her muscles tense, her mind spinning with images of what Lord Devlynn would do to her if she woke to find her missing.

Dear God, help me, she silently prayed as she led the beast along the northward path until she was certain enough distance was between her and Devlynn's band, then she swung herself astride the beast's broad back and urged him into a quick gallop. With moonlight as her guide and the wind at her back, she rode through the thickets and over the streams, heading straight to the old inn where she hoped she would find Payton and the boy.

She felt a moment's relief to be away from the camp where she'd been held prisoner and didn't wonder why she'd escaped so easily yet again.

Nor did she realize that as she guided her stolen horse down the moonlit roadway her every move was being watched and tracked.

Chapter Fifteen

"Saints be damned," Devlynn growled to himself as he watched the woman steal the brown steed and ride through the night-dark forest.

To Yale.

His smile was pure evil. She'd reacted just as he'd expected, just as he'd baited her, and he had no doubt that she would lead him straight to his son. 'Twas all part of his plan.

Though, he had to admit as he straightened from his hiding spot behind a rotting stump, falling under Apryll of Serennog's spell had not been what he'd intended. And yet he'd found her irresistible. Ah, she could be charming, and sensual, and even amusing. *And deceptive. Do not forget who invaded your castle, burned the stables and stole your son. Whether by intent or association, she is a murdering kidnapper, make no mistake!*

Angry with his conflicting emotions, he stealthily gathered a few of his things—weapons, a bit of food, a bedroll. 'Twas evident enough that one, mayhap several of the men who rode with him were traitors. But who? He eyed the sleeping men who'd been with him for years, soldiers he'd trusted, some he'd called friends.

Orwell was stretched out near the sorry lot of tethered horses, his face in repose, his aquiline nose prominent over a scruffy black beard. Friend or foe? Loyal or a traitor?

Lloyd, a big bear of a man with reddish hair and an odd sense of humor, a man who more often irritated than appeased, was now wrapped in a cloak, snoring loudly, his head propped on a mossy pillow. Was his heart true, or black as the night? Would he defend the honor of Black Thorn or gladly slit Devlynn's throat?

How could Devlynn sort out the true from the false?

The other men in this group were of no consequence, even the fool of a guard who was slumped near the fire, dozing.

Who were the traitors? *Who?* No doubt there was one, perhaps more, in this small band. But there were others who had split from him at the crossroads, and still more within the walls of Black Thorn, those who had welcomed the invaders into the castle, who had helped them escape, who had even gone so far as to release Apryll from the tower.

Someone was leading the enemy, someone who would profit from Black Thorn's fall, someone he had trusted.

'Twas his lot in life, he thought angrily as he glared at those sleeping around the campfire. He could sneak around, tie and gag each one, threaten with a blade at each lying throat, but he had no time. Each man would be stubborn, the truth not easily lodged from his lying tongue.

Nay, 'twould be better to ride alone, take the best

horse and the lead bitch and follow Apryll's trail by himself. 'Twas ironic he thought with a sneer, he, the lord, responsible for hundreds of lives, with an army of men whose sworn allegiance had come easily, now without anyone he could trust. Leader of hundreds, friend to none.

His thoughts were as dark as the stygian night as he took a short path away from the glowing embers of the fire. With a soft, nearly soundless whistle to the dog, he saddled the finest steed—a pathetic creature when compared to Phantom, one he'd tethered apart from the rest—and took off alone, urging the black steed into a quick lope to keep up with the hound, a bitch so well trained by the kennel master that she would not bay unless Devlynn gave the order.

The night was damp, thick with mist, the horse's hoofbeats muffled in the mud and leaves. Cold air pressed against his face as he leaned forward, eyes straining in the moonlight. He watched the dog silently race through the forest, nose to the wind. Within minutes, she had found the main road where instinctively she turned due north.

To Serennog.

Had Apryll told the truth? Was his child already shivering in the dungeons of that old, crumbling castle? The thought chilled him to his very core. And he didn't believe anything Apryll had claimed. He could trust her no more than any of his own men.

Someone was conspiring against him. Someone he trusted. Someone who had formed an alliance with Apryll of Serennog. His first thoughts were of his brother, as he remembered Collin dancing with Apryll, remarking on her beauty, causing jealousy to spurt through Devlynn's blood on the night of the revels.

His own brother.

But had Collin not betrayed him once before? And had it not been over a woman? Glynda's face appeared before his eyes, flashing brown eyes, white skin and straight red hair that caught in the wind. Devlynn's fingers curled more tightly over the reins. Aye, Collin could easily be a traitor.

As could Miranda. His loving sister had never approved of his leadership. And she had her own secrets to hide. Firstborn and ignored by a father who only wanted sons. Would she be so bold as to defy him?

Or Rudyard, captain of the guard and forever sullen? There was insolence in the man's eyes and disrespect as well.

Scowling, he urged the horse onward after the fleeing hound. The wind slapped his face and the moon was hardly visible, but Devlynn was determined to find Apryll and his son. Until he did, 'twas madness to try and sort it out. As soon as he caught up with Apryll again, he would find a way to force her to reveal the truth. The thought of the last time he'd been with her, how warm and lush her body had been, how the heat between them was a living, breathing thing. Oh, 'twould be a pleasure loosening her tongue.

His cock grew hard at the thought of kissing her and touching her breasts, of feeling her moisture deep inside, of hearing her soft moans . . . by the gods, he ached for her and he was suddenly uncomfortable in the saddle as he rode, the smooth, rhythmic gait of his mount forcing the leather pommel to rub against his stiff member.

What the devil was wrong with him?

He couldn't allow lust to interfere with his purpose. He had to find Yale and ensure his safety. Nothing else mattered. Certainly not bedding Lady Apryll.

For the moment, he had only to track her to the lair where Yale was held.

Yes. First he had to catch the wench.

Then, if she did not lead him to his son, God help her. He'd force the truth from her beautiful lying lips, or die in the ecstasy of trying.

At last! Through the wisps of early morning fog, Apryll spied the old inn. Firelight glowed through the windows and Devlynn's big gray destrier was tied beneath the sheltering branches of a tall pine tree. At least her brother had not altered this part of the plan, she thought as she swung off her smaller horse.

Her bones ached from her long ride, but she couldn't think of the exhaustion that threatened her, nor would she let her thoughts wander to the man she'd left in his tent, the Lord of Black Thorn, who by this time had probably awoken and discovered she'd duped him again.

With chilled fingers she tied her horse next to the stolen steed, then, squaring her shoulders and ready for battle, she marched through the sagging door of the old inn.

Payton and the boy were inside.

A doeskin robe pulled close around his neck, Yale sat near the fire while Payton poked at the embers with a long, charred stick.

At the sound of her footsteps, he whirled, free hand on the hilt of his sword.

"Sister!" His face split with a relieved grin.

"Aye, I'm alive," she spat, crossing the hard earthen floor. "No thanks to you."

"You were following me and disappeared," he argued, straightening, the flames behind him crackling hungrily over a piece of mossy wood.

The boy stood, a crude wooden sword in his hands. "Who are you?" he demanded.

Payton's eyes narrowed. "This is my sister."

"She is with us?" the boy asked, hitching his chin at Apryll.

"*Us?*" she repeated.

"Aye, she is on our side." Payton nodded.

"Wait—whose side—what side—what the devil are you talking about?"

"The game." Yale's eyebrows slammed over eyes the same silvery hue as those of his father.

"I was beginning to think that you would not arrive," Payton said quickly, dismissing the boy.

"Where are the others?"

"Not here yet."

"Captured?" she asked, thinking of the men who had risked their lives for her, for her brother.

"I know not. What happened to you?" Payton asked as the boy continued to glower at her suspiciously and the fire crackled and spewed smoke up a chimney, missing many stones.

"I was . . . detained."

"By my father!" the boy guessed, his eyes brightening expectantly. He turned on Payton and twirled his crude sword in the air. "I told you, he is coming for me."

"He's on the other side," Payton said, only confusing Apryll further.

"What the devil are you talking about?"

"The game," the boy explained, making no sense whatsoever. "What's your name?"

Her brother snapped his fingers. "Ah, forgive my manners. You two haven't met yet." One side of Payton's mouth lifted as if amused at the situation, while Apryll was ready to grab him by the throat and shake some sense into him. She shot him a look meant to warn him that they would share words later, when alone, but his cocksure grin only grew wider at her obvious vexation.

Later, she reminded herself, she would deal with him and insist they return the boy. For now, she tried to act calm. She turned her attention to her brother's hostage.

"I'm Apryll, Payton's sister."

"Lady of Serennog," Payton clarified with the hint of a sneer.

"Lady?" The boy gave her a quick once-over, eyeing the muddied huntsman's breeches and tunic. "You look not like any lady."

"It's her disguise." Payton turned toward the fire again, poking at the logs with the charred stick, and Apryll stepped closer to warm her hands. Truth to tell she was chilled to the bone, tired and hungry.

The boy wasn't impressed. "No lady I know would wear man's clothes."

"Well, I'm not like other ladies," Apryll said.

Yale snorted. Agreement or contempt? His gray eyes, so like his father's, were suspicious and his dark hair fell forward over his forehead just as Devlynn's did. Apryll felt a curious tightness in her chest at the resemblance and she hated to think what would happen should Devlynn catch up with her before she'd executed her plan to free his son.

Yale stepped closer to her, dragging the doeskin, his gaze focused upon her cheek.

"What happened to your face?" he asked impudently. "Were you in a fight?"

She touched the spot beneath her eye where Payton had struck her and sent her brother's curved back a withering glance. "Of sorts."

"And you lost?"

For the time being. Apryll's stare was as cold as death, but Payton, tending to the coals, didn't so much as glance over his shoulder. "'Twas not a contest." Apryll walked closer to the boy. "But a mistake."

"Still, you lost."

Payton's shoulders tightened and he finally dusted his hands and straightened. His face was a mask of irritation. "It does no good to ask questions!"

"He's just curious."

"He's a pain in the arse, that's what he is."

"But you brought him here."

A muscle worked in her brother's jaw. "Mayhap a mistake."

"Then—"

"No!" He flipped up a hand, cutting off her thought. "He stays. 'Tis all we have to bargain with."

The boy's eyes narrowed on his captor. "You would sell me?"

"Without a second thought," Payton snapped. "To whatever thug would pay a decent price."

"You would not!" Apryll was outraged. She once thought she knew her brother, understood what drove him, but she'd been fooled, for he was far from the boy she'd grown up with, the sibling she'd trusted. Payton had hardened over the years to become this harsh, bitter man consumed with a need for vengeance.

A vengeance you accepted when you agreed to be a part of his plan to raid Black Thorn. How could she have been so blind? So foolish? Payton had killed several men already. He wouldn't think twice about getting rid of the boy if it served his purpose. She had only to feel the bruise upon her cheek to realize how ruthless her half brother could be. Yet she couldn't allow him to bully her or the boy. She managed a smile for Yale. "You are safe with us."

The boy seemed unconcerned. "I can take care of myself."

She doubted it but thought it time to turn the conversation. "What has happened to Bernard and Samuel?"

Payton shook his head. "I know not. They should have angled back this way and arrived last night."

"And Melvynn, Isaac and Roger? Were they not to ride the direct route along the ridge? Or did you alter the plan again?"

"Aye, they should be here," Payton said, striding to the doorway to glare into the morning as if he could will them to appear. "And nay, the plan remained the same. They were to lure the soldiers of Black Thorn into the hills, then douse their torches and ride here." He rubbed the back of his neck in frustration.

"You think something happened to them," she guessed and again felt an icy stab of dread.

"I know not."

"But one of the parties should have made it."

"Aye." He shrugged, but tension was visible in the

set of his jaw as he turned to face her again. "We'll wait."

"I'm tired of waiting," Yale complained. "And hungry and thirsty. So what is this band of yours, eh? What kind of outlaws do you have? Are they lazy? Lost? Or—" He brightened considerably. "Mayhap my father has found them. Oh, if he has, they are in trouble. Deep trouble."

"He hasn't found them," Payton argued, obviously irritated. "Hush."

"But he is powerful and he is quick with his sword and even quicker with bow and arrow. Aye, your men are in danger if they've met up with him!" The boy was on his feet, dropping the blanket and taking his wooden sword to swing it wildly. As if he heard an enemy's footsteps behind him, he spun on a toe, then crouched to face an invisible enemy.

Payton's lips flattened over his teeth and he rubbed a temple as if a headache were forming behind his eyes.

"If I were an outlaw, no one would catch me. Not ever." Whoosh! Yale's thick sword sliced through the air as he twirled on one foot. "I would kill them all." He slammed the blade of his wooden sword into an old bench. Whack! Whack! Whack! "Die, cur!" he commanded and Payton glared at Apryll with eyes that had aged over the past few days.

"This goes on all the time. *All* the time. There is no rest. I'm thinking of gagging him and tying his hands and feet."

"Ach! Try it and die!" the boy said, whirling and jabbing, slashing the air with his weapon.

"No." All too vividly Apryll remembered her own wrists being bound with the cords from her tunic, the feeling of being completely vulnerable. "Come," she said to the boy as she realized her brother was about to explode. She offered Yale her hand to stop another argument or worse. "If you be thirsty, Yale, there is a creek where you can drink your fill."

"You can call me Death," Yale announced.

Payton shook his head as if at a great folly. "'Tis his new name. One he chose."

The boy nodded vigorously. "If I am to be part of this band in the game, I need a fitting name. As do you. What shall I call you?"

"Her name is Lady Apryll," Payton cut in, adding to Apryll, "As we discussed, the boy believes this is a game because of the Christmas Revels. He also thinks his father will come and rescue him."

"Oh, he will and when he does he will kill you all," Yale agreed. "But if I am one of you, mayhap I can save your worthless skins."

Apryll, tired as she was, swallowed a smile. This son of Black Thorn was giving Payton something to think about.

"Now—outside!" Death, née Yale, pointed his crude weapon at the broken door.

"Wait—"

He ignored Payton's cry. As swift as an arrow shot from a taut bow, Yale streaked through the sagging portal.

"I don't let him go outside, nor do I leave him alone," Payton said, striding to the door to glare at the boy.

"I'll watch him."

"See that you do, sister, for if we lose him as a hostage we will have nothing. All we have done to this point will be a waste! Surely you don't want that. Much worse will be the wrath of Black Thorn."

"At least we agree on something," she muttered, casting a scathing glance at her brother before slipping through the rotting timbers of the doorway. Outside, fog still shrouded the trees and crept upon the hard ground, adding a sense of gloom to the forest.

Apryll's mind spun with ideas of escape, for now would be the perfect time, before her brother knew what was happening, but Payton, as if he expected her to try and thwart him, strode outside.

"We must not let him out of our sight," he said, his lips barely moving, his eyes trained on the boy as Yale slid down the bank to kneel on rocks where ice collected near the shore. "And think not of taking him away from here, sister, or I will hunt you down and kill the boy as easily as if he were a stag in the woods."

"And suffer further the wrath of Devlynn of Black Thorn?"

"Gladly." Payton's hatred ran deep; his need for vengeance was as dark as Satan's soul. 'Twas more than Geneva's visions that drove him. 'Twas more than a need to save Serennog that compelled him. 'Twas a need to prove himself, a burning desire to be recognized and be no longer cursed as a bastard.

"Watch yourself, brother. I am still the ruler of Serennog," she reminded him.

Payton barked out a cold laugh. "Are you? And who is watching your keep while you're away?"

"Sir Brennan, of course," she said staunchly as she watched Yale lying flat on his stomach and peering into the clear water of the creek.

"And you trust him? He's an idiot."

"He's loyal. And he has the steward to aid him," she said with far more confidence than she felt.

"Andrew? Come, Apryll, surely you know the steward to be a weak, miserly man. He has no backbone whatsoever."

"Let's not forget Father Benjamin."

"He's blind, Apryll! For the love of Jesus and so are you," Payton said over the caw of a raven hidden deep in the woods.

"I'm not so blind that I can't see a brother turned traitor."

"A brother who is trying to save your castle," he reminded her harshly as his eyes scanned the woods. Worry etched the corners of his mouth. "Where the devil are Bernard and Samuel? Even if Black Thorn took the bait and the others had to elude his army, Bernard and Samuel should have made it here by now."

Apryll shook her head. "Are you so foolish? Black Thorn's army split into small groups and each group followed a different course at the crossroads." When his eyes narrowed suspiciously, she added, "I was captured, Payton, that's what took me so long to catch up to you."

"By Black Thorn?"

She nodded.

"Again? After the time in the castle?"

"Aye," she admitted, embarrassed.

"And yet you escaped?" He frowned skeptically, his gaze searching the patches of fog that refused to dissipate.

"'Twas not easy," Apryll said, though in truth, it had been accomplished without much trouble. That worried her. Gnawed at her. Had Devlynn let her go? Nay . . . and yet . . . Payton was staring at her, expecting an explanation. "I waited until the guard had dozed and the wind was high so that the dog didn't hear me, then I stole a horse."

Payton's eyes moved to the brown stallion with its distinctive white stockings. "You were not followed?"

"Nay."

Anxiously he rubbed his jaw, scratching at the reddish stubble. "You're sure?"

"No one has appeared, have they?"

"Yet." He glanced back at the boy and his lips tightened with renewed worry.

"Be careful, Payton," she warned, her blood turning to ice as she recognized the hate in the narrowing of her brother's eyes. "If you so much as lay a hand on the lad, Black Thorn will do everything in his power to destroy not only you and me but our entire keep. No one will be safe."

"It matters not," Payton growled as Yale scampered to a tree near the old inn and swung from a low-hanging branch.

"It does matter. Lives depend upon it," she said vehemently. "The only way they will be saved is if we return the boy to his father."

He stared down his nose at her as if she were a fool. "The only way lives will be saved is for us to ransom the boy back to Black Thorn and strike a deal. He is all we have with which to bargain."

"Then you best see that he's unharmed," she said, closing the few feet of distance between them. "For our safety and your stupid vengeance. Elsewise everyone will have died or been tortured in vain and you will not have achieved your goal of retribution." She had to appeal to him at the only level she knew. "The boy must stay alive."

"Bloody Christ."

"Think, brother," she said, laying a hand upon his sleeve, her fingers curling in desperation around the coarse fabric. "Do not let your temper get in the way of your dreams."

But as she said the words, she knew that it was already too late. There was no reasoning with Payton.

She had no choice but to deceive him.

Chapter Sixteen

Payton alternately watched Devlynn's son and searched the surrounding trees. His fingers curled nervously over the hilt of his sword, his eyes scoured the woods as if he expected the Lord of Black Thorn to burst from the cover of the brush, sword drawn, at any moment.

Yale dashed back to the creek, fell onto the bank and then tried to grasp a fish that wriggled past. "I need a spear," he said, slanting Apryll a knowing glance. "Then I'd catch one sure. Have you a knife?"

"Nay," she shook her head.

"Ah, but I had one. Last night." He bolted toward the old building and returned seconds later with a dull-looking short-bladed dagger. He flopped on the cold bank, his eyes searching the water.

"That was only for whittling. You're not to have a weapon!" Payton stormed to the creek bed and reached forward to snatch the knife from the boy's fingers.

Yale's eyes took on a wicked gleam as he hopped lithely to the balls of his feet. The wind caught in his hair and brought color to his cheeks. He danced away, holding one hand palm-out as if to ward off a blow, the fingers of his other gripping the knife and wiggling it menacingly. "But 'tis a game, and you've got a sword and bow." He hitched his chin toward the horses and his eyes narrowed. "And, though you admitted it not, you stole Phantom. Oh, my father will be displeased."

"I care not what he thinks."

"You should."

"But, Death," Payton cajoled not very convincingly, "this is how this game is played. I am your captor."

"Then I should have a weapon," the boy insisted.

Payton gritted his teeth. "Give me the knife."

"Take it from me."

"Nay, don't test him," Apryll said to the boy, her heart nearly stopping. She could not bear the thought that Devlynn's son might be harmed.

"This be your fault." Payton threw his angry remark her way. "You've encouraged him. Now, *boy*, give me the knife." His lips had thinned and showed white in suppressed rage as he and Yale circled.

Apryll stepped between them, facing her brother. "Leave him be!"

"Not with any kind of weapon. I swear, lad, if you don't give up the knife I'll be forced to tie your blasted hands behind your back and stuff a gag in that loud mouth of yours!" He pushed Apryll aside and advanced upon Yale, but the son of Black Thorn was agile. He ducked and sliced the air with his blade, nicking Payton's sleeve and slicing the fine leather tooling of his mantle.

Payton wanted to strangle the insubordinate pup. "Christ Jesus, are you daft?" he demanded. "I could kill you as easily as not."

"And what then? My father, he would not be satisfied with your death. Nay, he would torture you, twist your heart out slowly, spill your guts and let the castle pigs feast on them."

Cold dread drizzled into Payton's blood at the image. Had the cocky lad no fear?

"Nay, I think you'll not kill me," the boy said with a knowing, arrogant grin, his blade flashing in the pale morning light.

Damn Apryll for allowing the boy outside! Payton wanted to rant and rail at his fool of a sister, but he didn't dare throw her another glance. He kept his eyes trained on the little dagger. Every muscle strung tight, he was ready to pounce upon the boy the second the lad's attention was diverted.

"This is not part of the game," Payton said.

"It is now."

Apryll, curse her, didn't do anything to stop the display. "Take the knife from him," Payton ordered.

Slash, slash, slash.

The boy wielded the dagger in the air. "My father will have you beheaded. Even now he is coming for me and when he finds you, you'll wish you'd never defied him!" Yale's eyes held a wicked gleam and in that second Payton saw his own death . . . nay! He wouldn't let a mere boy scare him. Quickly, he drew his sword.

"No!" Apryll sprang between them again. "Enough. There is to be no more bloodshed!"

"No more? Was someone hurt?" Yale asked and some of his spirit evaporated. He didn't know what to believe, 'twas obvious.

"Not hurt. Dead. Killed," Payton explained, thankful to finally witness a tremor of fear in the lad's face, some of his cocksure mien slipping. "A guard or two and a stableman who didn't want us to take the horses."

"At Black Thorn? Seth?" The boy's Adam's apple jerked. "Is this true?" he asked Apryll.

"Aye. Sadly."

Confusion contorted Yale's young features.

"This . . . this be not a game?" he whispered and looked for the first time at the horses pulling at their tethers. The gray let out a nervous nicker and tossed his great head, tugging at the leather straps holding him fast. "Phantom," Yale whispered to himself, as if suddenly putting the pieces of a difficult puzzle together. "My father's steed." His head snapped around and he glared at Payton as dry leaves rustled in the near-naked branches of the oaks. "So you really did steal my father's horse. I—I thought it all a game . . ." His voice fell away.

"And I stole your father's son."

At last the daring youth was beginning to understand his dire plight. That was good, but also a worry.

The boy might try to escape and Yale, though he was finally showing some signs of concern, was a bold one, the baron's son, a reckless boy. Like his father, and grandfather, Payton thought bitterly. Like himself.

A branch snapped in the woods. Payton whirled, hand on his weapon, his eyes searching the copse of trees to the west.

He saw a movement. A dark shadow leaping. Heart in his throat, he watched, certain death was upon them.

Ears twitching, a doe sprang over a fallen log to disappear into the mist-shrouded forest.

God's teeth, he was wound tight. What he needed was a mazer of wine and a fine, hot wench, not this gloomy, eerie forest, deteriorated inn and impudent hostage who didn't know when to shut his mouth.

And then there was Apryll. She was another worry; 'twould have been better had she not escaped Black Thorn. Payton couldn't trust her; he was certain of it. He saw the fury in her eyes, knew she'd thought he'd abandoned her. Twice.

Bloody hell, what a mess!

Where was Roger? Samuel? *Anyone?*

For a second his thoughts slid to Geneva with her pale, all-seeing eyes and her lush, willing body. Oh, that she were here . . . or, if not her, some other hot-blooded woman.

Rubbing his arm where Yale had sliced his jacket, he watched the wayward boy, who, after casting a furtive glance over his shoulder to ensure that Payton wasn't following, made his way back to the creek's bank, where he tried vainly to spear a fish. He was quick, determined, the set of his jaw reminiscent of his father.

No doubt he would try to escape.

It was only a matter of time.

But Payton had a few more drops of the drug Geneva had concocted for him, the same combination of herbs that had been used on the night of the revels. One of the traitors at Black Thorn had doctored Yale's mazer, causing the boy to tire and fall asleep earlier than usual, allowing Payton to kidnap him.

It had been so easy. Almost too easy. But then the Lord of Black Thorn was a fool, Payton thought, remembering the weight of Black Thorn's treasury in the leather pouches he'd filled. He'd carried them here, upon Devlynn of Black Thorn's finest steed, then hidden the pouches beneath a stone in the old inn. Yes, he'd bested Black Thorn. He leaned against the corner of the inn and watched his sister.

Apryll walked to where the boy was playing and as she passed, he saw the welt on her cheek, the bruise yellowing and healing, but a reminder of what it meant to cross her brother.

Inwardly, Payton cringed when he thought of striking her, of deceiving her, and yet it had been necessary. He knew there were times when his temper got the best of him. 'Twas a burden, not only for him to bear but for those who dared defy him.

Eventually he would apologize to her. When the time was right. When she understood and accepted the extent of his ambitions. However, for the moment, he would keep his plans to himself.

Silently he vowed never again to raise his hand to her.

'Twas cowardly to hit a woman . . . he knew it, and yet the fury that ofttimes burned within him was a beast he could not cage. His jaw clenched hard and he pushed his guilt deep into a far corner of his mind. There was no time for it.

With a flap of great wings, the owl circled, landing upon the roof and glaring down at Payton as if he were an intruder. 'Twas nothing new. Payton had always felt as if he didn't belong.

Soon that would change. A restless breeze pushed the fog around and rattled the naked branches of the trees surrounding the small clearing. Payton squinted at the looming shadows of the forest and wondered where the hell his soldiers were. Had they been detained? Taken prisoner? Even now leading Black Thorn's soldiers to this old inn?

Apprehension gnawed at his gut. From the corner of his eye he saw Apryll tending to the horses. He couldn't trust her; she was too insistent upon returning the boy to his father. If given the chance, she would certainly steal him away.

Or Yale would escape himself. There were many ways for a clever boy to slip out of the decrepit building and disappear into the forest. Then all would be for naught—his years of planning, of dreaming of a chance to claim what was his by right. Nay, he couldn't lose Yale of Black Thorn now, not when all he wanted was so close at hand.

Payton crossed the cold ground to the creek bed where Yale was vainly trying to catch a fish. Clear water splashed over stones and a fox peered between exposed roots on the far bank only to disappear in the mist. Payton rubbed his arms at a sudden chill, for he felt, rather than saw, that he was being observed.

Squatting near the imp so that he was eye to eye with the lad, he said, "For the moment, boy, you must remain prisoner." Payton reached into his pocket, quickly withdrew a leather thong and slipped it easily over Yale's wrist.

"Nay!" The boy whirled, nearly toppling, his knife slashing, but Payton was quick, caught Yale's small wrist, squeezed hard and the knife fell, clattering against a rock. Payton swept it upward and wiggled the point beneath Yale's freckled nose. "You'll stay quiet and obedient and tied until your father comes for you."

"For the love of St. Jude, what do you think you're

doing?" Apryll dashed across the short distance separating them. She was about to say something else, probably order him to unhand the boy, but she stopped dead in her tracks. Her skin took on the color of pale milk as she stared at the blade near the boy's throat. "Aye, Yale," she amended, her voice barely a whisper. "You must do everything we say so that we might win the game."

"There is no game," Yale spat, and wiped the back of his mouth with the sleeve of his free hand while Payton kept the leather strap taut.

"You know that not," she cajoled but she was worried. "You need not tether him like a mule," she said, turning to Payton.

"He acts like one."

"Let me go!" Yale cried, pulling at the leash.

"Later. If you behave yourself."

"My father will have your head!"

"Your father isn't here!"

"Release him," Apryll ordered.

"When we return to Serennog."

Yale pulled on his tether, then fell onto his rump, trying to use his weight to upset Payton.

"But—"

"I said, when we return, sister. For now, I can take no chances." With a swift yank, Payton drew Yale to his feet and though the boy struggled, swore and spat, Payton wrestled him and quickly managed to wrap the strap over his free wrist, manacling the lad.

"This isn't necessary! Payton, please, let the boy be free!"

"And take the chance of losing him? I think not." Payton skewered her in his cold glare. "Now, there are

supplies inside. Salt pork and the like. We'll prepare a
meal and celebrate by opening a cask."

"This be not the time," she said.

"Nay?" Payton snorted. "'Tis the perfect time. I've
brought the baron of Black Thorn to his knees."

"Never," the boy snarled, pulling at the leather cutting into his wrists. "Let me free."

Payton laughed mercilessly as clouds crawled over
the pale winter sun.

Tossing his hair out of his eyes, Yale stiffened his
spine and thrust out his hands, drawing the leather
thong tight. "Cut me free," he ordered. "I be the lord's
son and I order you to cut me free or suffer the consequences."

"Not yet."

"I command you."

"And I command you to hell. I, too, be a lord's son,"
Payton said, and the fire that had raged in his heart
from childhood burned ever brighter.

The boy had the nerve to lift his chin, to somehow
seem to look down his nose as he stared up at the man
who had dared bind him. "You will rue this day," he
said calmly and Payton knew a second's fear.

"I think not."

"My father will cut you to your soul."

"Mayhap I don't have one."

"Then he'll settle for your liver."

"Enough," Apryll said. "Untie him."

"I think not." Payton shook off his discomfort and
breathed deeply. He wouldn't let the boy unnerve him,
not when victory and retribution were so close at
hand. "So tell me, *Death*, like you not the game?"

"The game," Yale repeated. His eyes narrowed on
his captor with such intensity Payton wanted to slap

him. "And what be the prize for the winner?" Yale asked.

Justice, Payton thought, glancing toward the sky where a hawk circled beneath thin clouds. Finally, at long last, sweet, sweet justice.

Leaving his horse and dog tied farther into the forest, Devlynn crawled on his belly up the far side of the creek. He hid behind a small mound of earth where the roots and branches of a pine tree offered cover.

Peering through a low-hanging branch, Devlynn felt a mixture of relief and rage. Yale was alive. Healthy. Impudent as ever. And he was being restrained by the bastard who had the audacity to place a blade at the boy's throat.

"God in heaven, no!"

Every muscle in Devlynn's body grew taut. It was all he could do to restrain himself from vaulting over the deep stream and running his sword through Payton of Serennog's heart. But he couldn't risk it. Not with the wicked dagger angled against Yale's soft and oh, so vulnerable throat.

Apryll flung herself at her brother, then stopped short as she noticed the blade. Fear shone in her gold eyes and she tried cajoling both Payton and Yale, trying to stave off any bloodshed.

Do not fight him, son, Devlynn silently thought, as if in prayer. *I will save you, I swear it.*

The bastard yanked his son to his feet and bound both his wrists as Apryll sprang at her brother, arguing fiercely against Yale's manacles. But Payton was relentless. Unmoved. Yale, as if he didn't realize how dire the situation was, argued and jeered at his captor, throwing himself against his restraints. For once Devlynn wished his son would still his impudent tongue. Taunting Payton might make him react violently.

Again Devlynn silently rued the very night on which he'd met Apryll of Serennog, when his head had been turned, his defenses let down and his son stolen from him.

Devlynn's teeth gnashed in frustration. His fingers itched to strangle the bastard. And yet he waited. As mist clung to the forest floor and the branches dripped with the thick fog, Devlynn considered killing the bastard here and now. With his bow and arrow. The trouble was, in the shifting, foggy light there was a chance he might wound either Yale or Apryll, for Payton held the boy close.

Apryll stayed close to her brother, alternately yelling at him and whispering in his ear. Nay, it was too hazardous. He could not risk either life.

But there was a chance things would improve and he might get a clean shot. Slowly he reached behind him, withdrew an arrow from his quiver and strung his bow while lying upon a bed of dead pine needles. He could stand quickly, step away from the cover of the trees, draw back his deadly weapon and fire within a matter of seconds. His aim was true enough . . . if Yale or Apryll did not step into the arrow's deadly path.

His gaze never leaving the unlikely threesome, he started to roll to his feet. At that moment Payton lowered his blade and, with a hard glance over his shoulder, shepherded the boy into the building. But Apryll paused, standing at the doorway, her golden hair damp with the fog, her eyes turned in his direction.

His heart nearly stopped, for he was certain she'd seen him, sensed his presence; then, she shook her head, as if to dislodge a silly notion, and hurried through the sagging entrance to her brother's lair.

Devlynn silently cursed himself for hesitating.

The opportunity to save his son had slipped through his fingers.

But only for a moment.

The next time, he would not fail.

Chapter Seventeen

Collin waved the sentry into a chair near the fire.
The man was half-dead from the looks of him,
pale, nearly trembling, dirty as sin. "Sit, Sir Dennis, and
tell me of my brother," Collin said as Miranda, blast
her, had the audacity to enter the great hall.

"Is there word from Devlynn?" she asked, her fingers wringing nervously. "And Yale? What of the lad?"

"I know not of the boy." Dennis's dark eyes were
sunken far into his skull. "But Lord Devlynn rides
with Sir Lloyd, Sir Rearden and a few others. At the
crossroads just north of the old mill, we split into three
groups, each searching for the outlaws."

Collin settled back in his chair, resting a boot heel
on a stool, his eyes narrowed as Dennis explained
what had happened in the ensuing days. Miranda listened intently and snapped her fingers, ordering a
page to fetch the soldier food and wine from the
kitchen. While Dennis was explaining Devlynn's strat-
egy, the nervous page deposited a jug of wine and
three mazers, while a serving girl brought a tray of
cheese, smoked meat and bread.

"Does Devlynn not know that 'tis better to keep the

army together, that there is strength in numbers?" Collin poured three cups, handed them about, then took a long swallow from his mazer. With a snort he added, "Our brother may be a warrior, aye, there is proof enough of that in the battles he's won, but he is no general."

"Let Sir Dennis finish," Miranda snapped. She sat upon a bench and leaned forward on her elbows, eagerly drinking up every word the soldier reported, as if she wished she were riding with their headstrong brother through the dark forests and rugged cliffs while searching for the enemy. Collin had always suspected his sister would much rather have been born a man. Oh, she was a good enough woman, he supposed, if not a devoted wife to her old grunt of a husband, an adoring mother to her child. But whenever there was rumor of a battle, Miranda's eyes would gleam and she would ask intricate questions, demanding details that most women of her station would find either boring or distasteful. Not so Miranda. Oftentimes Collin wondered if, given the chance, his sister would don a warrior's armor and ride into battle herself.

". . . So when the Lady Apryll of Serennog was captured, the lord was furious. He sent me here to warn you that there are traitors within the walls of Black Thorn. Someone aided the enemy into the keep as well as helped her escape." Dennis eyed the platter of meat and cheese and quickly Miranda nudged it his way. "Eat. Please." Dennis tore off some of the bread and sliced a thick slab of cheese.

Collin scowled, rested his foot on a stool near the fire. "We have yet to find the Judas."

"Lord Devlynn will force Lady Apryll to talk," Dennis said, eating hungrily.

"How?" Miranda asked.

"I know not, but he told me he would interrogate her himself, find out who was betraying him. When he returns, his justice will be swift."

"And deadly," Collin muttered as he glowered into his mazer. Was it his imagination or did he hear a quiet cough behind one of the curtains? He glanced behind him but saw no movement, no indication that someone was listening from the shadows, and yet the hairs on the back of his neck raised.

"What of the others—of Rudyard and Spencer?" Miranda asked, trying to sound casual, though, Collin suspected, she was more interested than she feigned. He'd seen her in the company of Spencer, where she transformed from a determined, unhappy woman to a silly lass whose eyes sparkled and whose cheeks blushed. 'Twas scandalous as she was married to another—an old codger who was Lord of Clogwyn, a man who spent his days warming his feet by the fire, feeding his pigeons or waxing philosophic about the tense state of affairs between the bastard English and the righteous Welsh. Lowell of Clogwyn hadn't bothered to leave his keep for the revels and scoffed at any sort of celebration. 'Twas no wonder that Miranda found life with him dull and had returned here to live and, it seemed, find a different life from that of her husband.

Lowell of Clogwyn made Aunt Violet seem youthful. Collin had often wondered how his niece, Bronwyn, had been conceived and had speculated that Sir Spencer might be the girl's father. Bronwyn looked so much like her mother, 'twas hard to tell, but he couldn't imagine that the old man had the fortitude to sire a child.

"Are the men who rode with Devlynn safe?" Miranda asked.

"I know only what I have said," Dennis admitted. He'd polished off his first portion and was cutting another slice of bread.

Miranda turned serious, worried eyes to her brother. "We must send troops to help."

"And leave the castle defenseless? Nay," Collin disagreed. "Our best men are with Devlynn. They will prevail." With a glance to the hungry soldier, he added, "Did Devlynn ask for more men?"

"Nay." Dennis shook his head. He ate heartily, piling meat and cheese upon his bread and washing each bite down with a swig from his mazer of wine.

"But we should send some troops to help," Miranda insisted.

Collin wouldn't budge. "Until he requests fresh soldiers, we will stay here and defend Black Thorn."

Miranda didn't argue any further but silently seethed, defiance sparking in her green eyes. That was the trouble with his sister, always thinking she knew more than he or Devlynn, which was ridiculous. For the love of St. Peter, she was a woman. A *woman*!

In a whisper of velvet Aunt Violet appeared in the archway near the base of the stairs. "Is there word of Devlynn?" she asked hopefully, as a serving girl scurried over the rushes carrying a second tray filled with boiled eggs and slices of winter apples. The girl deposited the tray on a table while a page appeared to refill each mazer.

Collin and the weary soldier climbed to their feet as Violet made her way into the room. She used a smooth walking stick to aid her balance, then dropped into a chair.

"Sir Dennis has come from Devlynn's camp," Collin said.

"Has he found Yale?" Her old eyes brightened at the prospect.

"Nay, m'lady." Dennis plucked up an egg from the tray Miranda held for him, then plopped it into his mouth nearly swallowing it whole. "Not yet."

"Oh." Crestfallen, Violet sighed and pursed her lips. Her fingers linked together over the top of her walking stick. She was the eldest woman by far within the keep, yet she had no ailments other than a knee that twinged with the cold weather and a mind that sometimes betrayed her with spells of forgetfulness and fancifulness. Nervous fingers tapped against the knot at the top of her cane. "Has no word of ransom been brought here?"

"Nay." Collin shook his head and settled back into his chair by the fire. A lad of eight or so brought in more wood and tossed a few mossy logs onto the iron dogs. Flames hissed and spat and smoke spewed up the chimney.

"The poor boy," Violet thought aloud. "I hope he is all right . . . all that blood in his chamber." She sighed and shook her head, small teeth pressing into her lower lip. "We must do something."

"We can do nothing but wait," Collin argued. "As I promised Devlynn."

"'Tis enough to drive one mad, all this waiting," Miranda complained.

"Devlynn will find his son."

"If the boy's alive." A strand of Miranda's hair had

fallen from its braid, but she ignored the wayward curl and sipped from her cup, her eyes dark with worry.

"He is alive," Violet said, tapping her cane on the cold stones of the floor. "He has to be." But her eyes were troubled, her bravado slipping visibly, and she seemed to sink within the chair. The tapestries upon the wall appeared dull this day and even with the candles lit, the hall was gloomy.

Ever since the raid on Black Thorn, Collin had been tense, seeing the suspicion in the eyes of the servants and peasants, sensing the worry that troops would be called to war, aware that many within the castle walls didn't trust him, had pledged their allegiance to Devlynn and considered Collin nothing more than a figurehead, a man incapable of ruling the keep.

Well, they were all wrong. Dead wrong.

"All we can do is pray," Violet said, "and put our trust in the Father."

Collin didn't argue, but thought the old woman a twit.

Prayer had nothing to do with what would be the fate of Black Thorn.

The boy sat glowering at the fire, his back propped by a sack of supplies, his bound hands dropped between knees drawn nearly to his chin. "He'll kill you, you know," he said as he glowered at the fire where a rabbit and dove were roasting on a spit. "My father, he'll kill you all."

"You mustn't think of it." Apryll cast a glance over her shoulder. Payton, full into his cups, was adding wood to the fire, and settled on one knee, his attention, for a few seconds, averted.

He'd asked Apryll for another mazer of wine and

she'd agreed, feigning disapproval and knowing this
was her one chance for escape before the others in Payton's band joined them. While Yale stared at the sizzling carcasses, Apryll turned her back to the fire and,
using her body to cover her actions, hid the fact that
she was rifling through the pouch Payton had left unguarded in a corner. Though the air within the drafty
old building was cold, her fingers were sweaty, her
skin prickling at the thought that she could be caught
any second.

She found the vial and retrieved it, pulled out the
stopper and poured the clear liquid into Payton's
empty mazer. Then she filled the cup with wine and
sent up a quick prayer that the concoction had no
taste, for as drunk as her brother was, he might discern
a change in flavor and toss the wine out before downing it.

"Where the devil are they?" Payton growled. "We
can wait here only another hour and then we must be
off."

Mother Mary, help me, she silently prayed, pouring
water from her cup into the vial, stopping it and dropping it into the pouch again before glancing over her
shoulder. Her hands sweated and every muscle in her
body was tightly drawn.

"The longer we tarry here, the more likely Devlynn
and his troops will arrive." Nervously Payton plowed
stiff fingers through his hair. "Christ Jesus, what could
have happened?"

"Mayhap they were captured."

"Yes, that's it!" Yale cried. "My father found them
and beheaded them all!"

"Enough!" Payton snapped. "I'm sick to death of
hearing about your father. 'My father this, my father

that.' Well, where is he, eh? He hasn't shown up here, has he?"

"He will."

"Oh, for the love of bloody Christ! Have you got that wine?" he demanded of Apryll just as she turned with the doctored cup.

"Aye, but I think you should only have one more," she said, hoping to sound stern and disapproving so that Payton wouldn't change his mind. "This is no time to lose your wits in drink."

Adjusting his breeches, Payton cast a glance around the bleak room and sent her a mistrustful look. "I'll drink as much as I like."

"But we both need to keep our minds about us," she argued, lifting the mazer to her lips. "Mayhap I should drink this last one. You've had enough."

"'Tis not for you to say," he argued and crossed the room swiftly.

"But, we have the boy to think of—"

"He's fine." Payton cast a glance at Yale and a smile of satisfaction stole across his beard-darkened face. "You just need a meal in you, don't you, boy?" he asked.

"What I need is to be unbound." Yale held up his fists, stretching the leather manacle taut.

"In time. All in time." Payton snatched the cup from her fingers and glared down at her suspiciously. "Bloody ingrate. I give the lad a new adventure, and what does he do? Complain." He laughed, took a swallow, and Apryll held her breath as his brows slammed together. "What be this?" he muttered, running his tongue over his lips and frowning. "The wine—"

"Would you rather have water?"

He snorted and scowled into his drink.

"Can we not eat now?" the boy cut in, glaring darkly at Payton through a fringe of shaggy hair that had fallen over his brows.

"In a minute," Payton growled.

"If I eat not now, I'll surely starve and die and then my father will—"

"Stop it! Didn't I just tell you I'm sick to death of hearing about your damned father?" Payton swore roundly and Apryll, hoping to stay his anger, stepped in.

"Don't bother yourself with the boy. I'll handle him."

"Will you now? What of all that talk of taking him back to his father?"

"'Twould be impossible. I hate to admit it, brother, but you're right. Devlynn of Black Thorn would slit our throats in a minute if we did not have something to bargain with and the boy is his weakness."

"He's not weak!" Yale cried, standing, his face red with indignation.

"Just do as Payton says," Apryll told Devlynn's son, hoping her brother wouldn't see through her ruse. "You are our prisoner now."

"You're as bad as he."

Her heart stung but she managed a cool smile. "Mayhap he's as bad as I am, for I'm the ruler of Serennog." Was it her imagination or did she see a gleam of something unholy in her brother's eye? "He does what I say."

"'Twas your idea to kidnap me?" the boy asked, disbelieving.

"Nay. But now that it's done, I understand the wisdom of it. Be good and no one will harm you."

"And if I'm not?" he asked boldly. Oh, he was a brave one. So much like his father.

"Do not even consider it," she said in her sternest voice. She had to convince both her brother and the boy that she intended to keep the son of Black Thorn hostage. "Do as you're told and all will be well."

Payton's eyes narrowed. Obviously he didn't believe her quick change of heart, but the boy was more gullible.

"Then my father will kill you as well. And then . . . and then he'll gut you and roast you like that rabbit and cut off your head and . . . and he'll feed you to the vultures and—"

"Enough!" Payton finished his wine in one swallow. "The lad makes my head ache. Give him something to eat." Then, with a devious, self-satisfied smile, he walked to the corner near the wine jug, retrieved his pouch and withdrew the vial. Apryll's heart thudded. Dear Lord, would he see that she'd double-crossed him? "And I have something special for you, boy," Payton said.

"What?" Yale asked suspiciously.

"A little wine." He filled the mazer again and winked at Apryll, who held her breath as he dumped the contents of the vial into Yale's drink. "Now, a toast to our success," he said, slurring his words. "And to Serennog."

"I want nothing from you," Yale spat. Shaking a small, manacled fist, he refused to drink. He kicked at a tiny pebble, shooting it into the fire. Sparks erupted and wafted up what was left of the chimney. Overhead the owl flapped his great wings and a few feathers fell, like long, drifting flakes of snow, from the rafters.

"Drink."

"I'll not!"

"Listen, boy, you'll do as I say."

The heir to Black Thorn leaped to his feet. "No."

Payton's fingers touched the hilt of his knife.

"Come, Yale, be not unreasonable," Apryll suggested quickly. "A little wine with the rabbit and fowl would not hurt."

"But—"

"If you don't do as I say," Payton cut in, "you'll go hungry, for we ride after we eat. We can wait no longer. The rest of the men will have to catch up."

"You would leave them?" Apryll asked.

"I have no choice. No doubt by now Black Thorn is tracking you with that dog of his. So we eat and break camp," he said around a yawn. "By the saints, I'm tired." He stretched, then poured himself another drink and Apryll, after cutting up the charred rabbit, offered a leg to Yale. Upon prodding the boy actually sipped from his mazer, satisfying Payton, who sat near the fire, gnawing on a dove's wing and tossing the bone into the fire.

"So, this be not a game?" the boy clarified as he bit into the meat.

"No. 'Tis very serious," she said.

"Do you plan to kill me?"

"Never!" Apryll was emphatic.

"Of course we will, if you don't hold your tongue," Payton said, yawning and blinking hard as if trying to stay awake, while the boy sucked the meat from the small bones and took a second piece of meat.

"Then you are a thief," he accused Apryll. "And a murderess."

"She killed no one." Payton was stretching out in front of the fire and yawning.

"But she is the ruler, did she not say so? It was on her word that people were killed."

"Bloody hell, what does it matter who did what?" Payton snapped. "You are the prisoner. That is all you need to know. Now, quiet down. We'll all rest for a few minutes and then we'll break camp." He turned a groggy eye on the boy. "Sleep. You'll need it."

"'Tis the middle of the day."

"And we will ride long into the night."

"Payton is right. You should rest."

"But I be not tired."

"You will be . . ."—Payton's brow furrowed—"or you should be . . ." And then, as if he'd finally understood what was happening as the boy hadn't become drowsy from his wine: "By the gods . . . Apryll . . . you did not . . . you would not have . . ." He looked into his mazer, then over the rim at his sister. "If you have betrayed me, you will regret it for the rest of your life."

"I would no more turn against you than you would against me," she said and he seemed as if he wanted to argue further, but the potion took hold and within seconds he was sleeping soundly, snoring like an old man, not knowing that the Lord of Black Thorn, from his hiding place on the other side of the rotting walls, had heard every word.

Chapter Eighteen

Devlynn tightened the cinch on Phantom's saddle. Then, assured that all the horses were ready for a long ride, he coiled his fingers around the hilt of his sword in a death grip. Noiselessly he slunk through the gray drizzle and around the perimeter of the old inn to the entrance where a door hung open. Weapon drawn, he slipped inside, where a fire blazed and the smell of seared meat was heavy in the air.

Payton was sleeping soundly, his body stretched in front of the grate, his mouth hanging open. Apryll, still wearing the huntsman's clothes, had her back to him as she bent over his son, adjusting Yale's bonds. Devlynn crept in the shadows, easing closer, and she didn't notice, but the boy, peering around her slim hips, started to speak. His gray eyes sparkled and his mouth curved into a triumphant smile.

With a quick, silent shake of his head, Devlynn, moving silently as a lion after prey, pressed a finger to his lips and Yale understood, immediately shutting his mouth and shifting his attention to the woman working with the straps surrounding his wrists.

But she'd already caught his change of expression

and turned, just as Devlynn crossed the room and grabbed her from behind. She started to scream. His free hand clamped over her mouth. His other arm still holding his sword, fastened securely over her waist.

"Not a word," he breathed into her ear as she stiffened and struggled, fighting him tooth and nail. The scent of her reached his nostrils and the position of her backside, drawn so close and thrashing wildly, threatened to arouse him. With a nod over her shoulder, Devlynn met Yale's gaze and hitched his chin toward the doorway. Yale shot to his feet and dashed toward the door while Devlynn struggled to drag Apryll with him. He backed toward the opening, his gaze nailed on Payton, the bastard, sleeping as if he didn't have a worry in the world.

Wrong, Devlynn thought as Apryll struggled. "If you do not come quietly, lady," he warned in a deadly whisper, "I swear I will slay your brother as he sleeps."

She bucked, writhing and twisting, trying to bite through his glove.

Devlynn's grip tightened. "You seal his fate. He's already killed some of my men and kidnapped my boy. Do you think I would not enjoy running him through?"

At that she stopped fighting him and he was able to draw her out of the smoky dark cave of a building and into the winter-cold air where Yale, still rubbing his wrists, was waiting.

"Untie me," he ordered his father.

"You do it," Devlynn said to Apryll, for he wasn't loosening his hold upon her. Not yet. "Set him free."

Thankfully she didn't refuse. Without any show of rebellion she unknotted the leather straps surrounding Yale's small wrists and within seconds he was free.

Yale grinned widely as he rubbed the skin of his wrists and shook his hands to get the blood flowing again. "I knew you would come," he said to his father. "Even when I thought 'twas only a game, I knew you would rescue me. I told them so."

"Shh! This is no time to crow," Devlynn cautioned. "There are others to worry about." His ears strained, for he thought he'd caught the sound of hoofbeats gathering speed, but he heard nothing now. 'Twas only his imagination getting the better of him. "Now, Yale, you must help me if we are to escape."

"Aye, Father." The boy was suddenly sober. Intent.

"Good. Bind the lady's hands. Use the leather straps that she removed from your wrists."

Apryll shook her head and jerked against him.

"Do I have to warn you again?" Devlynn growled, wrestling her and clenching his jaw, for the feel of her back and buttocks against his body heated his blood and his thoughts were turned from the moment to memories of touching her late at night—hot skin against fevered flesh. Angry with himself, he added, "'Tis not too late to go back. Mayhap it's time to send Payton's pathetic soul straight to hell." Her resistance melted. She stopped fighting.

Somehow it was a hollow victory.

"You want me to tie her?" Yale asked, reluctance heavy in his voice, as if he couldn't believe his father would order him to bind a lady.

"Yes. Now! Quickly." Again he thought he heard the muffled sound of hooves trampling the forest floor. The dog sensed it, too. Her nose was to the wind, her eyes locked toward the forest to the south; she growled low in her throat and the fur behind her ears raised.

The boy did as he was bid. Apryll twisted her pretty neck so that she could skewer Devlynn with a gaze filled with pure loathing.

"Now, you watch her—here." Devlynn handed his son his sword. "And if she so much as moves, shout to me." His gaze held the self-righteous fury in hers. "Do not cross me," he admonished as he ducked quickly into the inn.

Her heart thundered. Did he mean to go against his word and slay her brother? No matter what crimes Payton had committed, Apryll couldn't stand the thought of Payton being murdered as he slept. Though Devlynn had left his sword with the boy, he had only to use a knife he'd hidden upon himself, or Payton's own weapon. She took a step after him, but Yale blocked her way.

"Do not make me call him," the boy suggested. "'Twould be a mistake."

"Not my first," she said, ignoring his sword.

"Father!" the boy cried as she swept into the old building and found Devlynn with Payton's sword at her brother's neck. "Wake up," he ordered.

Payton, on his back in front of the fire, groaned in his sleep.

Devlynn nudged him with the toe of his boot. "Rise, cur!"

"He can't!" Apryll was soon across the room and kneeling at her brother's side. "I put a potion into his drink, the same drug that he gave Yale on the night he was kidnapped."

"Why?"

"Because I was trying to get the boy back to you. Without any more bloodshed."

Yale appeared in the doorway. "Horsemen approach."

"Damn!" Devlynn drew back his sword, but Apryll flung herself on her brother.

"Kill him and you'll never know who within your keep betrayed you."

A muscle worked in his jaw. He turned away from her brother. "Hurry!" he ordered Yale. "Run to the other side of the creek. There is a horse waiting!" He grabbed Apryll roughly and pulled her toward the door.

Glimpses of men astride racing horses flashed through the barren trees and drizzling rain. Hard faces etched with determination were close enough that Devlynn recognized his captain of the guard. Rudyard, riding hard, was following the lead of a man Devlynn didn't recognize, a tall man on a reddish horse.

Traitor! A man he'd trusted with his men, to guard his family. A dark-hearted Judas. And only the first of many.

"Now," he said, pulling Apryll toward the horses he'd already saddled. He forced her onto the destrier she'd stolen just as he heard shouts over the thunder of hoofbeats tearing through the forest.

With the reins of Apryll's mount in his fist, Devlynn vaulted onto the gray's back. Phantom bolted. The dog followed. Icy water splashed upward as the horse plunged into the swirling current. Devlynn glanced over his shoulder and saw Apryll, wrists bound, clinging to the pommel of her saddle to stay astride. Nose lifted, her horse trailed the gray.

Rebellious gold eyes clashed with his for a heartbeat. Devlynn spurred his mount on. If the lady of

Serennog was foolish enough to fling herself into the icy water and hard stones, so be it.

Phantom scrambled up the rocky bank and Devlynn's arm felt as if it would be ripped from its socket as Apryll's horse balked. He yanked hard on the reins and the brown horse plunged up the embankment, white-stockinged hooves flinging mud. The dog caught up with them and shot forward through the stark trees. Birds squawked and scattered, rain dripped from the gray skies and behind him he heard shouts.

No doubt they'd been spotted.

He urged Phantom ever faster and spied Yale upon the black steed. The boy was already heading south along the path and smiled triumphantly as Devlynn caught up with him.

"Home?" Yale asked, and Devlynn, his heart swelling with pride for his courageous, reckless son, nodded.

"Fast. As if Satan himself is on our heels."

Yale grinned widely. "Hiya!" he shouted, leaning forward as the black shot ahead.

Devlynn followed, his eyes scanning the horizon in all directions, for, though the boy seemed not to know it, his words were not idle. The Lord of Black Thorn was certain that, in the guise of Payton or other traitors he'd not yet identified, Lucifer himself was searching for them, intent on dragging them both through the portals of hell.

Horses.

She heard horses.

Dozens of them from the sounds of it.

From the knoll, Geneva looked through the bare

trees and saw riders approaching a sagging, weathered building where she sensed Payton was hidden. Alive. *Oh, love,* she thought, her heart aching, *the sins I have committed for you.* She had to face him, to tell him she'd lied. But all the horses and soldiers—they were a ragtag bunch, led by a man with an unfamiliar face.

The hairs on the back of her neck raised and she feared for Payton's life. But before the soldiers reached the old building in the weed-choked clearing, she heard a shout.

"Hurry!"

It came from a tall, dark-haired man . . . the baron of Black Thorn . . . she'd seen him in her visions, for he was the death of her beloved Payton, the devil incarnate, the man she'd agreed to help destroy.

He was holding a sword in one hand and dragging Apryll out of the inn. A boy raced across the creek as the lord threw his captive onto the back of a sleek brown horse, then climbed astride a gray destrier and escaped across an icy stream just as the soldiers, shouting and milling, seeming about to give chase, burst into the clearing.

Payton. Her heart froze. *Where was he?* She had the sense that he still lived and yet would the beast of Black Thorn leave him alive?

Nay. Her heart froze in fear and she started toward the ancient building. Mayhap her vision was muddled, or perhaps she'd angered the gods that had given her the curse of her "sight" by lying. Could she be wrong? Even now, was Payton lying in a pool of his own blood, mortally wounded by Devlynn of Black Thorn?

On wooden legs she began to run, faster and faster, down the knoll, through the trees, ignoring the brambles that tore at her gown or the rain that dripped from the sky and spattered her face, dripping down her neck in freezing rivulets.

No! She thought. *He can't be dead.*

She stumbled, her ankle wrapped by a vine, but she caught herself, hands splaying in the mud. Nausea rose quickly, her stomach churning from the lack of food and sleep.

Sweat poured out of her forehead despite the cold. She retched. Violently. Emptying the bit of juices from her gut, leaving her feeling weak. Yet she pushed herself upright and as the nausea faded, she made her way through the forest to the clearing.

The horses were now free of riders. Men's voices sifted through the cracks in the walls.

"Bloody Christ, wake up, will ya?"

"Where's the boy? Bloody hell, did he get away as well?"

"What happened here?"

"Wake up!"

"Did you see Devlynn of Black Thorn? 'Twas him or his ghost and the Lady Apryll. He threw her onto a horse and they took off across the stream. Even now they ride farther from us. By the saints, can we not wake him up?"

"Is he dead?"

Payton! Her heart twisted and tore. She flew through the door, where she found a bedraggled group of men standing around the fire and the prone body of a man, the man she loved.

"Nay," she cried. The smell of sweat, horses and rain mingled with the odors of burning fat and charred meat. There were more than half a dozen men gathered together and each of them turned suspicious eyes in her direction. Several reached for their weapons, but she paid no heed. Pushing her way through the small crowd, she stared at Payton, motionless on the dirty floor. He couldn't be dead. Not vibrant, brave Payton. She flung herself to her knees and quickly tore open his mantle. Her hands were on his throat, her fingers searching for a pulse. "Payton, oh, please . . ." He couldn't be dead. He had to live. To meet his unborn son.

Her fingertips encountered the steady throb of his heartbeat and she felt the shallow whisper of his breath from his nostrils and open mouth. "He's alive," she whispered, feeling tears of relief fill her eyes.

"Then he sleeps the bloody sleep of the dead!" one man, a short, hefty soldier wearing the black and gold colors of Black Thorn, snorted. A traitor.

"He's been drugged," another growled. He, too, she'd never seen before. Tall, with crooked teeth and the eyes of a coward, he glared down a hooked nose at her. "Who are you?"

"She's the sorceress," Isaac said. "Geneva."

"What's she doing here?" Bad Teeth asked, as if he had some kind of authority. The men she recognized, Isaac, Melvynn and even angry Roger, seemed to defer to him.

"Bloody hell if I know, Sir Rudyard," Isaac, the most vocal, said.

Melvynn lifted a shoulder and Roger, forever the rebel, a man whose bloodlust was far too strong, added, "It's not a place for a woman, especially one who practices the dark arts and prays to the devil."

"Is that what you are? A heathen?" Rudyard's eyebrows lifted and he studied her with new interest. "A witch, then, one who can see into the future?"

"Aye, Sir Rudyard," Isaac agreed, bobbing his bald head while overhead the owl in the rafters glowered down. The tall man was interested, giving her a quick appraisal with his close-set eyes.

Payton moaned and rolled over before she could answer.

"Wake up!" Rudyard commanded, pushing the muddy toe of a boot into Payton's side. "For the love of God, wake up. We've no time." He glanced around the dark interior, then signaled to one of the soldiers. "You—Roger, take two men and give chase. We'll follow."

"And if we catch him?" Roger had his hand on his sword, his eyes filled with anticipation, his lips curving beneath the coarse hairs of his beard.

"If you're that lucky," Rudyard said thoughtfully, "then kill him."

"Nay!" Geneva sprang to her feet.

Roger's eyes gleamed. He ignored Geneva's protests. "What of the woman? Lady Apryll?"

"There is to be no death," Geneva said as icy fear gripped her heart. Is this what she'd started, a war of death and destruction, all because she fell in love with a bastard whose only desire was to rule?

"Kill her as well," Rudyard ordered, then added, "unless you would rather bed her first."

"No!" Geneva's blood ran cold. To what kind of hideous ogres had Payton allied himself? "Is not Payton the ruler here?" she demanded. "You must wait until he awakens and hear what he has to say."

Rudyard's eyes met Roger's.

"What about the boy?" Roger asked, his eyes gleaming in evil anticipation.

"Well, of course, slay him."

Geneva let out a strangled cry. "No, you must not. He is but a lad."

"Born to the wrong man." Rudyard cast a disgusted glance at Payton lying listlessly on the floor and once again, Geneva feared for her beloved's life. "What the bloody hell good is the boy to us if his father is already dead?"

Chapter Nineteen

Apryll clung to the saddle for dear life. Her horse sped after Devlynn's destrier, galloping wildly as rain spat from the dark sky. The woods opened to a road and Devlynn turned unerringly southward.

To Black Thorn.

Her heart turned to ice at the thought of returning to the keep where only a few short nights ago she had distracted him, played the tease, dressed in her mother's wedding dress. They'd laughed, danced, flirted and kissed and it seemed like it had happened in another lifetime.

Her bones jarred and she slid in the saddle, her balance upset as she had no reins to control the horse, no sense of the animal. She could, when they slowed, fling herself to the ground, but what then? Where would she run with her wrists tied? Even if she did manage to dupe Devlynn again, which she seriously doubted she could, how far would she get on foot? Surely he would not be trusting enough to untie her and let her steal a horse again, should they ever rest.

It had been hours since they'd left the old inn and night was closing in. She was cold and hungry and needed to relieve herself, yet she refused to complain and gritted her teeth against her fate.

What would become of her, she wondered, watching Devlynn's broad shoulders as he rode so effortlessly. Her heart twisted as she remembered how it felt to touch him, to kiss him. Well, that was long over. Any thoughts she had of lovemaking were foolish memories. Now, she knew, she was his enemy. Nothing more. Would he throw her in prison? Keep her hostage as Payton had Yale? Ransom her?

With what? The coffers of Serennog were empty. That condition was what had prompted her upon a course of lies and deception, steps she would gladly retrace if only she could. She thought of those in her keep, those who had trusted her with their lives, those she had sworn to protect. She'd failed them, every last one. From the grouchy wheelwright to the girls who collected eggs, or the stingy baker or apple-cheeked Edwynn the jester . . . or Mary, pregnant with her twins. Had they been born? Had they survived?

Darkness had descended and Yale had begun to complain about being tired and hungry. Devlynn insisted they ride on, only stopping at a creek to refresh the horses and relieve themselves. To Apryll's mortification, he never left her side, only giving her a bit of privacy for a few minutes behind a small bush for her ablutions.

Finally he gave in to his son's complaints and, no doubt, his own fatigue. At a farmhouse alongside the road he stopped and bargained for a hot meal and a bed of sorts with a huge bear of a man who offered them a spot in the hayloft.

The farmer's groggy wife was as skinny as he was fat. At her husband's behest, she heated a thick soup in a pot suspended over the fire. She glanced at the straps binding Apryll's wrists but didn't say a word, just bustled about her task.

Apryll and Yale warmed their hands at the fire while chickens roosted in the woodpile and a cat with suspicious eyes sat on the windowsill. Inky black with green eyes, it stared at the dog and hissed if the bitch dared come too close.

The hut was simple. Tools hung on the wall near the fire and a large table was pushed away from the heat. Two stools and a bench surrounded the fire and a simple bed was tucked into one corner. A few pieces of clothing hung from hooks near a back door that, from the sounds of bleating and mooing, was attached to the shed where the animals were kept.

Apryll sat on the bench and tried to draw the woman into conversation, but whether she was still half asleep or scared to death of the looks sent by her husband, the wife kept mum except to say that her name was Mina.

Once her husband had disappeared with Devlynn to tend to the horses, Mina seemed to relax a little. Yale explored the single room, causing the cranky hens to squawk in protest and flap their wings. The dog took up residence by the fire, her nostrils twitching at the pungent aroma steaming from the big black pot.

"In trouble are ye, lass?" Mina finally asked as she glanced at Apryll's hands.

"Of a sort." Apryll's wrists ached from the tight laces and her stomach rumbled at the scent of food.

"Ye be a prisoner?"

"For the time being."

"Ach, aren't we all?" She tsk-tsked and stirred the soup. Her face, illuminated by the flames, was weathered and wrinkled, the hair peeking out of her scarf a coarse, springy gray.

The back door opened and Devlynn strode in, bringing with him the odors of horses, dung and dust.

"Your husband said to tell you he'll be in as soon as he's tended to the horses."

Mina lifted a bony shoulder, then ladled the soup onto thick slabs of bread. They ate at the table, Apryll struggling with her manacles, Devlynn not offering to set her free. Even when Yale suggested that she could eat more easily if she wasn't tied, he was silenced with a deadly, warning glare from his father.

And Apryll had too much pride to beg. She caught Devlynn's glance once, saw the anger burning in his gray eyes, and inched up her chin, refusing to play the role of the subservient. She'd rot in hell before pleading with him to release her.

Yale and Mina threw scraps to the dog while the chickens clucked back to sleep and the cat leaped onto the cross beams, sitting aloft, his tail twitching as he stared down at the ragged guests.

The thick gravylike soup was divine. Hot and flavored with onions, it warmed a path down Apryll's throat. She washed it down with ale and afterward the farmer offered them the hayloft in which to bed down. It was a slope-roofed space positioned over the pens holding two cows and a nanny goat.

Mina gathered several tattered blankets and, embarrassed that they were so ragged, offered her apologies. "'Tis sorry I be, but this is the best we have."

"Don't worry, the blankets are fine," Apryll assured her and the woman glanced at Devlynn who, along with the farmer, was scattering hay into a manger.

"Is he . . . is he good to you? He claims he's a baron . . . that's he's Black Thorn himself."

"He is," Apryll admitted.

Mina frowned. "Black Thorn," she repeated under her breath as if the words were evil. "He's a dark one, he is," she whispered, making the sign of the cross over her nonexistent bosom. "His wife and unborn babe were killed . . . many think he was to blame." With another furtive glance toward the men, she added, "She was a headstrong woman, Lady Glynda was. A match for him with her fiery temper." Swallowing hard, Mina looked pointedly down at Apryll's wrists again and added, "I wish I could help ye, but if I cross me Sam, he'll beat me sure."

"You've been more than kind."

The wife's dark eyes skittered from the manger to the loft and deep lines of worry furrowed the brow beneath her scarf.

"Woman! What're ye gossipin' about? Don't you have work to do, now?" her husband, a mountain of a man with a bulbous nose and thick lips, growled. His face was illuminated by two candles flickering on a bench near the watering trough. The only other light came through the open doorway, a reddish glow from the fire. Sam shook a finger at his wife. "Just tend to the guests, Mina, and don't be botherin' 'em with any of yer chatter, now." He turned back to his work and muttered something about stupid, ungrateful females.

Mina sent his backside a scathing look, then said to Apryll, "You'll be needin' a wet cloth to wash up. I'll bring it up to you." Rotating on a worn heel she bustled into the house as her husband grunted in satisfaction that she'd obeyed him.

"Can't treat 'em too well," he muttered, "Or they

get a swelled head and expect it all the time." His laugh was ugly and punctuated with snorts as if he thought himself the most clever man in the land.

Apryll would have liked nothing better than to put the big mule in his place but she held her tongue and climbed the ladder to the loft. Yale had already wrapped himself in one of Mina's blankets and had curled himself into a corner where the sloping roof met one wall. He'd made a nest for himself in the loose hay and was snoring softly, dead to the world.

Apryll clumsily threw her blanket on a pile of straw near the top of the ladder. From her vantage point, she could glance over a single rail and see the dark shapes of the cattle, goat and now three horses packed into the small shelter. There were grunts and lows and an occasional snort, and the animal smells were strong, but the rain and wind no longer lashed at Apryll's face, and despite the farmer's stupid remarks, she was grateful for the food and shelter.

Boots rang on the ladder and Mina's head appeared over the edge of the loft. She balanced on the top rung and handed Apryll a wet, folded rag. "'Tis not much, but will make you feel better to clean up," she offered.

"Thank you." Apryll's fingers brushed the older woman's as she attempted to retrieve the cloth. Suddenly Mina clasped her fingers around the leather manacle surrounding Apryll's wrists. "No woman should be bound," she said in a barely audible whisper. "No woman." In the darkness her voice was harsh. "There are many prisons, lass, many ways men have to keep a woman from her freedom and 'tis accepted, but I'm tellin' ye, 'tis wrong. Always. It makes no difference whether ye be a lady, a peasant or a whore."

Then, hearing her husband's heavy gait below, she scurried down the ladder and disappeared into the darkness.

Apryll leaned against a post and listened to the sound of the animals feeding. Where was Devlynn? She was surprised he'd left her alone for so long, for he surely expected her to try to escape again. But then, where would she go?

You could steal a horse. As soon as the farmer goes inside and Devlynn falls asleep.

Oh, but she'd tried that and she'd only ended up leading him to Payton.

Devlynn had let her escape from the camp. Then followed her. She was certain of it. No, she couldn't try the same ruse. Closing her eyes, she heard the sound of rain drizzling down the roof and Yale's steady breathing. Wind battered the roof and a horse nickered softly.

Soon Devlynn would climb up the ladder. What would the next few hours bring? They would be together, essentially alone, as Yale was fast asleep. What then? She remembered their last night together, the passion, the feel of his fingers upon her flesh, the way she'd ached for him, wanted him, had nearly begged him to take her virginity.

Even now, at the thought of it, she blushed. No, it wouldn't happen again. He would never trust her enough to untie her, nor would he want to touch her or kiss her . . . nay, if he had any appetite left for her it would be purely animal, a man's lust for a woman, a need to conquer and tame, without any affection or love.

At that thought she froze. Love? 'Twas a silly notion. Foolish. There was no love between them, only distrust and wanton desire, a carnal ache that she would consider no longer. Nor would she think of escape. Not tonight. She was too tired, she needed rest and then, once she awakened, she would find a way to outfox the damned beast of Black Thorn, a way that would somehow benefit her own keep.

Oh, Serennog! With a heavy heart she thought of her home and felt a deep-seated and desperate longing. Aye, the tapestries were torn and threadbare, and yes, there was hardly enough food to go 'round. The castle walls were crumbling, the rushes old and stale, but Serennog was home, a haven, her place on this earth. And the people who lived there depended upon her. Somehow she would find a way to bring it back to the grandeur it once held.

Without stealing.

Without kidnapping.

Without killing.

Curse Payton's blind ambition!

Damn his thirst for revenge!

To hell with his need to prove himself as worthy!

What had happened between Morgan of Black Thorn and Apryll's mother two decades past should be long buried. Aye, Apryll understood why Payton would feel a need to prove himself. Even after Apryll's father, Lord Regis, was dead and Lady Rowelda had been close behind, her lungs rattling with the disease that had claimed them both, Payton had been unable to forgive their mother.

"'Tis sorry I am," she'd whispered, trying to take Payton's calloused fingers in her own dainty, blue-veined hand. She'd been lying in her death bed, her pale face having lost all of its joy, her eyes as dull as her thinning hair. "I have done you an injustice. I should have sent you away from Serennog, to some-place where you were not always reminded that you were another man's child."

He was stunned. "Why? Did you not want me either? Then why didn't you just get rid of me before I was born as everyone believes you should have?" he asked, searching her face.

"No! I wanted you despite . . . but Regis, he . . ." She glanced from one of her children to the next. "He never forgave me for having borne another man's child."

"But you were forced," Apryll said.

Rowelda's thin lips twisted into a cynical smile. "I suppose I *should* have taken my own life. Honor, you know." She drew in a raspy breath.

"Instead you bore a bastard and left him to be taunted and humiliated his entire life." Payton's face, once ashen, was quickly suffusing with color as anger surged through his veins.

"I saw to your needs," she said softly.

"But never had the spine to defend me."

"No." Her head moved heavily against the pillows propping her up. "'Twas cowardly of me, but Regis, he wanted his own son and . . ."

"And the children you did have were bitter disappointments to him," Apryll had finished. She, too, was disquieted. Although she had not been ignorant of the circumstances of Payton's conception, they had never before spoken of it.

"Aye. But the fates stepped in and you, daughter, will be the ruler. You must marry and soon. Serennog needs a strong baron and an heir."

"What of me?" Payton had demanded, stepping

close to his mother's bed and leaning down to view her more closely. "What's to become of me?"

"You shall continue to live in the great hall and advise your sister."

"I could rule. I have the blood."

"Not of Serennog," their mother said, sitting up before dissolving into a coughing fit and ending up retching into a small pail at her bedside. Her serving woman was quick to be in attendance, retrieving the pail and leaving another.

"She tires," the woman insisted and the smell of oncoming death was heavy in the air.

"Yes . . . leave me . . ." Rowelda had whispered, her forehead shining with beads of sweat, her pale lips cracked. She looked at her children and forced a sad smile. "I did my best," she said softly. "'Twas all I could do." It was the last time Apryll had ever seen her mother alive. Within the hour, Rowelda of Serennog was dead.

And Payton's ache for bloodlust had just begun.

Apryll had been too blind to see it for what it was. Grateful to have some little piece of family left, she'd allowed him too much power, too much authority, too much say in the decisions regarding running the keep. His appetite for authority had only been whetted. His hunger for vengeance had only increased.

He'd never forgiven Rowelda for keeping him. And his feelings for the man who had sired him, the warrior who had raped his mother, impregnated her and never claimed Payton as his son, had only festered over the following years. That the man was dead was of no consequence.

And Apryll had been foolish enough not to see his need for vengeance.

She pulled a blanket about her and opened up the cloth to wipe at her face, but there was something bulky hidden in the wet folds. Something hard and long. In an instant she realized it was a knife, a simple, bone-handled knife with a long, deadly blade. A weapon. Means of escape. From the wife of the big farmer.

As Apryll turned the sharp weapon in her fingers, the wife's words ran through her mind. *No woman should be bound. No woman.*

At that instant she heard the ladder to the loft creak, then the ring of boots as someone heavy began the short climb to the hayloft. Hurriedly she tucked the knife into the loose hay beside her blanket and began washing her face with as much grace as was possible considering that her hands were tied. Oh, Lord, she couldn't let him see the knife.

Her heart banging wildly in her chest, she felt the weight of Devlynn's gaze upon her, yet she went about her cleansing as if she couldn't sense him in the dim light, as if she couldn't hear the sound of his breathing, or smell that now-familiar musky scent that clung to him.

And yet she could. 'Twas as if all her senses were attuned to his every movement.

From the corner, Yale gave off a soft, drowsy sigh. Devlynn hesitated only a moment and then he was in the loft, bending low to avoid hitting the ceiling, moving toward her. She pretended not to notice, didn't so much as glance up as he stood over her, bit her lip when she realized the toe of his boot might at any second scrape against the knife, her only hope of escape and salvation.

"Well, now, Lady Apryll," he said, lowering himself

into a squat so that his head was but inches from hers, "what are we going to do about sleeping tonight?" His breath fanned her cheek. "I don't dare let you sleep by yourself or you'll disappear by morning light, and if I sleep with my hands upon you there is no telling what might happen."

She felt his fingertips lift a strand of hair off her face and push it behind her shoulder. The loft seemed to shrink, the animals below were suddenly far away.

"You tempt me, Apryll. Like Eve did Adam."

"I'm offering you no apple."

"Nay? Mayhap then I'll be forced to steal one from you."

She swallowed hard, knowing far well that he wasn't speaking of fruit but of her virtue.

"You are in no position to deny me," he reminded her and his hand settled possessively on her shoulder.

"I have no apple . . ." she whispered.

His fingers slid down the slope of her breast, idling at the nipple beneath the rough fabric of the tunic. To her dismay, the wayward bud puckered in anticipation and her breast seemed to fill. Slowly he traced the hard bud through her tunic. "Oh, but you have sweet sin to give," he said. "Sweet, sweet sin. The kind a man could lose himself in, the kind a man would gladly give up his soul for."

Heat raced through her bloodstream and deep inside she felt an awakening, the ache she'd tried to deny. He reached beneath her tunic and his fingers scaled her ribs. She held back a moan, resisted the urge to fall against him, but her breast responded and as he touched the very tip of her nipple, hunger swept through her. His finger skimmed that sensitive skin, then withdrew. She couldn't breathe. He pinched her then, teasing and playful, but with a sharp little bite that made her want more. She imagined his weight upon her, and in her mind's eye she viewed his naked body, all hard sinew and muscle, skin shiny with sweat and stretched taut as he parted her legs, thrust into her and claimed that which he called sin for his own.

"I should wring your neck for all that you've done," he said and she was brought quickly back to the here and now. "But I think instead I've found a much more pleasurable way to punish you."

Chapter Twenty

*D*on't *do this.*
    Devlynn heard the voice in his head, knew he should stop, that touching the woman, even being close to her, was dangerous.

Punish her, indeed!

Who would pay the price if he were to bed her now? Was there any chance that he could have his way with her and forget her? Nay, he thought not, and yet he could not resist the temptation of her lips or the dark seduction he'd seen earlier in her gold eyes.

Here in the darkness with the rain tapping on the roof and the soft bed of hay and straw, how could he withstand the warm seduction of her body?

Was she willing? She had been only last night. He leaned forward and brushed his lips over hers. She trembled. Didn't draw away. Nor did she kiss him so ardently as she had the night of the revels.

"Untie me," she whispered.

"So that you can escape?" He was so close he could smell her, taste her. His blood ran hot.

"Nay. I would not."

"And you, my lady, are a liar. A beautiful, bold liar. Nay, your bonds will stay for the night. Come morning I may change my mind."

"Morning is but a few hours," she said.

"Then you won't have long to wait." His body ached for her and it would be so easy to strip her of her clothes, to pry open her legs, to bury himself in her moist, enticing warmth . . . what would it hurt? God knew it was time he had a woman. Right now, just thinking of it, his manhood was as stiff and hot as newly forged steel.

But not this woman. Not now.

He pulled her tight against him, heard her gasp as he rolled them both in the blankets.

"Sleep," he said.

"That is my punishment?"

Had she the nerve to taunt him? She was shameless. And seductive. And a tease.

"For now."

"And later?" she asked, her voice breathless.

"Later, we shall see." It wasn't chivalry or nobility that kept him from taking her but something far deeper. 'Twas fear. Fear that he might lose his Judas of a heart to her—*A kidnapper! A liar! His enemy!*

'Twas insanity.

Disgusted with the turn of his thoughts, he curved his body around hers, cupping her smaller frame with his, feeling her buttocks pressed against his cock. He held her manacled wrists in one hand, his other arm surrounded her waist. She was tense. Unsure. Her breasts spilled over his arm while her rump pressed intimately to his crotch. So supple and rounded. So firm. An invitation.

By the gods, he wanted her. Ached for her.

But not tonight.
Not tonight.

"'Tis as you said," the boy, Henry, whispered into Father Benjamin's ear as they walked past the bee-keeper's hut in the bailey at Serennog. "Father Hadrian is living in the great hall. He sleeps in the lady's bedchamber."

Benjamin sighed, though he'd expected the news. Henry was his eyes, though Benjamin was not as blind as many thought. For some reason they believed that his blindness had affected his hearing, his ability to smell, his touch and most certainly his mental prowess.

To his dishonor, he hadn't disavowed anyone of their perception. Let them think they were hiding from him when he heard their footsteps, let them shout at him that they had given up drink when he smelled the ale upon their lips, let them swear that they had been at mass when he had not sensed them in the chapel. Let them think him slightly dithery and addled.

'Twas his only weapon and sad as it was, these days all men needed a defense. He knew that treachery abounded. He feared that Lady Apryll was in danger and he realized that those who had plotted against her also pretended to be her most devoted servants.

The very ones who lied to him about attending mass. One day, the Father would see to their sins.

Hadrian was the worst. Wearing the vestments, pretending to be a messenger of God, when he was evil incarnate, indulged in the pleasures of the flesh and lied through his supposedly devout teeth. 'Twas a travesty.

"We must leave the keep," he told the boy as he listened to the sounds of the night. Somewhere nearby guards were playing dice, laughing drunkenly, while the wind creaked through the sails of the windmill.

Henry was an orphan, both his parents having fallen ill to the sickness that had swept through the castle three years before. Since Apryll had left, the lad had no one but Benjamin to see to him. "We will need some supplies, Henry, and a horse or a mule. I will procure the animal and you will find a way to weasel an apple or two from the cook and, mayhap, some dried eel?" A jug of wine would help, but he thought it best if he didn't ask for too much. He didn't want to raise any more suspicions than was necessary and these days no one within the keep trusted the other.

"I will try."

Benjamin grabbed the boy by the sleeve. "Do not fail me, Henry. I fear the lady is in grave danger and it is up to us to save her."

"Really? An adventure?" Henry was suddenly eager.

"Aye. Now, off with you. Come back at dawn and as soon as the gates are lifted we shall leave. I will tell Hadrian that I must visit those in the village who are too weak and old to come to mass."

"You would lie?" The boy was awestruck and it bothered Benjamin. Not only the lying, but the fact that the lad was impressed.

"All in the name of God," Benjamin said, then cringed, for he wasn't certain he was doing God's will . . . and yet he felt as if he had no choice. The fate of Serennog appeared to be in his old, tired hands.

* * *

Payton groaned. He felt as if his head had been flattened on a rock, beaten with a stick, then pounded to a pulp. Rolling over, he blinked and saw a ring of men standing around him. In their midst was Geneva and for once her placid expression had turned to worry. "Christ Jesus," he swore, rubbing his eyes with his palms and wishing something would stop the painful banging in his brain.

"Here, drink this." Her voice was a balm, her hands cool as she touched him and offered him a mazer. He took a sip. Water!

"Wine," he muttered and pushed himself to a sitting position. "I need wine." He eyed the men surrounding him—nearly a dozen of them, men whose allegiance he had bought and others, traitors to Black Thorn, who had their own reasons for joining him.

He could not be seen lying here like a pig wallowing in mud. His spine snapped to attention and he stood so quickly he nearly fell over. "Where are they?" he demanded with a sickening feeling as he surveyed the empty old inn.

"Your hostages?" Rudyard, the thin, shifty captain of Black Thorn's guard, asked.

"Aye." He was walking now, striding through the decaying, drafty building, searching the cobweb-infested corners, his gaze scraping every nook and cranny where a boy might hide.

"They're gone," Rudyard said. "Black Thorn stole his son and your sister."

"No—" But the reality set in and the pain in his head increased. By the gods, no! No longer caring what the rest of the men thought, he strode to his hiding spot. Dread took a stranglehold on his heart as he removed the stone. The hollow beneath it was empty, the pouches missing. "Damn!"

"That's right," Rudyard said, his voice irritating over the murmur of the rest of the men. "Black Thorn took back the gold you wrested from him. Now you have nothing. No money. No hostage. Not even his steed."

Rage fired Payton's blood and burned out the last of the cobwebs in his mind. How could this have happened? How could he have become so careless? He remembered sitting at the fire with his sister and that impudent boy, eating the charred meat and drinking a cup or two of wine, and then he'd become so sated and drowsy that he hadn't been able to keep his eyes open, that rather than ride out, he'd insisted they rest. "Damn it all to hell," he muttered, then swiped at the air with a fist, for he understood the depths of Apryll's betrayal. She'd drugged him rather than the boy. Cursed, cursed woman! He swore under his breath.

"What?" Geneva asked, walking up to him, her serene expression once again in place.

"I was drugged," he growled, casting an embarrassed glance over her shoulder to the men he'd banded together. One found a jug of wine and began passing it around. "With the potion you gave me."

"How?"

Again Rudyard's grating voice as he stood at the fire, declining a drink from the communal jug. Payton's gaze fixed on the heavy vessel and he remembered Apryll offering him "one last cup." Oh, she was a clever one, his sister, but not clever enough.

"I don't know, I thought I gave it to the boy, but now I think Apryll slipped some of the potion into my cup and somehow filled the vial with something else—or mayhap she split the last dose . . ." Why had he trusted her? Why hadn't he tied her as he had the boy?

"Then you failed," Rudyard said with a lift of his palms, as if it was a simple fact anyone should understand.

"I made a mistake. 'Twill be soon fixed." Payton glowered down at the gaping hole where he'd hidden his pouch of stolen gold, coins and gems.

"You failed," Rudyard repeated and this time his voice was much closer. His breath brushed Payton's back.

"'Tis not a failure but a misstep." Payton spun quickly, just in time to see a flash of a blade.

Geneva screamed.

Payton ducked but wasn't fast enough. Rudyard's sword plunged deep into his stomach. Twisted. White hot pain burst through his gut. He couldn't believe it. The coward had run him through? A satisfied smile contorted Rudyard's lips, showing off his crooked teeth.

"God in heaven, no!" Geneva cried.

Payton's legs trembled, couldn't bear his weight.

"Nay, nay, nay!" Geneva threw herself upon him as he fell to his knees. "Payton, oh, God, nay. Please spare him, please . . ." Tears streamed from her eyes. "I love you . . . I carry your child . . . do not die . . . do not!" He gasped, his breath rasping, and he knew the fight was over.

With a horrid sucking sound Rudyard retrieved his blade. "You failed. A leader has but one chance."

Geneva's tortured face swam before his eyes, the entire room spun. "Payton, oh, love, your son needs you."

A father? He was to be a father? He reached out and she took her hand in his and, as if understanding what he needed, placed his palm on the flat of her abdomen. Blood streaked her tunic—his blood, he realized as his gaze shifted to the man who had double-crossed him.

Rudyard, the unfaithful captain of the guard, was not his ally after all. The world shifted, became blurry.

Geneva, holding Payton, rocking slowly, glowered up at Rudyard. "A curse upon you."

"There may be many already, woman."

"I'll see you in hell," Payton rasped, fixing his eyes upon Rudyard's bony face. 'Twas that of a skeleton already. Darkness threatened from the corners of his vision.

Rudyard laughed and the sound was like dry leaves crushed under a destrier's sharp hooves. "Don't wait for me."

Geneva sobbed, or was it another woman? Apryll? His mother? His mind was foggy again and, by the gods, he was cold, bitter cold as if he were buried in the snows of winter.

"What shall we do with her?" a deep voice asked as the woman holding him was dragged away, her warm arms no longer about him. Payton tried to locate the owner of the voice, but his gaze was fixed and dark; he knew he should try to stop what was about to happen, but his body wouldn't move. Couldn't.

"Do whatever you want with her. I care not," someone—Rudyard, aye, Rudyard—said heartlessly.

Somewhere a woman screamed, crying, begging . . . "Nay, do not do this . . . nay, nay, nay, oh, Mother, do not make me suffer so . . ." Payton couldn't reach her or say a word. There was laughter, men's drunken laughter, and the sound of rutting and a woman's terrified howls . . . and then nothing but a soft buzz in his ears. Nothing.

As the lifeblood seeped out of him, Payton of Serennog, born a bastard, raised by a lord who hated him, never realizing that one woman had loved him, gave up his battle.

Chapter Twenty-one

A rooster crowed so loudly that Apryll started. Blinking, she tried to rise, but was held fast by a strong arm.

Devlynn. He was lying beside her, pinning her against him, his breathing soft and gentle against the back of her neck. It felt so natural, so warm, so right to be snuggled against him.

He is your enemy, Apryll, her mind taunted. *Forget it not. Has he not bound your wrists, kept you prisoner? Did he not promise to punish you for your sins against him?*

She thought of the knife buried somewhere beneath the matted hay. Where had she hidden it? Slowly, moving with painstaking deliberation so as not to awaken him, she explored the area around her with her hands, gently patting the straw, probing carefully with the fingers of both hands. She'd tucked it away quickly but had barely moved from this spot. It had to be nearby. Was it stuffed in the hay beneath Devlynn's body? Or somewhere else? It was still dark in the loft, though the animals were stirring and she heard the creak of footsteps in the house. Again she sifted through the dry hay and her fingers brushed against something cold and sharp.

At last! Pretending to stretch in her sleep she managed to grab the hilt and draw it downward as she lifted her leg so that she could slide it down the inside of her boot. There was no time to use it now—the farmer was already up, his gruff voice filtering through the thin wood walls.

"Mina! Up with ye! There's milkin' to be done and me breakfast to see to!"

Devlynn shifted. Pulled her closer still.

Barely daring to breathe, Apryll slid the knife into the side of her boot and prayed it wouldn't slice her skin.

The door to the house banged open and light from the fire streamed into the shed. Chickens cackled, the goat bleated and the farmer grumbled under his breath.

Devlynn raised his head as she pretended to be asleep. She sensed his gaze upon her, felt his hand steal up beneath her tunic to find her breast. Calloused fingers brushed her nipple but she dared not move, could hardly draw a breath. She longed to snuggle closer to him, to press her body against his, but she resisted and, as if he realized suddenly what he was doing, he jerked his hand away.

"For the love of God, woman, why do you tempt me?" he grumbled, then rolled away. He was on his feet in an instant and said more loudly, "'Tis time to rise. Now."

Apryll sighed loudly, then opened an eye to find him towering over her. She stretched languidly and forced herself to a sitting position just as Yale, from the corner, roused himself. His hair was filled with straw, his eyelids still heavy with sleep.

"Must we get up already?" he complained.

"Only if you want to get home today," his father said and a smile played upon Devlynn's harsh features. "Mayhap you would rather stay here with the farmer and his wife. I'm sure they have plenty of work for a lad your size."

"Aye, that we do!" the farmer called up from the floor below. "Mayhap he would like to milk the goat, or clean out the dung in this shed, or stack firewood."

Reluctantly Yale climbed to his feet. Yawning widely and holding the blanket about his shoulders, he made his way to the ladder. "Will we really make it back to Black Thorn this day?" he asked Devlynn.

"Only if we hurry." Devlynn grabbed the boy and hugged him fiercely. "Wouldn't you like to see Aunt Vi and Miranda and Collin and Bronwyn?"

"Not Bronwyn," Yale said, shaking his head. "I *never* want to see her. She's a *girl*."

"So she is and there will be a time soon when you'll want to be around her because she is a girl."

"Never." Yale made a face and then dropped his blanket to scramble rapidly down the stairs. Devlynn's gaze followed after him, his smile only fading when he pivoted and leaned a hip against the post. Folding his arms over his chest, he pinned Apryll in his cold, silver stare. "And it's time for you, too, lady. Black Thorn awaits."

"You're telling me that Devlynn abandoned you?" Collin tapped his fingers on the arm of his brother's chair. Seated in the great hall, warming his backside by the fire and sipping wine, he glared up at the ragged group of soldiers who had returned a few hours after the sun had risen.

Lloyd, the heavyset, foulmouthed knight, seemed to be the self-appointed leader. "That's right," he said, nodding as he did to the rest of the ragtag band. "He and the hostage took off in the middle of the night without a word. In the morning the two best steeds were missing. We waited for nearly a day, then reasoned that he'd brought her back here, so we broke camp and returned."

"Why would he leave with her?" Collin asked as Miranda, imperious as ever, swept into the room. Though she hadn't appeared until this moment, Collin suspected that his sister had been listening from the other side of the doorway. But then he always suspected that she, or persons he had yet to identify, were spying on him, watching his every move, hoping that he would make a mistake ... he took a swallow from his cup and the wine soured his stomach.

"Are you certain that the prisoner did not escape and that Lord Devlynn gave chase?" Miranda eyed the soldiers as if they didn't have a brain between them.

"Why not wake us?" Lloyd asked and Rearden nodded. "Would we not be more likely to catch her if we all searched? Are not ten eyes better than two?"

Miranda glanced thoughtfully at the fire. "Mayhap Devlynn didn't think so."

"Or mayhap he wanted to be with her alone," Collin thought aloud. He'd seen how taken with the woman Devlynn had been from the moment he'd first seen her in this very hall.

He remembered the night well, and there were still

remnants of the revels scattered about the hallways and chambers, swagged greenery and candles burned nearly flat, to remind him how short a time had passed. The last of the guests had left yesterday and with Devlynn's absence and Yale's life in question, the keep had become somber and dark, servants, knights, peasants, all mistrusting the other. No one knew who was enemy or friend.

"Lord Devlynn could be at Serennog," James offered as if he'd thought about it long and hard. "If he was chasing the lady, she might lead him back to her keep."

"And overpower him with her army?" Miranda asked.

"*If* he was chasing her." Collin stood abruptly, tired of the waiting. The idleness. The not knowing what to expect. "Dennis returned yesterday," he advised the men. "He told me we were to send an army of men, horses and weapons to Serennog, but before I have amassed it, you arrive and tell me . . . what? That Devlynn has abandoned you and his keep and has taken off with a woman who helped deceive him? A woman who stole his son? Is that what you would have me believe?"

"'Tis what happened." Lloyd rubbed the end of his nose with his sleeve and looked longingly at the jug of wine sitting on the table next to Collin's mazer.

"Where are the others?" Miranda asked. "Sir Rudyard? Where is the captain of the guard? And Sir Nathan? Sir Spencer?"

Ah, there it was again, her interest in Spencer. Though she might hide her concern for Spencer by inquiring of the others, Collin saw through her. She cared naught for anyone but the barrel-chested knight with a broken, aquiline nose and eyes as dark as obsidian.

Miranda wasn't all she seemed, Collin thought not for the first time. There was something she was hiding, some secret she held close. Not that he didn't have a few of his own.

"We must find them," she said impatiently as she stood and worried her fingers against her thumbs. "All of them."

"How?" Collin watched agitation form lines across Miranda's face.

"Go after them, of course."

"To Serennog?"

"Where else?" Her face lit with anticipation and her eyes took in the face of each tired soldier. "We'll scour the forests, search the fields and ask of them in the surrounding towns. Surely someone has seen them and would recognize the colors of Black Thorn."

"Even though Devlynn ordered us to stay here?" Collin asked, enjoying watching the flush of color climb up her cheeks. Miranda was beautiful and knew it, but she was a woman who depended upon her wits more than her beauty to get what she wanted.

"Did Devlynn not send Dennis back and ask for new recruits and weapons?" she demanded, crossing the short distance to Collin and staring down at him with bright, determined eyes. "What's the matter, brother? Be you a coward? Would you rather stay here, hidden deep within the castle walls, than brave the cold nights and harsh days searching for our brother?"

"I would do what's best for Black Thorn."

"And who decides what that is?" she asked, anger

radiating from her so intensely that Rearden actually took a step backward lest he become the object of her rage. "I am first born, am I not?"

"I've heard this before."

"And you'll hear it again. Just because I was born without balls, I was passed over by Father, looked upon as someone to barter with and marry off to the highest bidder or the best alliance, while Devlynn, because he was a boy child, was groomed to be lord and you . . . you are the replacement. Should Devlynn fail, then you will be lord. It matters not that you are self-centered, incapable of leading and hedonistic."

"While you are virtuous, is that what you're suggesting?" He glanced at the expressions of the men in the room. Some were amused, other disgusted, still others showed awe or fear.

"I'm suggesting that you are not cut out to be the ruler of Black Thorn. Testicles or no testicles."

"Devlynn asked me to watch the keep."

"Then he was foolish. 'Tis the same as suggesting that a thief watch the jewels."

Collin was tired of the argument. "I'm doing what I think is best for Black Thorn," he repeated.

She arched a dark, disparaging brow and sneered at the mazer he'd so recently emptied. "By sitting on your arse and drinking wine?"

He felt one corner of his mouth lift. "If that is what's best."

"Then I'll have to amend my opinion of you, brother. I thought you were only lazy, but now, it seems, you are cowardly as well." Proudly swinging her hair over one shoulder, she marched out of the room in a cloud of self-righteous disgust.

Collin decided if he were smart he would have a guard watch her, for Miranda, it seems, was more dangerous than he'd previously thought.

Women!

They were the most sought-after of his pleasures.

And the bane of his existence.

Father Benjamin heard the sound of a woman's moans and he sensed a great sadness in the universe. "Father be with us," he prayed, deftly making the sign of the cross over his chest. Astride the mule, the boy walking beside him, he was certain that a woman was nearby and in pain. The smell of the forest in winter filled his nostrils; dank, wet earth, rotting leaves, fresh rainwater, all carried on a brisk cold wind that bit at his cheeks and congealed his blood. Ach, he was too old for this. Riding the mule caused his legs to ache and walking hurt his feet.

He heard the chatter of a squirrel and the flutter of wings, and beneath it all the woman's moans. They were getting closer.

"You're certain this is the way?" he asked the boy.

"Aye. I listened to Payton and Father Hadrian and Sir Brennan when they didn't think anyone was about, the night before Lady Apryll set off for Black Thorn. Sir Payton insisted that they would split up on the way back to confuse Black Thorn's troops, then, once they'd lost those following them, they were to meet at an old inn on the road that forked to Pentref, east of the new bridge. This be the road."

"It's old—overgrown?"

"Aye."

"Have there been horses here recently? Is the grass trampled, the earth turned?"

"Aye, Father, many horses from the looks of it."

Benjamin squared his shoulders. Shook off the damp cold. "Then we'll carry on." The mule plodded forward and within a few minutes the boy stopped dead in his tracks, the beast pausing as well.

"What's that?" he asked, trepidation in his young voice, for the woman's sobs were more distinct, her moans whispering eerily through the forest like a bad omen.

"Let's find out."

"But—"

"It sounds as if someone needs our help. Now, come along, Henry, you must be my eyes."

Benjamin heard the boy gulp and tug on the mule's lead and within minutes, he said, "By the saints, Father, 'tis Geneva!" And then his footsteps were hurrying away. "She's hurt, oh, God."

Benjamin slid off the mule and, using his walking stick, hurried as fast as he dared through the long, wet grass toward the sound of her sobs. "I'm here, child," he said, wondering what had happened to her. She'd left the keep but two days before to search out herbs, but she'd not returned to Serennog and he'd been worried.

"Are you all right, Geneva?" Henry asked, then to Benjamin, "She's just lyin' here on the grass, cryin' and lookin' like she don't see me. She's shiverin' cold and her face is bruised and . . . and there's blood."

"Where?" Benjamin asked as the tip of his walking stick encountered something on the ground.

"Careful, or you'll step on her."

Praying softly, Benjamin kneeled, his stiff knees meeting the frigid earth. He reached forward and touched Geneva's shoulder. "Geneva, 'tis I, Father Benjamin, what happened, child?"

She moaned incoherently.

"Tell me what's wrong with her," Benjamin said to Henry.

"Her face, 'tis black-and-blue and there be scratches on her arms and . . . blood, lots of blood."

"Where?" Benjamin asked again, but started to understand.

A pause.

"Henry?" Father Benjamin asked sternly.

"On her skirts. I think . . . I think it might be from her privates, Father."

God be with her. "And the inn, it's nearby? Could we take her inside to shelter?"

"Yes—"

"Nay!" she screamed. "Nay, nay, nay! Oh, Payton . . . oh . . . the baby, the baby . . . precious baby. No! Please. Stop!" She was crying and shivering and as Father Benjamin tried to hold her she thrashed. "Bastards! Horrid monsters! A curse on you, on all of you!"

"Shhh. I'm here, Geneva, and the Lord is with you. Shh, be still . . ." But he understood her cries as he listened to the undertones of her words, felt her quivering in fear and rage. That she allowed him to touch her was a miracle, for though his eyes were blind, he saw that this woman had been raped and, during the heinous act, had lost a child.

"Go into the inn. See if there is anyone inside," Benjamin ordered Henry.

The boy took off running, his footsteps and breathing fading as the priest turned all of his attention to the woman trembling in his arms. "Now, Geneva, we must take you back to the castle. To Serennog. You need help."

She was shivering, her skin icy, her hair matted from the dirt and rain, her teeth chattering either from the cold or her ordeal.

What monster lived within men to force a woman?

In all his years Benjamin had recognized his own lust, he'd experienced a mind-numbing want of a woman, he'd felt desire run hot through his veins, but never had he given in, never had he let temptation overrule his vows. He'd spent hours on his knees on the hard stone floor of the chapel, praying to God for forgiveness for his wanton, carnal thoughts, and the Lord had helped him, given him strength, showed him the path. Too many men gave in to the sins of their bodies—too few spent hours in prayer.

And this poor woman, good-hearted Geneva, had paid the price, as had the poor little innocent growing within her. He prayed for the baby's soul, for though it was conceived beyond the sacrament of marriage, it was a person nonetheless, a child of God, a pure little being who should not be punished for the sins of his parents.

Ah, 'twas a dark world at times. "Rest easy," he said, stroking Geneva's cheek. "We will find a way to get you home."

"AAAAAHHHHHHH!" The boy let out a cry that shook through the forest. Geneva screamed. Father Benjamin flinched. He was struggling to his feet when Henry's quick footsteps returned.

Breathing wildly, he was stammering and making no sense whatsoever.

"What?" Father Benjamin snapped, for though

Henry was a good boy, a true heart, he was a bit of a coward and tended to be overly dramatic.

"'Tis Sir Payton," the boy said.

"Get him."

"Nay, I cannot. He's dead. Stabbed to death."

Benjamin's old shoulders sagged. Sadness and despair overcame him. "You're certain?" he asked, now understanding Geneva's rantings.

"Aye. Oh, aye."

Geneva let out a pained wail. "Murderer," she cried. "Murderer. Black Thorn. May the gods curse your soul . . . oh, oh . . . Payton . . ."

"Shh, child, 'tis time we pray, for Payton's soul," Father Benjamin said, crossing himself, and ignoring the fact that Geneva had defied the teachings of the church, had trusted in the dark arts. Mayhap this was God's way of punishing her, for He was a vengeful God as well as a loving Father.

"Pray with me." Benjamin closed his sightless eyes. "In the name of the Father, and the Son and the Holy Ghost . . ."

The castle loomed before her, a behemoth of gray stone turrets and wide walls perched high on the hill, a forbidding fortress of bleak, formidable rock. From the highest towers the black and gold standards of Black Thorn snapped in the winter wind. Apryll's heart sank as she eyed the banners so proudly displayed. Her fingers felt like ice as they gripped the pommel of her weary mount's saddle. The straps holding her wrists were tight, the winter air raw against her cheeks, the knife tucked into her boot cold against her leg.

Trepidation stirred in her soul.

Less than a week before she'd been in this very spot.

She'd remembered shivering as she'd dressed in the forest, working at the fastenings of her mother's white gown, her fingers numb with cold. She'd managed to finger-comb her hair and lace it with ribbons, then, forcing a poise she hadn't felt, slip past the drunken guard at the main gate. Carefully holding her skirts above the puddles and mud, she'd picked her way to the great hall, knowing that she was to distract the lord while Payton and the others crept through the keep, stealing from the treasury, taking the horses, getting back some of what Morgan of Black Thorn had stolen from Serennog two decades earlier.

When she'd spied the lord, sitting high on his dais, glum and spiritless despite the music and revelry, she'd been caught by his handsome despair, the secrets in his gray eyes, and when he'd approached her and asked her to dance, she'd been wary, but intrigued. During the dance, as he'd held her in his arms, she'd lost herself in some silly romantic vision—an illusion she'd helped create.

Even now as she rode behind him she stared at the width of his shoulders and the proud bearing with which he rode. She noticed the way his dark hair fell over his collar and her silly heart skipped a beat. She was being brought back to Black Thorn a prisoner and still she dreamed of loving him.

Payton was right. She was foolish. A woman unfit to reign. A female who sometimes let her heart rule her head.

And so it had come to this. She was prisoner and half in love with her captor. Silently she cursed her fate and remembered Geneva's prediction. *'Tis about destiny, m'lady. Your destiny.*

You will marry the Lord of Black Thorn.

'Twas a joke.

A vile trick.

For once, it seemed, the sorceress was wrong. Completely and utterly mistaken.

Chapter Twenty-two

Bells pealed throughout the bailey.

A sentry yelled, "Lord Devlynn has arrived! He brings his son!" People dropped what they were doing.

As Devlynn rode through the gates of Black Thorn, shouts rang out. The carpenters repairing the stables put down their hammers, the smith abandoned his forge, the armorer ignored the weapons he'd been cleaning and the boys netting eels in the pond looked away from their catches. Women carrying laundry and girls with egg baskets and water buckets stopped their tasks as the Lord of Black Thorn returned to his keep.

"Welcome home, m'lord," one man said as he yanked off his hat and bowed slightly. "We've missed ye. I see ye've got yer son." A smile of crooked teeth peeked out from behind his red beard. "'Tis good that ye're home."

"Aye, welcome," a big-bosomed girl with braids and doelike eyes said, curtsying. Her lips curved into a suggestive smile and she batted her eyelashes slowly. Suggestively. Apryll felt a ridiculous spurt of jealousy.

"Yale!" Bronwyn screamed in delight as she flew

out of one of the huts and dashed across the bent grass and mud. Her face was alive, her brown curls flopping and streaming behind her. "There are new puppies in the kennels and yesterday Mother let me ride with her into the meadow and Uncle Collin said that he would take me on a hunt when you returned. Come!" she cried breathlessly, so excited she actually clapped her hands and jumped up and down.

With a quick look to his father, Yale slid off his mount and chased after his cousin through the throng that had gathered. Laughing and chattering, they ran together along a muddy path that twisted past the well and a broken wagon.

Apryll's heart twisted as Devlynn reined in. How she envied Devlynn his family. Brother, sister, Aunt Vi, a niece and child, while all she had was Payton, one half brother, who was as close by blood to Devlynn and his siblings as he was to her.

But for the sets of adoring eyes looking at their lord there were others as well, malevolent, shifty gazes, hard-set jaws, flared nostrils that were impossible not to notice. For the most part the angry glares were sent her way, but she was certain she saw more than one tight-lipped, hostile gaze taking in the baron's return. Who were the men and women who hated him? Were they the traitors who had aided Payton in his raid? Or was she imagining things, she wondered as dogs barked from the kennels and sheep bleated in the fields. Mayhap it was her own despair, her own sense of guilt, her own anxiety about being away from her castle and the people who depended upon her.

Laundry flapped in large, open sheds, smoke curled upward from chimneys, carts and wagons brought wares and the windmill's sweeps turned in the cold, chill breeze.

"Look at her—sitting upon her horse. As if she was the damned Queen of England!" The shrewish whisper was loud enough for Apryll to hear. She steeled herself. She was regarded by everyone within the keep as an enemy of these people, a threat to Black Thorn, the woman responsible for death and destruction. She refused to meet their eyes but sat proudly, chin high, shoulders level, spine stiff, ignoring the whispers that swept through the crowd, conjectures about her.

"Who is she?" a fat laundress carrying a basket of filthy clothes asked her smaller companion, a birdlike woman with a beak for a nose and small, pinched features, certainly the source of the harsh whisper.

"She called herself Lady Apryll of Serennog." Yes, the same ugly tone.

"That one? Nay. I saw the lady of Serennog on the night of the revels. A true beauty she was and dressed so fine, all in pure white silk—Lady Violet likened her to an angel."

"An angel straight from hell!" The tiny woman made a swift sign of the cross over her chest as if to ward off any evil spirits lurking nearby.

The laundress's small eyes lifted and she stared straight at Apryll upon her muddy mount. "But . . . but this one . . . the same woman? Bah!" She shook her head side to side and her short little nose wrinkled as if she smelled something putrid. "She's so filthy and thin and she's wearing a peasant man's clothes."

"A disguise, you idiot," bird-woman explained with a sniff. "And she's not to be trusted. Look there"—bony fingers pointed at Apryll's hands— "she's a prisoner."

The fat woman stared at the reins running from the bridle of Apryll's mount to Devlynn's gloved hand.

"And well she should be. She's deadly. If not for her, young Yale would not have been kidnapped, the stables wouldn't have burned and poor Grace wouldn't have buried Seth and be a widow today, I tell you. That one"—she cast a hateful nod at Apryll astride her weary horse—"she's heartless, she is, and deserves whatever fate Lord Devlynn has for her."

"Look at her face. See you not a bruise beneath the mud? Do you think he had to beat her?"

"'Tis possible. The baron has a temper and this one would sorely test it, taking his boy. Remember what happened with poor Lady Glynda."

Apryll closed her ears to the gossip, though her heart was as heavy as if it were weighted with stones. As long as she was a prisoner within the walls of Black Thorn she would be hated. Mistrusted. Accused of every foul deed that happened.

"Brother!" Collin dashed out of the great hall and down the steps to Devlynn, who was still holding the reins of Apryll's horse. Collin slung an arm around Devlynn's shoulders and hugged him fiercely.

As he had never done before.

Devlynn's throat tightened and not for the first time in his life he felt a deep deceit, the kind of rift that can only be wrought by one you love.

"Welcome!"

"'Tis good to be home," Devlynn admitted, though he glanced at the charred stables and remembered the men who had died for Payton of Serennog's greed.

"Here, George, tend to the horses," Collin ordered a gangly stable boy as Devlynn extracted himself from his brother's embrace. "We were worried," Collin ram-bled on. Devlynn slapped Phantom's reins into the stable boy's hands but held tight to the straps leading to Apryll's mount. "Miranda wanted to search for you, but I told her you would return." He smiled and clapped Devlynn on the back. "And you've found Yale and Lady Apryll!" 'Tis time for a celebration! Come, come, no reason to stand out here in this bloody weather; let us have a cup."

Devlynn didn't feel like celebrating. Not yet. There was much to do. He glanced back at Apryll and saw her elevate her chin even higher as she sat, waiting, upon her horse. Devlynn noticed the curious eyes staring at her, heard the whispers, and though they fired his blood, he ignored them. He could not defend this woman who had put his entire castle at risk. "Have the others returned?" he asked Collin.

"Some. Not all." Collin cast a glance toward the heavens where dark-bellied clouds promised more rain. "Come, Devlynn, let us have a cup by the fire." His gaze traveled to Apryll and a smile of appreciation curved his lips. "What of her?"

"She is to be locked away."

Apryll stiffened.

"In the dungeon?" Collin asked and Devlynn saw his hostage pale beneath the mud upon her face. He walked to her steed. "Come on," he said, offering to help her off the animal, but she refused his aid, clasped the pommel with her tied hands and swung her leg over the horse's back to land a little ungainly upon the soft ground.

"Oh, for the love of God, what is this? Lady Apryll is to come inside and be treated as the lady she is." Miranda was standing at the top of the steps to the great hall. Her arms were folded under her breasts, her hair catching in the wind, the glint in her eye unmistakable.

"She's an enemy." Devlynn was pulling Apryll toward the keep.

"And you may lock her away, but not in some foul-smelling dungeon, brother, oh, nay. She can be kept in one of the chambers within the keep, a decent chamber with a fire and bed."

"So she can escape as she did the hermit's cell?"

"Only if you're foolish enough not to guard her with someone you trust implicitly."

And who would that be? Devlynn wondered, for now he understood that deception and treachery ran deep within the thick castle walls.

"How about you, sister? Would you have her be your charge?" he asked.

"Why not?" Miranda eyed Apryll with a blend of fascination and awe. "But I'll not keep her caged like an animal."

Devlynn hesitated. Could he trust his sister? "She is not to leave the upper chambers," he said. "And she is to be under your watch unless she is with me. If she disappears again, I will hold you responsible."

"I would expect no less." Miranda turned her gaze to Apryll. "Come along, you must be tired and hungry. 'Tis time you had some time away from my ogre of a brother."

"And you, lady," Devlynn said, his eyes drilling deep into Apryll's imperious gold orbs. "You are to obey me. Do not try to escape, for your very life and the lives of your brother and the men who rode with him are at stake." He placed a hand over her upper arm. "I will tolerate no insubordination, do you hear me? You are my prisoner and if you try to escape again, I swear to you I will take my vengeance not only upon your skin, but on that of everyone in Serennog. No one—not a man, woman or child—will be safe from me, do you hear? You are to obey me."

"And should I bow down and lick your boots as well? Or mayhap, you should trade in this manacle for a leash and I will follow after you and sit at your side like some faithful, stupid dog." A few men coughed. Women tittered.

"You test me, woman."

"As you test me." She took a step toward him and seemed not to notice that several people watching had gasped. "Now hear this and hear it well, Devlynn. I will never bow down to you. I will never give you my pride. I will never act the poor, beaten animal, do you understand? You can threaten me, torture me or kill me, but I will never beg, nor will I kneel at your feet."

By the gods, she was spirited. Her eyes gleamed with conviction, her jaw hoisted her chin heavenward, and even in the filthy, stolen huntsman's tunic and breeches she managed to appear regal.

The muscles at the back of his neck tightened. "Take her away," he growled at his sister, "but do not take your eyes from her. She's as slippery as any eel in the sea."

"Ah, but far more fetching, don't you think?" Collin said as Miranda led Apryll into the great hall. "Even in rags she's a beauty."

Jealousy raged through Devlynn's blood, but he held his tongue. It infuriated him that he would feel anything but disgust for the woman. But his feelings for her were complex. Throughout the long ride to Black Thorn, he'd watched her, seen her smile kindly at Yale, even joke with the boy when they'd stopped for food or water. Once he'd spied her rumpling Yale's hair affectionately with her bound hands, as if she truly felt some fondness for the child.

And yet she'd been a party to kidnapping the boy. He remembered listening at the old inn, hearing her conversation with her brother. *I would no more turn against you than you would against me.* That had been her vow to Payton. At the time Devlynn had heard the words he'd thought she'd meant that she would do anything for Payton and that Yale's fate mattered not, but during the ride to Black Thorn she'd displayed tenderness, even laughed at some of Yale's antics, her gold eyes shining with something akin to caring for the boy.

Was it all for show?

Mayhap.

Probably another ruse so that Devlynn would forgive her, a ploy to save her own pretty neck. Well, it wouldn't work. He knew her too well.

Disturbed, he walked into the great hall, expecting to feel elation and relief at being home; instead he felt only apprehension.

His life since the night of the revels had changed. Forever. All because of the regal, feisty woman who was now his prisoner.

Nothing would ever be the same.

"You're in love with Devlynn." Miranda's words echoed in the wide chamber on the second floor. Apryll stood by the fire, warming the winter chill from her bones. Two boys of ten or so were filling a large tub with steaming water while a girl with curly red hair and freckles spattered over a short little nose was adding fragrances to the bath.

"In love?" Apryll shook her head violently though a part of her acknowledged the fact. A silly wayward part of her heart crumbled at the sight of the monster.

"I can see it in your eyes when you look at him," Miranda said with a knowing lift of one eyebrow. "'Tis an expression I've seen far too often. Many have loved my brother."

"Have they?" Apryll attempted to sound disinterested, when, if the truth be known, her heart ached at the thought.

"Aye, but he rarely returns the favor."

Water splashed into the tub and steam rose to the ceiling. "Enough, be off," Miranda ordered the boys and to the servant girl she said, "Leave the soap and towels. I will tend to the lady."

"But me mother, she said I was to bathe her and get her dressed."

"Then go down to Bessie and see if there are dresses within the keep that will fit the lady. Mine are too large, but Lady Glynda's before she was with child might work. And we'll need a chemise and something for the lady's feet. Bessie should know where Glynda's things are stowed."

"Nay!" The thought of wearing Devlynn's dead wife's gowns was loathsome and seemed indecent somehow. "I . . . I can wear these again, if they are but washed."

"Don't be silly." Miranda shooed the girl out the door and insisted Apryll strip from her dirty breeches and tunic, then settle into the basin before the water cooled.

Apryll laughed without any mirth. "I think I'll need some help," she admitted, holding up her bound hands.

"Devlynn is such a beast! What was he thinking?" Quickly Miranda slid a wicked little dagger from her pocket and sliced the leather bindings. As if she'd been a serving girl all of her life rather than the daughter of a lord, Miranda helped Apryll out of her clothes and into the tub. The water was so hot it stung, but within minutes Apryll's muscles had loosened, she'd washed her hair and skin with the lavender-smelling soap and she'd managed to rub the feeling into her wrists and hands. She leaned her head against the tub's rim, smelling the fragrant scent and sighing.

Miranda walked to the window where she peered through the slats of the blinds, looking down to the bailey. "You know," she said thoughtfully, "Devlynn cares for you."

Apryll's heart jumped but she snorted her disagreement. "I think not."

"Oh, he tries to hide it, but I saw his anger, his passion, the way he looked at you. He's never looked at a woman that way, not even Glynda."

"His wife?"

Miranda nodded and her lips compressed.

"What happened to her?" Apryll asked.

Sighing, Miranda glanced at Apryll, then walked to the fire as if suddenly chilled. "She was a headstrong woman, Glynda was. Beautiful and playful, but willful, as well. She and Devlynn had many rows. He wanted a castle full of children, but she did not. She'd had one son, 'twas enough."

"But I thought . . . I'd heard she was with child." Apryll laved her arms with the fragrant soap, letting the warm bath water rinse away the lather as Miranda gnawed her lower lip.

"She was. The babe died when Glynda did." She

closed her eyes for a second and shivered as if reliving
the day of her sister-in-law's death. "She and Devlynn
had quarreled and she'd taken off not on her little jennet, but upon the wildest steed in the stable, a sorrel
stallion. Devlynn had been beside himself and rode
after her, giving chase, but Glynda took it as a compe-
tition. She pushed her horse faster and faster and
when he balked at jumping over a fallen tree, Glynda
was thrown off. She landed on the back of her head,
breaking her neck. She was dead by the time Devlynn
reached her." Miranda rubbed her arms and shivered.
"He blamed himself for her death and has never forgiven himself."

Even in the warm water, Apryll's blood chilled.

"It's only been a few days since he tore off his
mourning band. Such a waste," she thought aloud and
then glanced at Apryll as if she'd given away a great
secret. "To be in an unhappy marriage . . . oh, I know
'tis a sacrament, one that must be upheld, and that
love has no place in marriage, but it seems foolish to be
forever yoked to the wrong man."

"And you think Glynda was not in love with Devlynn?"

"Of course she wasn't," Miranda said. "She was too
busy being in love with herself."

"And what of you?" Apryll asked suddenly.
"Where is Bronwyn's father?"

Miranda hesitated, opened her mouth to speak and
shut it again. She handed Apryll a towel. "He is away."

"Is he returning soon?"

There was a rap on the door and the serving girl
appeared toting a heavy basket and three fine dresses
before Miranda could answer. The girl held up each
dress for Apryll's appraisal. There was a pale gray wa-

tery silk, another heavy blue damask trimmed in fur, and a rich gold velvet with a low neckline and fitted bodice. Miranda tossed the first two onto the bed.

"This'll do," she said of the gold gown as the girl handed her a basket filled with underthings. "You've done well, Anne," she said, extracting a pair of black leather boots, and pattens. "Thank Bessie for finding them."

"She said there are more, if you need them."

"We might. But not today. Tell her to make sure they are washed and pressed and have these cleaned." She scooped up the huntsman's outfit, then dropped the dirty tunic and breeches into the girl's outstretched arms. "Now, send up Ginny to dress the lady's hair."

"Aye, m'lady," the girl said before disappearing through the heavy door.

"I don't need my hair tended to."

"Of course you do," Miranda said with a small, knowing smile. "The next time you see Devlynn you will look every bit the lady you are."

"Why?" Apryll stood and wrapped a towel around herself as she climbed out of the rapidly cooling water.

"Because I want him to view you as you are, his equal, not as a peasant or prisoner."

"He views me as his enemy."

Miranda smiled slyly. "Then you'll just have to convince him that you aren't."

"No messenger has returned with word from the group led by Spencer?" Devlynn asked as he and Collin strode through the bailey during a break between the bursts of rain. Dark clouds roiled overhead and the winter wind gusted, knifing through his mantle and tunic. Frowning, he surveyed the damage to the stables. Blackened beams were still visible though a crew of carpenters had been working day and night to replace the charred logs and strengthen the structure.

"There has been no word from Spencer."

"Nor from Rudyard's band?"

"Nay. Only Dennis, quickly followed by Lloyd and those who rode with you."

"They must have gone on to Serennog." 'Twas odd, Devlynn thought, alarm bells ringing in his mind. He'd ordered each group to send a messenger back to Black Thorn. Even if Rudyard had turned traitor, the others should have reported in.

"We'll send a search party out in the morning," Collin said as they headed into the great hall. Evening was closing in and the clouds had started to unburden themselves again, a few drops of rain falling from the black sky.

Devlynn didn't reply. Something was still awry, he was certain of it, but his son was safe, at least for the moment. He'd asked two of his most trusted men to watch after the boy. And every so often he'd checked on Yale himself, only to find him playing with Bronwyn or some of the other children in the keep, or talking with the kennel master. Devlynn had ordered the gates to the castle closed and no one was to pass in or out without the sentry first checking with him.

No matter what else, Devlynn would not lose his son again. Payton of Serennog and anyone else who tried to steal the boy be damned.

But what of the traitors within your own keep?

With no answer to that question, he strode through the bailey. All seemed calm. Serene. The everyday tasks being accomplished. Some of the cook's helpers were plucking feathers from two dead geese, the dye makers were boiling fabric in a huge vat, turning the fabric with wide paddles, and the candle maker hustled into her hut carrying a pail of tallow. A loom clacked while a potter's wheel whirred and the sounds of barrels being rolled into the wine cellar were just as they should have been, but Devlynn wasn't satisfied with the normalcy of the sights and sounds of Black Thorn, not while he was certain there were those plotting against him.

But who? Which of those who had pledged their lives to him had betrayed him? Which would do so again?

As he walked up the steps to the great hall, he worried again for Yale's fate. Would someone in the keep risk killing the boy right under his nose? At the door, he growled at the guard. "Find my son and bring him to me."

"We just saw him at the quintain," Collin protested.

Devlynn ignored him. "Get him," he commanded the guard. "Until the traitors have been uncovered, Yale stays at my side."

"You cannot run a castle if you are to play nursemaid all day—"

Devlynn's temper snapped. He grabbed his brother by the front of his tunic and slammed him up against the wall. "Who is lord here?"

"You are, of course," Collin answered though his hands clenched into hard fists.

"Then I'll run this castle any way I see fit!" Nose to nose, he glared at his younger brother and wondered if he could trust Collin. Once before they'd been at odds. Over a woman. Devlynn had won. He'd married Glynda of Prys and had never felt a moment's peace from the day the marriage banns had been posted. Slowly he uncurled his fingers.

"Mayhap we should make a fight of this," his younger brother said, glowering at him.

"Mayhap."

But Collin's anger seemed to melt as he stared over his brother's shoulder to the staircase. "Christ Jesus," he whispered under his breath.

Devlynn glanced behind him and his heart nearly stopped. Descending the steps, her head held high, dressed in a deep gold that matched her eyes, was Apryll of Serennog, his sworn enemy, looking as regal as any queen. He was reminded of the first night he'd seen her and his heart twisted. God, she was beautiful. Too beautiful. Her hair fell past her shoulders in soft yellow waves and the tops of her breasts were plump over the scooped neckline of the gold dress.

His mouth turned to dust.

God in heaven, what was he to do with her?

Send her to the gallows for her betrayal?

Or bed her?

Chapter Twenty-three

She felt like a fool dressed in Devlynn's dead wife's dress. The bodice stretched tight across her bosom and the hem dragged a bit on the floor, but worse than the fit was the idea that Glynda of Black Thorn had worn the gown. Cheeks flaming in embarrassment, Apryll descended the stairs and saw Devlynn with his fist bunched in the front of his brother's tunic.

He glanced over his shoulder and something flashed in his eyes, some dark emotion she didn't want to analyze too closely, something dangerous she didn't want to consider. Slowly, he let his hand fall to his side.

"Are you two at it already?" Miranda demanded in exasperation. A step behind Apryll on the stairs, she shot forward, stalked across the great hall and wedged herself between her brothers. "Enough of this! You two are as bad as two rutting stags in the forest. We have no time for this . . . this nonsense!" She beseeched both her brothers with her wide, green eyes. "'Tis time we sent a search party for the others. What if they have been killed, or wounded in battle? Even now they could be rotting in the dungeons of Serennog!"

Devlynn ignored Miranda's plea, his gaze centered

on Apryll. "What is she doing down here?" he demanded, his face grim. "She is to be locked in my chamber."

"*Your* chamber?" Collin asked, one side of his mouth lifting. "How convenient."

"Oh, stop it." Miranda looked as if she wanted to slap both her brothers. "I thought she should come down for a meal. Mayhap she can tell us where the rest of our troops are. She might know of Payton's plans."

"We've been over this," Devlynn said, white brackets surrounding the corners of his mouth. "Why didn't she wear her own dress, the one she left here during the revels?"

The back of Apryll's neck burned but she met his eyes and said evenly, "I wasn't offered it, m'lord, elsewise I would gladly have donned it."

"Would you?"

"Especially if it were to please you," she mocked, the air between them crackling as servants began preparing the table. Apryll felt curious eyes upon her, heard whispers rustling behind the thick curtains, hushed conversations punctuated by her name. With all the pride she could muster, she somehow managed to hang on to the threads of her poise.

"You look magnificent," Collin said, earning a suspicious glare from his brother. "But we are all on edge because some of our men have not returned, men who were searching for Yale and who are presumably still following some of the outlaws from Serennog who so boldly raided this keep." He was pacing between the base of the stairs and the main door and the tables where serving girls were placing knives and mazers. From the kitchen the smells of roasting meat and warm bread seeped into the great hall. "Mayhap you might be able to help us locate the men."

"I know only what I told Lord Devlynn," she said and repeated her insistence that she didn't realize Yale would be kidnapped or lives taken. ". . . the only thing that is odd is that my brother, too, was waiting for his soldiers. He was about to break camp, as they hadn't met him, when I managed to drug him. He fell asleep just before Lord Devlynn arrived. As we rode off, a few soldiers, some from Black Thorn, appeared."

"Who?" Miranda asked quickly.

"I don't know their names."

Disappointment reflected in Miranda's eyes and Apryll finally realized that she was in love with a soldier, one of the missing men. That was what all her talk about an unhappy marriage was about. She was tied to a man whom she didn't love. Apryll understood Miranda's plight. Had not she been urged to marry anyone who would ensure Serennog's good fortune? Payton had been all too ready to have her wed Lord Jamison or Baron William of Balchdar without any regard for her own desires.

Collin began shepherding them toward the lord's table. "Mayhap they'll return soon. Now, come , let us eat. As I said, we'll send troops in the morning if they have not yet arrived." Apryll forced herself not to limp. Lady Glynda's boots were a little too tight and the knife she'd managed to swipe from the huntsman's footwear and tuck into the new boots while Miranda's back was turned earlier pressed against her calf.

Yale bounded into the room and leaped over a small bench. With a squeal of delight Bronwyn chased him and the castle dogs barked.

"Slow down," Miranda warned.

Yale was breathing hard, but he still was able to duck under a table with Bronwyn on his heels. He scrambled to his feet and ran past Aunt Vi's vacant chair and received a sharp glance from his father. Unconcerned and flush-faced, he took his seat and Bronwyn plopped down beside him, sharing a short bench wedged between Devlynn and Miranda.

If they realized they were in any trouble, they didn't show it, laughing, joking and jabbering like crows in an apple tree on a sunny afternoon.

Though she was starving, Apryll could barely eat a morsel of the succulent salmon and roast goose. She listened to the buzz of conversation, heard her name spoken from the tables below the dais and wished the ordeal was over. Being seated next to Devlynn, as if she were his wife instead of his prisoner, made her want to squirm away. Sharing a trencher with him seemed laughable, yet she somehow found her dignity and even when his hard thigh brushed against the folds of her skirt, skimming her own leg, she didn't show the tiniest bit of notice.

Pages and serving girls stared at her, knights and freemen ogled her as they slowly chewed their food at the lower tables, while maids and villeins avoided her gaze. Over the clink of mazers and knives she heard the gossip that whispered around her like a dry, brittle wind.

"Look at her, sittin' next to Lord Devlynn, as if she has the right, as if she's his bloody wife," one soldier seated next to Lloyd muttered.

"And isn't that the lady's favorite gold gown?"

"Aye, but she fills it out nicely."

"Some nerve of her, after what she did. She's lucky

the baron hasn't had her drawn and quartered." Lloyd offered a greasy-lipped smile at her, then lifted his mazer in a mock toast.

"Yes . . . there still be time. The baron may yet mete out his punishment."

"Aye, she's locked in his room, I hear."

Both men laughed their evil laughs but Apryll leveled Lloyd with a haughty, cold stare. Oh, she would love to start chanting again, as if she were conjuring up a spell, just to watch his reaction and show him for the fat coward he was.

More laughter and sneers, titters and jeers, were made at her expense. The air within the great hall was tense and filled with hatred and suspicion, most of it aimed at her, though again, she sensed a darker presence in the castle, an unhappiness. There were undercurrents of unrest at Black Thorn and even Devlynn was not immune to those who, she felt, were plotting against him.

Those very souls in league with Payton.

At the thought of her brother, she wondered what he would do. Would he mount an outright attack? Try to free her? Convince the traitors within Black Thorn to rise against their lord? Oh, God, what then?

She glanced at Yale, who, plopping a date into his mouth, tossed Apryll a happy smile. Her heart warmed for just an instant, until she caught Devlynn's stern glare. 'Twas enough to shrivel her appetite.

She looked away and gathered herself. She could not let him intimidate her. She would not allow anyone in the castle to see that she had any fear.

She nibbled at a bit of buttery-crusted plum tart and silently swore that she would leave Black Thorn as soon as she was able. If Devlynn didn't free her then, once again, she would find a way to elude him.

Someone within the castle was a friend of Serennog. Someone had helped Payton sneak through the gate and past the guards. That same someone had helped her escape through a sally port a few nights earlier.

Who?

Would he show himself again?

How could she contact him?

'Twas impossible, she realized as she glanced around the large room at the sea of unknown faces. Knights. Peasants. Freemen. Servants. None so much as offered her a smile. Nay, she could not depend upon an unknown ally, she had to use her own wits if she was to escape. Feeling Devlynn's gaze upon her, she attempted to hide her thoughts and quickly turned her attention to a platter of dates drizzled with honey.

"See any traitors within my castle?" Devlynn asked as he reached for his mazer. Was she so transparent that he could read her mind? "Mayhap someone who will help you escape again?"

"I know no one here," she said as she bit into a piece of warm bread. "Only you."

"Then you are in trouble, lady."

That much she already knew, though she kept her thoughts to herself. She had her wits, the knife the farmer's wife had given her and a bit of knowledge of the keep, enough to mayhap find the same sally port that had been her escape route once before.

But this time you'll have to find it on your own.

This time there will be no horse waiting for you.

And this time you will have to evade the lord himself.

Her heart sank. The fates seemed against her.

Well, destiny be damned, she decided. Apryll was a

woman who had grown up believing in herself. For the moment, she could rely on no one else.

"Call for the physician and the midwife," Father Benjamin ordered the guard at the gate of Serennog. The portcullis rattled shut behind him. Geneva was weak. Losing blood. Softly moaning as Henry helped keep her astride the mule. With every step of the beast's hooves she'd whimpered and Benjamin worried that, despite his prayers and fumbling attempts to bind her wounds with the hem of her skirt, her soul would pass out of this world and on to the next.

"I'll find 'em!" Henry's voice and footsteps faded as he ran ahead just as Benjamin sensed the guard coming closer.

"Help me get her down," he told the man.

"For the love of God, 'tis Sir Payton," the sentry said as he examined the body draped over the backside of the mule. "He's dead."

Geneva choked back a sob.

Did the man have no brains? "Aye, I've offered up my prayers for his soul. Now, man, help me with the woman."

"Oh, right." Together they managed to help her to the ground. She leaned heavily against Benjamin and he felt her shiver, though he doubted it was from the bite of the winter wind. Nay, she was cold from the inside out. Not only had she witnessed Payton's death, but she had endured a horrid rape and, finally, been forced to ride next to the body of her beloved. "We're home, lass," Benjamin whispered to her as quick, sharp footsteps accompanied by the rustle of skirts hurried toward them.

"What's this? Oh, for the love of Mary—forgive me,

Father—'tis Geneva. Come on, Charles, help Father Benjamin git her into me hut, I'll see to her," Iris, the mason's wife, ordered. "And what is this? Heaven help us. Sir Payton . . . what happened?"

"I'm not certain," Benjamin admitted.

Iris was a devout woman, mother of three boys, and she worked in the kitchen, oftentimes kneading bread dough or skinning eels or boiling eggs. "Millie— Millie, over here, help me with Geneva."

"Wha—? Migawd," the twit of a laundress said. "She's bleedin' she is, omigawd, she's—she's—and—" She let out a tiny squeal. Benjamin assumed it was that she'd laid eyes upon the slain man. "Sir Payton! What in God's name—"

"Shh! Geneva needs help, that's what she needs. As for Sir Payton, there's nothing we can do for him but pray. 'Tis in the Father's hands now," Iris insisted and as Henry came back with the midwife, Father Benjamin followed the women into the mason's hut, where the smells of warm bread, ale and goat cheese made his mouth water.

The midwife was clucking her tongue. "She's lost a babe, I'll tell ye that much. Now we'll need to clean her up, lay her on the bed there, and we'll see what we'll see." Thankfully Geneva had stopped moaning and Father Benjamin, though he was blind, excused himself to allow the women privacy. "I'll be outside," he told Iris and slipped through the door, nearly running into Henry, who had returned after, he claimed, reaching Sir Brennan and giving him the news of Payton's death. Brennan would come straightaway.

"How's Geneva? Will she be all right?" the boy asked, concern tinging his words.

"If God allows it. Sometimes He calls us home before we think we're ready." Benjamin pulled his cloak around him. He was cold to the marrow of his bones, hungry and tired.

"Like Sir Payton?"

"Aye." Benjamin placed a hand upon the lad's shoulder. "We must pray, shall we, for Sir Payton's soul." Without waiting for the boy's reply, he forced Henry's head into a bent position and offered up a short prayer. ". . . Amen."

"Amen."

Benjamin felt the boy's right arm move as he quickly made the sign of the cross. "Now, run along. See that the mule is taken to the stables and put up proper, then get some sleep, 'tis late."

"What about him?" he asked and Benjamin knew he was speaking of the slain man.

"Leave him to me."

"Aye, Father," the boy said gratefully and slipped into the night, the sound of his footsteps diminishing as the wind picked up and the cold breath of winter blew over the priest's round face. He thought of the chapel and his warm chamber but didn't move except to rub his hands together and shift from one foot to the other. Who had killed Sir Payton? Where had they gone after slaying him and defiling Geneva? Was it the soldiers of Black Thorn, or Payton's men who had turned against him and the sorceress? But why? For gold? For the woman? Out of anger? Oh, who could understand the ways of men? He rubbed his fleshy arms and felt the turn of the wind, bitter cold, sharp as the bite of an asp. Where was Lady Apryll? Why had she not returned? His kind heart bled at the thought that she, too, was in mortal danger. Would she endure the horrid trial that Geneva had faced? Oh, this winter night did not bode well, not well at all.

He thought of Geneva, with her serene voice and noiseless footsteps. She'd always been a calm one and though he disapproved of her use of the dark arts, he'd found her to be kind and intelligent—a woman, he was certain, who, given enough time, would understand and accept the one true God. Oh, how he'd hoped for the day when she would step over the chapel threshold, renounce her sins and accept God as the Father.

Again he deftly made the sign of the cross, then prayed for Geneva's life.

He heard men approaching, boots crunching against the cold ground and short bursts of angry conversation over the rise of the wind.

"Father Benjamin," Father Hadrian said and the older priest's shoulder's sagged. "Where have you been? I thought you were going to visit the bedridden who were not able to attend mass. Oh, no. 'Tis Lord Payton!"

"Sir Payton," Benjamin corrected, attempting not to show his disgust at the younger man.

He sensed the younger priest bending over the body and heard another man—Sir Brennan?—swear under his breath. "Murdered. Run through."

"For the love of our Father, what happened?" Brennan's deep, worried voice.

"I know not," Benjamin admitted but sketched out what he had gleaned.

"You did not find him while you were 'visiting the bedridden,'" Hadrian charged.

"That is true. I decided to go onward into the forest."

"Why?" Hadrian demanded and, when Benjamin was not forthcoming, added, "You lied to me and lied to Sir Brennan, whom Lady Apryll left in her stead. This will not go unnoticed, you know, when the lady returns. I assume you saw no evidence of her, or the others who left with Payton?"

"Nay, only Geneva."

"The witch!" Hadrian spouted in contempt. "God has seen fit to punish her for her pagan ways."

"Nay, I do not believe—"

"You will have to explain yourself when Lady Apryll returns," Hadrian interrupted.

"And so I shall," Benjamin agreed.

"Now, you said the sorceress survived? Where is she?"

"Geneva is inside, being tended to by Iris and Britt."

"As I said, the holy Father has struck her down for her heathen ways."

"I think not."

"Bah! What do you know, old man?" Hadrian charged. "You have no backbone to stand up to the heathens, now, do you?" As Benjamin opened his mouth to protest and point out that Jesus often walked among the sinners, Hadrian added, "I'll hear no excuses. You have a position here at Serennog, a position that comes with responsibilities. What kind of example are you setting, Father Benjamin, by leaving the castle, lying to me and Sir Brennan, and returning with Sir Payton dead and an ailing sinner who herself lied her way out of the keep and forever flaunts her pagan ways? What have you to say for yourself?"

"I ask no forbearance for my behavior. I will speak to the lady when she returns. As for Geneva, she was with child, Father. The babe is lost."

"God's vengeance for a child conceived outside of the sacrament of marriage. It, too, would have been a savage and God saw fit not to let it live, to strike it down before it defiled our earthly kingdom."

"'Twas but a babe," Benjamin argued.

"The devil's spawn. And with original sin and the sins of its mother. 'Tis a blessing it didn't live."

He swept into the hut and Benjamin leaned against the exterior wall. There was no stopping Hadrian once he started ranting about the wages of sin or the suffering of those condemned to hell.

"What do you think happened?" Sir Brennan asked. He was a calmer man, one who took his responsibilities to heart, and had a level head. Some called him weak. Benjamin considered him thoughtful, a cautious knight not quick to make rash decisions.

"I am not certain, but I think she saw Payton, who was the father of her child, mortally wounded, and then the men who killed him took their turns with her and she lost the child."

"Where is Lady Apryll?" Brennan asked.

"I know not." Benjamin turned his face to the knight in whose charge Serennog was left and though he could not see Brennan's reaction, he felt the man's sadness, sensed his fear. Brennan was far from the strongest of the knights within the castle, though surely one of the most loyal and kind.

But Brennan was unable to stand up to the likes of Father Hadrian, and the young priest used the man for his own purposes, even taking up residence in the lady's chamber within the great hall. Something was very, very amiss.

From inside the hut, Geneva, who once was stoic and silent, let out a horrid scream. Benjamin shivered.

"We must find the lady," Brennan said, as if to himself.

"Aye . . . and soon." But in Father Benjamin's heart, he was afraid it was already too late. Serennog and the woman who ruled her were already lost.

This thought had barely passed through his head when he heard the sound of hoofbeats and bridles jangling. The guard at the gate shouted, "Who goes there?"

"'Tis Isaac. Open the gates, I've got some wounded men with me."

Hadrian was out the door of the hut as fast as if he had Satan himself at his tail. "Open the gates! Draw up the portcullis! These men left with Payton."

There was hesitation and Benjamin felt a movement beside him. "What's happening?" Henry whispered, suddenly at Benjamin's side, as if he'd been lurking in the shadows all along.

"Open up!" Brennan ordered as he swept past the priest on his way to the gate.

Ancient gears ground and the heavy metal grill clanged upward. The feeling of foreboding in Father Benjamin's heart bored ever deeper. The ground shook as if dozens of horses raced into the bailey.

"Is it really Isaac? Has he returned with Payton's soldiers?" Benjamin asked the boy.

"Aye. And Sir Melvynn. And Sir Douglas and others."

"Soldiers you know?" the priest clarified.

"Some, but not all, and the leader, he is a scarecrow of a man. And he wears the colors of Black Thorn."

"A traitor," Benjamin whispered and held back his other thoughts, for they were dark indeed. "Is Lady

Apryll with them?" he asked, though he knew the answer.

"Nay."

"You must be my eyes, boy," Benjamin said softly. "So watch carefully." He pulled Henry closer to the side of the mason's hut, hoping to melt into the darkness.

"Who are you?" Brennan shouted.

"Rudyard of Black Thorn. My men and I are in alliance with Payton and Lady Apryll. Though we wear the colors of Black Thorn, we have pledged ourselves to Serennog." Benjamin heard Geneva moan from in the hut and he drew the boy farther away, around the corner.

"Then you have not heard," Brennan said. "'Tis sad news. Payton is dead. Father Benjamin brought back his body along with one of our women who herself is near death."

"Aye." Hadrian this time. "The witch, Geneva."

"She lives?" The stranger's, Rudyard's, voice.

"For the moment."

"'Tis Black Thorn's doing," Isaac charged. "He and his soldiers must have come across Payton, defiled her and killed Payton when he tried to stop them."

There were gasps and cries, as more people had joined the crowd that was gathering near the mason's hut. Men grumbled while women whispered quiet outrage.

"This is but conjecture," Brennan cautioned.

"Aye, but I know Devlynn of Black Thorn." Rudyard again. A few of his men mumbled their agreement.

"Each of these men with you has turned against Black Thorn?" Brennan asked, clearly skeptical.

"Aye."

"That's right."

"All of us."

Different voices chimed in. All in agreement and yet Father Benjamin felt the discord among them, the lies that were unspoken, deep currents that ran beneath the words. 'Twas Satan's doing.

Chapter Twenty-four

Miranda tucked her daughter into her bed. Leaning over, she kissed Bronwyn's smooth forehead. The girl sighed and rolled over, her lips moving in her sleep. She was an angel, a perfect child.

Except for the fact that she'd been born female. Hence, she was as cursed as her mother and grandmother, born to serve and breed. Oh, there were those who believed it was women who ran the world, that with their charms, seduction, gentle urging or blatant bribery they could make a man do what they wanted. Women had but to be smarter, to scheme, to plot what they desired and simply trick a man into doing their bidding. Some believed women got exactly what they wanted.

Miranda knew differently.

Had she not been married off to a man older than her own father, a man who had wanted a young wife to bear him an heir? Had she not been told that her sole purpose was to bear Lowell of Clogwyn a son? Even though the elderly man's infirmities had rendered it impossible for his cock to remain hard enough for penetration, Miranda was required to give him an heir. 'Twas folly. Fortunately the old coot was full of himself and drank himself into stupors often enough that he believed he'd got his young wife with child. His biggest disappointment had been that the baby had been a girl. He had no thought that the child might not be his.

And so Miranda, a woman who had always held her virtue and principles high above those of her brothers, had compromised herself and passed this precious child off as Clogwyn's daughter when she was actually fathered by a dark-haired knight.

Oh, Spencer, where are you?

How had she come to love a man so deeply, a man who would never be able to claim her?

Sadly, Miranda brushed a curl from Bronwyn's cheek and sighed. It was a wonder that no one saw the resemblance, though she had purposely picked a man who had the same coloring as her aged husband had in his younger years.

How foolish she'd been to fall in love with him. 'Twas an impossible situation. One even she couldn't rectify.

She thought of Lady Apryll, one of the few women who ran a castle on her own. Now she was a prisoner to Devlynn, though, Miranda suspected, Devlynn was falling in love with his hostage.

Well, it served him right!

But Apryll, how could she have been so foolish as to have been duped by Payton? Miranda admired the lady and yet pitied her. Devlynn's temper and wrath had no bounds. Aye, even as a ruler of a castle, Apryll would now have to bow to the demands of a man. 'Twas always the same.

It would be no different for Bronwyn.

"Good night, little one," she whispered to her daughter.

Assured that the girl was fast asleep, Miranda crossed the room and pulled off her tunic. She was the only daughter of Morgan of Black Thorn, his eldest child. Yet she had been passed over in favor of her younger brothers time and time again. "No longer," she thought aloud as she slipped into her lonely bed. "No longer."

Apryll was alone. In Devlynn's chamber. Standing near a raging fire burning in the grate, wondering about the jug and mazers that had been left upon a small table, knowing that guards were stationed at each door, including the seldom-used one that led to the chapel.

Yale was sleeping in the room next door and there was an anteroom connecting the two chambers, but his door to the corridor, too, was watched by a man Devlynn trusted.

She walked to the window, the long skirt disturbing the fragrant rushes covering the floor. Peering outside, she saw no ledge to walk upon, no ladder left carelessly by the opening, no rope conveniently tucked in a corner of the sill. No, 'twas a sheer drop of three stories that did not end in a rick piled high with soft, cushioning straw but in the ground itself, muddy in the moonlight. Clouds had dropped their icy raindrops and scudded along, leaving the night clear and crisp. Silvery starlight shimmered on the eel pond and the puddles near the creek. She eyed that dark ribbon of water. The stream ran past the mill, where it deepened into a pond.

Mayhap that was how she could escape, by following the stream to the other side of the mill where it ducked beneath the heavy curtain wall and dumped into the river, a natural moat that surrounded the castle on three sides. No doubt there would be a grate or heavy screen, but she was a strong swimmer and might be able to wedge her body through or around the mesh.

But first you have to escape this room and the castle, get past a dozen guards who had been scolded and warned about leaving their posts. Tonight it would be the most difficult to leave.

Mayhap if she were to stay a fortnight or longer the guards would become lazy again and fall back into their ways of dozing or drinking . . .

A fortnight?

Dear God, how could she last so long under Devlynn's suspicious glare? Dealing with the barbs and looks of disgust from Sir Lloyd and the rest? Waiting for her brother?

Where was Payton?

Why had he not come for her?

Could he have given up the fight and returned to Serennog? Why would he bother trying to ransom her or help her escape, as he could rule the castle, appoint himself baron, saying it was but temporary? Perhaps his thirst for revenge and his need for his own brand of justice had been quenched.

Sighing, she watched the giant sweeps of the windmill turn and creak in the night. A few windows of the huts that surrounded the bailey were ajar, firelight glowing in the cracks, laughter or bits of conversation reaching her ears. Someone was singing, a clear, deep voice, another woman scolded her children and from the stables came the soft call of a nervous horse.

Oh, she longed for Serennog. Though not nearly as grand as this huge castle, 'twas home, where people needed her, depended upon her. What would become of them if Devlynn decided to keep her here?

But why?

To wait for trial?

To punish her?

To keep her as his whore?

She felt her cheeks burn at that thought, for she'd heard it in whispered speculation often enough since she'd arrived. Girls carrying eggs and buckets of water had tittered with the thought, soldiers had grunted their lusty approval, older women had glanced her up and down, then looked away, to their own husbands, some of whom had already undressed Apryll with their hungry eyes.

And yet, sleeping with Devlynn held much appeal. She knew of the things done between a man and a woman, had heard talk and gossip, but, heretofore, she'd experienced very little. Devlynn's hands had been the first to dare touch the skin of her abdomen, or brush over her breasts.

Deep inside she trembled, not with fear, but with that dark, desperate want she'd experienced at his hand only nights before, the touch of his calloused skin against hers, the feel of his wet tongue sliding over the curves of her body, the sear of his kiss on her lips and eyelids and every hollow in her flesh.

He'd sworn he would punish her and yet she was not afraid; instead she anticipated being alone with him. Oh, she was a fool. Her fists bunched in the folds of her skirt and she bit her lower lip. She could not have these wayward thoughts. Too much was at stake.

Again she wondered what had happened to her

brother. Where was the band of men who had ridden
with such wild abandon to the inn just as they were escaping? Apryll was certain a few of them had given
chase, but Devlynn had driven the horses hard and
taken seldom-used roads, doubling back here and
there, and never had a soldier appeared or accosted
them.

Nor had they been waiting at Black Thorn.

'Twas as if they'd vanished.

Or were waiting.

For what?

She heard footsteps outside the door and her heart
jumped to her throat. Her pulse leapt at the sound of
Devlynn's voice. She licked her lips nervously as he
pushed open the door, gave some muffled commands
to the sentry and slipped inside. In the past hour he'd
shaved and washed. His black hair glistened in the
firelight and the fresh smell of soap surrounded him.

She swallowed hard, watched as, without a word,
he took a seat in a chair by the fire, poured a mazer of
wine and while swirling it, crooked a finger at Apryll,
silently ordering her to come closer. She hesitated and
he crooked not one, but two, his jaw tightening at her
disobedience.

Slowly she stepped forward until she was standing
in the shifting circle of light from the fire. His eyes narrowed upon her and he let his gaze move painstakingly slowly from the crown of her head, down her
face and neck, past the rising swell of her breasts at the
low neckline to her waist and farther down, eyeing her
as if he could see through the heavy folds of velvet,
lifting an eyebrow in speculation as he would if he
were to buy a new mare for the stable.

"Take it off," he said.

"What?"

"My wife's dress. Take it off."

"Nay, I'll not—"

"Do it. Now."

She started to protest again, saw the glint in his eye and clenched her jaw. So this was how it was to be. Fine.

Spine stiff, she held back a hot retort and, feeling like an utter fool, unlaced the bodice as he sipped from his cup, his eyes never leaving her. *This is to be my punishment,* she thought, allowing the yards of lush fabric to pool on the floor at her feet. Feeling the flush of embarrassment climb up her body she stood before him wearing nothing but a thin, lacy chemise that held her breasts tight to her body and flowed downward around her legs. Well, so be it. She could endure this.

"The boots, too," he said without emotion.

"As you wish," she shot back at him and bent down to remove his wife's pinching footwear. She could either show him her rump, or her breasts, so she faced him and with some difficulty peeled off the boots, careful to leave her knife tucked inside the soft leather, aware that her breasts were falling forward, the nipples visible and hard against shimmering white silk.

He took a long swallow from his cup, but his eyes followed her every move. Kicking the boots aside, she straightened again, standing barefoot on the rushes, shorter than before, more naked and, she knew, more vulnerable.

He swirled a finger in the air, indicating that she should turn. Gritting her teeth, she did, but as she faced him again, he shook his head. "Slower."

"There is no reason—"

"Turn more slowly!" he instructed and she inclined

her head, lifted what she hoped was a saucy eyebrow and twirled around carefully, ever so slowly, feeling the weight of his gaze upon her. 'Twas meant to humiliate her.

"Satisfied, *m'lord*?" she said, knowing her eyes snapped fire, that her lips were slightly curved to show that she wasn't intimidated.

"Not yet, but I intend to be." He poured more wine and she thought his hands shook a bit, though she could have been mistaken in the half-light. Propping a booted foot onto the table, he leaned back and sipped from his cup. "Now the rest."

"The rest?" she repeated.

"The chemise. Remove it."

"Is it your wish to embarrass me? Is that how you will feel the victor, that you have punished me?"

"To start."

Had the man no shame? No sense of decency? Of course he didn't. The moments of tenderness she'd seen in his eyes were her imaginings, her fantasies. Nothing more. Her lips pursed as she glared at him and he raised both eyebrows, silently encouraging her.

Fine. She slid the straps of the chemise over her bare shoulders, then wriggled out of the tight garment. Blushing from the tips of her toes to her crown, she stood and tossed her hair over her shoulders, letting him view all of her, forcing her hands to stay at her sides when they wanted nothing more than to cover up her breasts and the juncture of her legs.

Before he could motion with his fingers, she slowly turned, offering him a view of her backside as well as the front of her, and finally faced him again.

"I heard rumors of you, Lord Devlynn," she said as the firelight played upon her skin, warming it and chasing away the goose bumps that the chill of winter caused. "I heard that you were cruel. That you were responsible for your wife's death. That you were truly a beast. I believed them all. Until I met you. Then my opinion changed. Over the past few days I've seen your love of your child, your conviction and concern for those you rule, and when I begged, you spared my brother's life. I had begun to believe that you were not the black-heart your reputation suggested. I even began to think . . ." Her voice failed her for a second, for she realized she'd almost admitted that she'd fancied herself in love with him.

He was staring at her over the rim of his mazer again, his flinty eyes unreadable, his expression stern. Waiting.

". . . to believe that you were maligned. That you were a kinder man, a truer heart, a stronger ruler than I had been told."

"And now?"

"And now I don't know what to believe, but I know no gentleman would demand a lady strip herself bare to embarrass her."

"I don't claim to be a gentleman." He set his cup aside. "So was it rumor that caused you to break in to my castle?"

"There was an old debt to repay for the ruin of Serennog."

"My father's debt. Not mine."

"And . . . the sorceress, Geneva, she told me it was my destiny."

"On that you invaded my castle? Upon your brother's need for vengeance, your belief in some pagan prediction, and because of an age-old injury, you dared breach the gates of Black Thorn?" He was angry now as he glared at her. "You risked your own life and took the lives of my guards and stable master, all because some witch told you 'twas in the fates?" Squeezing his eyes shut, he pinched the bridge of his nose and shook his head sharply as if to dislodge a painful thought. "We all be fools," he muttered, then motioned toward the chemise. "Get dressed."

She couldn't believe his change of heart. Quickly she gathered up the chemise and pulled it over her body before he changed his mind again. It was one thing to have him kiss and touch her, quite another to stand before him without a stitch of clothing.

"You won't need that," he said when she reached for the gold dress. He poured a second mazer of wine and offered it to her. "I should have you hanged," he said through lips that barely moved. "For the deaths of my men, and for stealing my boy."

She took the cup from his hand, careful not to touch his fingers, then took a sip of wine.

"Even if you were duped by your brother, you still plotted against me. That, in and of itself, is unforgivable."

"What would you have me do?" she asked.

"I haven't decided, but someone will pay." He frowned. "I intend to hunt down your brother. When I find him, I'll bring him back here and he will be charged for his crimes."

She bit her lip. "You would not kill him."

"That I cannot promise. Blood has already been spilt. If he wants to barter for his life, he will have to name all those who had plotted against me, the traitors within my own keep. After that I will expect you to step down as ruler of Serennog. Someone from my family will rule your castle."

"But—"

"I will not take a chance that this will happen again." His jaw was like granite.

Her knees threatened to give way. Lose her castle? What would become of the men, women and children who depended upon her?

As if he'd read her mind, he said, "All who reside in Serennog would have to bow to me, Apryll. They would have to declare their fealty. To me. If your brother is to live, he will be banished forever."

"He is your brother as well," she blurted, and he froze.

"What say you?"

She swallowed hard. Dare she tell him the truth? She saw the questions in his eyes.

"What, Apryll?"

"'Twas nothing."

"Nay . . . you said Payton was my brother." His eyes narrowed. His jaw was suddenly hard as granite.

She was about to argue, but saw no point. "Surely you knew," she said, holding his gaze. "Your father wasn't content to plunder Serennog."

"What are you saying, woman? That my father raped your mother and that . . . that . . ." She saw something change in his face, something dangerous. "You would say anything to save his miserable hide." He took a swallow from his mazer, then stood and leaned over the table so that his nose nearly touched her own and his breath whispered across her face. "You lie."

"I only say what you yourself have wondered. Tell me not that the gossip hasn't been whispered here, at Black Thorn, about your father's conquests, about the children he may have fathered, about the women he raped and discarded to be scorned by their own—Oh!"

He grabbed her wrist, his fingers clenching tight over her fragile bones. "Enough."

"Can you not face the truth?" she demanded. "Payton's your half brother, Devlynn, as much as I be his half sister."

His lips flattened over his teeth. "He is a bastard. Not by his birth, but by his actions," Devlynn snarled.

"He is your brother. Your flesh and blood," she threw back at him, and tried to pull her arm away. His fingers only held her tighter, a sinewy manacle that wouldn't let go. "If you kill him, you kill a part of yourself. Why do you think he's so angry? Why do you think he wants revenge?"

She saw a shadow chase across Devlynn's eyes and knew that she'd hit home. "Would you kill your own brother?"

"I believe you not."

"Now you be the liar, Devlynn of Black Thorn, for you know it to be the truth as much as I." She lifted her chin, met his angry glare defiantly and saw the denial in his eyes begin to fade.

"So this . . . all this destruction was because . . . of birthright."

"And rejection. Neither your father nor mine would claim him."

"Christ Jesus. My brother?" He dropped her wrist and shook his head, as if to dislodge a bad thought. "And so he would sacrifice you to gain revenge upon me."

"And all of Black Thorn."

A muscle worked in his jaw. He paced to the window, glowered outside, then returned to the small table, where he drained his glass. "If you be lying . . ." But he let his voice fade. He held her gaze as if searching for deception and yet his eyes darkened, not with rage, but with another, perhaps more perilous emotion. She sensed a shift in the room, as if it had warmed. The chamber seemed to grow smaller. Closer. More intimate. The air was suddenly thick and it was difficult to breathe.

Devlynn set his cup on the table, then extracted her mazer from her reluctant fingers. Her heart began to pound in wild anticipation as she recognized the seduction in his eyes. She noticed how thin his lips were, how the cords at the back of his neck were visible, how the hair on the back of his hands caught in the firelight. She licked her lips nervously. "There is no reason to barter tonight, lady," he told her, his voice low. "It's time for bed."

When she started to resist, he snarled, "Go now or I shall come with you."

Chapter Twenty-five

Devlynn felt a river of sweat run down his back. Sweat from denial. By the gods, Apryll of Serennog was an incredible creature. Her skin was without blemish, her pale hair curly and wild as it fell past her shoulders, her breasts high and firm with tempting pink nipples that puckered in the firelight and caused a man to lose all sense of reason, and Devlynn to push away the shock she had just delivered.

He was hard just from looking at her, his breeches suddenly much too tight. Swallowing what felt like a mouthful of sand, he had gazed at her front and back, taking notice of her perfectly rounded rump, her long legs and gold thatch of curls hiding the spot where they joined. God, he wanted her. Yet he had ordered her to get dressed, remembering all too vividly how taken he'd been with her at the revels, how he'd wanted her. He'd been foolish then, allowing his heart and mind-numbing lust to rule his head. Just as he was now. Oh, how easy it would be to give in, to kiss her and touch her and lose himself in her wicked, sweet warmth. Yet he didn't.

He could not be distracted. Too much was still at stake. He swilled the end of his wine and watched as she struggled into her chemise. The fine silk was little barrier, easily removed or torn with a man's passion.

Nervously, as if she expected him to lunge at her, she crawled into his bed and held the covers to her chin, like a frightened, trembling virgin. One side of his mouth curved into a smile, for he'd already tested her, known her to be hot-blooded and hot-tempered, a passionate woman easily roused to a fever pitch.

If he could trust himself.

Tossing a few logs onto the fire, he watched the flames crackle and spark, then made his way to the bed. Quickly he kicked off his boots. She followed his every move with her eyes, not averting them when he yanked his tunic over his head, not so much as blinking when he untied the laces holding up his breeches, laces that were stretched taut over the bulge in his crotch.

She was an enigma, strong one moment, fragile the next, willingly obedient and stubbornly obstinate. He let his breeches drop to the floor and caught her staring at his manhood, hard, stiff and ready. Rather than shrink away she lifted her gaze to his and raised a curious eyebrow while still clutching the coverlet to her chin.

What to do with her?

Make love until they were both sated and gasping for breath?

Leave her be and pray sleep would somehow come?

He threw back the covers and slipped into the bed. She was warm, her body smooth. It was natural to reach out to her, to circle her waist in his arms, to press intimately against the silken folds of the chemise and the warm flesh beneath it. She didn't recoil, but snuggled against him, as if she'd been expecting this, as if she wanted more. His blood fired and his damned erection ached painfully. She was so close, smelled so fragrant, hints of lavender mingling with that unique feminine musk.

He wanted to touch her and kiss her everywhere, he wanted to bury himself deep inside her and let go, he wanted to curl his fingers in her hair as he thrust into her again and again and again.

'Twould be such divinity.

And certain hell.

She was his sworn enemy; she'd lied to him and now tried to convince him that Payton was his brother. Could it be? Why not? Had he not heard the stories of his father's conquests, the snickers of the soldiers who had ridden with him, the talk of women who had been willing, others who had not? He closed his mind to that thought, but if Payton were his brother, could he not accept as family those he'd once thought were enemies? Could he not fall in love with a woman who had once betrayed him . . . who since had proved herself?

She let out a warm breath that ruffled the hairs on his chest. She flung one arm around his torso as he drew her close. 'Twas impossible not to kiss her, idiocy not to let his fingers slide down the smooth slope of her shoulder. He felt her tremble as his own heart began to pound.

With the fire hissing and popping, he slanted his mouth over hers. Welcoming lips met his. Eager. Anxious. Hot. She kissed him, letting her lips part, offering silent invitation. His tongue rimmed that silken edge, testing, tasting, probing deeper, flicking past her teeth.

Moaning softly, she arched against him.

All restraint dissipated. Lust fired his blood. Want throbbed with each beat of his heart. He ignored the warning screaming through his mind, the voice that reminded him that he dared not become entangled with this woman, that she had played him for a fool more times than not, that she was first and foremost his sworn enemy.

And sister to your brother . . . already a part of you.

He couldn't resist.

His hands found her breasts straining beneath the tight chemise. Her nipples were erect against his palms. She rubbed against him anxiously as he pulled her tighter, the silk of her gown a frail obstruction that rustled seductively.

His groin tightened. His cock felt as if it would burst.

She wriggled and writhed, drawing his head downward, and he kissed the hard buttons that were her nipples through the fabric, causing a wet spot that clung to her skin and only served to make her breasts more visible. She tasted of heaven and he pulled her tight against him, one hand on the small of her back, the other firmly around a buttock, the tips of his fingers exploring her cleft, massaging that sweet muscle as he suckled.

"Ooooh," she moaned, her fingers in his hair, her abdomen arching upward as he slid lower, bunching the fabric of the chemise and slipping beneath the soft folds to explore that most secret, moist part of her. She smelled of lavender and musk and tasted of feminine nectar. He parted her private lips with his tongue, nipped at her with his teeth, explored her with his fingers and mouth, sucking, tasting, breathing as she writhed above him. Her legs were upon his shoulders, the scent of her strong.

"Apryll," he whispered into that delicate, exquisite cave and she cried out. "Apryllllllll," he said again and she spasmed. He licked her, deepening his caress, hearing her gasp, feeling her heat. His own blood raged, pounding through his head, throbbing in his manhood, crying out for release.

Moving upward, parting her knees with his legs, he fastened his mouth over hers and nudged her gently, pushing, prodding, testing. She clung to him, her breathing as rapid and shallow as his own. Beads of perspiration ran down her face and caused her gold hair to darken. She looked up at him with wide amber-colored eyes and in that instant there was no turning back.

Despite whatever wrath this one act wrought, he had to have her.

He thrust hard, delving deep, feeling a moment's resistance as she gasped. "Oh!"

He pulled back and drove again. She melted around him, began to move with him, met each lunge feverishly, her fingers curling into the muscles of his back as she clung to him. His blood thundered and his body cried to release as he plunged ever faster, feeling the heat, fusing his body to hers, braced on his elbows and watching the color come to her face, her body convulse and her cry of release.

Then he let go. With a final thrust, lights shattered behind his eyes. His seed spilled and he fell against her, dragging in each breath, hearing his heart pound so wildly he thought it might explode, wrapping his arms around her and wondering if he could ever let her go.

Mayhap, he thought, his mind a blur of wine and sex, that he would keep her here forever, that she would become his love slave, that each night he would spend the hours ravishing her body, giving and taking of sexual favor. But the thought didn't sit right and he knew it was a foolish notion. Because, damn it, he wanted more. So much more from this woman.

You could make her your wife.

By the saints, where did that thought come from?

She is a lady.

But marriage? Nay.

She fascinates you.

And is she not more loyal than those you have called family? Remember, Payton is of your father's blood. Is it not time to heal the rift between the castles and . . . do you not love this woman?

He wanted to scoff at the thought. *Love? An enemy?* But she was no more his enemy than his own flesh and blood. She had redeemed herself time and time again and by the gods, he did love her.

Yet he could not admit this new emotion he felt, did not want to dwell on it.

She would give you more children.

Yale needed siblings, aye, but marriage? To this woman? What if she disagreed?

You could force her by promising no retribution would be made against her family or her castle. Serennog would be restored to the fine keep it once was. There would be prosperity for all and war for none. 'Twould be a marriage that would benefit both. A business arrangement.

Just business? That part left a bad taste in his mouth.

God in heaven, 'twas too much to think about, too much to consider when all he wanted to do was hold her close, kiss her and make love to her all over again.

She sighed and he brushed a strand of wet hair from her cheek. "You were a virgin," he said, rolling to his side and watching the firelight catch in her hair.

"You are surprised?" Flickering shadows played upon her face.

"Yes."

"'Tis not a sin," she teased.

"Nay."

"Some consider it a virtue."

"Yes, I know, but . . . you are the ruler of Serennog."

She laughed softly. "So I can command any man I want to sleep in my bed, is that what you think?" Levering onto an elbow, she stared down at him and shook her head, damp curls framing her face. Her color was high, her lips curved in amusement, a bit of mischief dancing in her eyes. "I am not a man, Devlynn."

"I noticed." He touched her breast, watching her nipples tighten and hearing her quick intake of breath.

"Nor an animal."

He lifted a disbelieving brow and she laughed gaily, the sound trilling off the rafters and walls.

"Well, not usually." Tracing the slope of his nose with one index finger, she added, "I seem to forget my sense of propriety with you."

"Do you?"

She was teasing him, her lips twitching in amusement. What was it about this woman that she could be such a feisty-blooded she-cat one moment and a playful kitten the next? Ah, she vexed him sorely. Mayhap when she tried to convince Lloyd at the camp in the woods that she was a sorceress, 'twas not a lie, for surely she had bewitched Devlynn.

She leaned over and kissed his lips playfully, just a light brush, followed by a giggle.

"Careful," he warned.

"Of what?"

"Me."

"Why?"

"Because I can have my way with you again."

"Is that so? Funny," she said, "because I was just thinking the same." She bit her lip and cast a glance at the ceiling. "That I might have *my* way with you. But then . . ."

"Then?" he prodded.

"Well, I was wondering how long it would take you . . . well . . . until you . . . until you would be able to . . . you know . . . pleasure me again."

"Pleasure you?" It was his turn to be amused.

"Yes . . . I, um, I've heard a man needs time to recover, to regain his strength before he is able to . . ."

"Pleasure a woman again," he guessed.

"Yes."

"Then you have heard a myth."

"Oh, I think not. I overheard Frannie, the seamstress, talking to Iris, she's the mason's wife, and there was much discussion about a man, even a healthy man, needing rest before he was able to . . . do his part in the lovemaking. I see no reason that they would make up stories."

"Mayhap they've just been with the wrong men."

"So all men do not have this . . . problem?" she asked, blinking her eyelashes in mock innocence. She licked her lips, the tip of her tongue darting from the recess of her mouth in a flirty gesture.

He was suddenly rock hard.

"Mayhap you should judge for yourself," he suggested, and pulled her tight against him, close enough that his resurrected shaft pressed deep into her abdomen.

"Oh," she gasped.

"Do you doubt me now?"

"Well . . . ?" There was the hint of a smile upon her lips.

"Vixen!" His mouth found hers and he kissed her until she was gasping for breath. And then, as the night wore on, he dispelled any of her doubts about his manhood.

"I want to ride with the men," Miranda announced as she walked briskly beside Devlynn through the bailey. It was early, the gray light of dawn barely streaking the sky, and a search party was being assembled. Collin and twelve men were about to set out to scour the fields, forests and towns separating Black Thorn from Serennog. Collin had selected those to ride with him and, of course, had not included Miranda, which had infuriated her. "I can ride as well as any man," she pointed out, her chin lifting as if expecting her brother to contest her claim.

"I'll not argue that," Devlynn said as he strode past a pen where newborn lambs were bleating plaintively and ewes shifted upon beds of straw. Miranda skirted a puddle swiftly, able to keep up with his longer strides. "But your place is here with Bronwyn."

"I'll be gone but a few days," she argued, her voice rising to the pitch that grated upon his nerves. "There are women who are trained to care for her."

"'Twould not be safe." He thought of his own son and how the serving girl meant to tend him had been drugged to sleep soundly so that Yale had been all too easily abducted.

"It is as safe for me as it is for the rest."

"Don't be a fool," he growled, whirling on her so suddenly that she nearly ran into him. The hood of her cowl fell away and a few strands of hair that had escaped the ribbon at her nape caught in the wind. She was a beautiful woman, tall and regal, and stubborn as an ox. "Aye, you are a good horsewoman, and no one can fault your aim, should you need to use your bow. I've seen you handle a sword with the dexterity many men have never achieved, but, my sister, you are not a man and you are not viewed as such. You would be a distraction to the rest of the search party and, God forbid, if you were captured by the enemy, 'twould not only be your life that would be in jeopardy, but your virtue as well."

"My virtue?" she repeated, color staining her cheeks. "You are worried about my virtue?" She laughed but there was no mirth in the sound. Folding her arms beneath her breasts as a cart pulled by a mule rolled past, she advised, "Leave my virtue to me, brother. Worry not."

"I won't worry. You will not be with the company."

"Please, Devlynn." Her fingers clenched in the folds of his sleeve. "I must." Her eyes begged him, her mouth curved into an unhappy frown, and he had the feeling that no matter what he said, she would do exactly as she pleased. Miranda, like all children sired by Morgan of Black Thorn, had been born with a will of iron.

"'Tis because of Sir Spencer," he accused and she did not argue her cause. "You are concerned for him. That is why you want to ride with the others. Need I remind you that you are a married woman? Mayhap you should return to your husband and Clogwyn."

Miranda snorted her disdain for the old man. "He misses me not nor has he ever loved me."

"Still, you are his wife."

"By no choice of mine. Tell me, *Lord* Devlynn. Would you marry without love?"

He didn't answer.

"You loved Lady Glynda, did you not—oh, that's right, you were besotted with her, offered her your barony, bested your brother to win her hand."

"Did I?" he asked angrily, and she paled. "Did I truly best Collin or was it the other way 'round?" For these past three years Devlynn had suspected that the babe that Glynda had been carrying was not his. The timing was wrong. He'd been long away and when he'd returned, not four weeks later, she'd begun to show . . . he'd never accused her of betrayal, had never known, but Collin's reaction to her death had been more emotional than his own.

"You killed her!" Collin had claimed. "You're a murdering bastard." He'd set upon his brother with fists and tears, actually drawing his sword as if to cut out Devlynn's heart before he'd dropped the weapon and fallen to his knees, weeping. Then the rumors had spread throughout the castle, towns and villages that Devlynn of Black Thorn, in a fit of rage, had murdered his headstrong, beautiful wife and unborn child.

Now Miranda was glaring at him with judicious eyes. "I think you should not lecture me of virtue and propriety, brother, when you are keeping a lady in your bedchamber. A *lady*. Of noble birth. Locked away as your personal whore."

He felt a muscle tic near his temple. "Careful, Miranda," he warned. "Lady Apryll is not—"

"I would hope not," she cut in. "Now for God's sake, Devlynn, allow me to ride."

"I cannot."

"You can do anything you bloody well want. You're the baron."

"And what I want, sister, is for you to stay in the keep. With the children. The search party will return soon enough. Besides, Clogwyn has written, asking for your return. I've not yet responded, but your duty is to him and your child." She started to open her mouth to protest, but he sliced his arm in the air to silence her. "No arguments. As you so aptly pointed out, I'm the baron and you will do as I say."

Defiance flashed in her green eyes as the morning sky lightened and the icy wind brought a promise of sleet. "You are baron because you were born with a cock," she said baldly, "and I was not so lucky. Remember that I am father's firstborn."

"And a woman."

"Aye. 'Tis the reason I'm not Lord of Black Thorn and the excuse for why I can't ride with the soldiers." With a toss of her head, she yanked up her cowl and swept past the carpenter's shop. Devlynn pushed her out of his mind. He was tired of her complaints, sick of hearing that if not for her cursed gender she would be the ruler of this keep. 'Twas enough to give him a headache and, as for that comment about Apryll being his whore . . . the thought was a stone in his gut. How close to the truth was it? He heard swords rattling and realized that, for the moment, he could not worry what Miranda or anyone else thought. Despite whatever gossip was whispered within the thick curtain walls, Apryll would stay with him, locked safely in his chamber with guards posted at the doors.

As the wind died, he followed a curved path to the stables where the soldiers were already mounted on spirited horses, saddlebags filled and creaking as the horses shifted, weapons rattling and ready.

Astride his bay destrier, Collin grinned down at Devlynn. The nervous horse, as if sensing battle, minced and sidestepped beneath Devlynn's younger brother. Steam shot from the bay's nostrils, sweat already dampened his dark coat. Other animals were edgy as well. Backing up, pulling at their bits, feeling raw, unbridled energy charging the morning air.

"'Tis time," Collin announced. There was something in his eyes that seemed odd, a smug gleam, and the smile he offered appeared false, as if he were holding a great secret. In an instant the arrogance was quickly hidden—or had it existed at all? Perhaps Devlynn was jumping at shadows, looking for traitors in the innocent. Aye, Collin had been in love with his wife, but that had been long ago. "I will not return without the rest of our soldiers," Collin promised. "Tell Miranda to worry not. I will find Spencer."

Devlynn nodded. "Godspeed."

His face suddenly serious as death, Collin tugged

sharply on his steed's reins. The bay reared, front legs pawing the cold air.

Collin gave the beast his head.

Quick as lightning, the destrier shot forward, galloping madly across the wet grass of the bailey to fly through the main gate. A dozen riders took off after him, shouting wildly as their horses gave chase. Legs flashing, eyes wild, hooves flinging mud, the horses tore away from the castle.

Devlynn motioned to the gatekeeper for the portcullis to be lowered as the rumble of hoofbeats faded. Behind a veil of clouds, a pale winter sun was struggling to rise in the east, but the sun held no ray of warmth and as the gate to Black Thorn was locked, Devlynn was left with the eerie feeling that somehow he'd just sealed his own doom.

Apryll stretched and sighed. She was warm beneath the furs and snuggled deeper into the blankets before she felt the ache between her legs and . . . her eyes flew open. *Oh, God.* She sat bolt upright, alone in bed—Devlynn of Black Thorn's bed.

What *had* she been thinking? Ever-changing vibrant images of the night before sped through her mind, each one more erotic than the last. Her cheeks flamed at the measure of her desire, the hunger she'd felt for this man, the wanton way her mouth had roved over the hard, sinewy muscles of his body.

Had she really thrown herself upon him? Held his mouth to her breast? Ran her tongue along the center of his chest and lower? She closed her eyes but the images remained. What must he think of her? How recklessly she'd tossed away her virginity. To a black-heart? Her enemy? Oh, for the love of God.

Flinging herself back onto the pallet, she stared up at the coved ceiling and cajoled herself. So she'd given herself to a rakish rogue, a man who didn't care for her. So what? Things could be much, much worse. And, really, as she thought about it, the things she'd learned last night had been deliciously indecent. If given half a chance, she would do them all again eagerly.

Oh, she was a wanton! And yet she wasn't ashamed. Nay, if the truth be known, she looked forward to sleeping with the Lord of Black Thorn again, to learning more in the ways of seduction and satisfaction.

Devlynn had not forced her, nay, other than not allowing her out of the room, he'd put no restriction upon her. Mayhap, after last night, he might change his mind upon keeping her locked and guarded.

She glanced at the door. Was it locked? Did he mean to keep her prisoner? Certainly not. Not after last night. She smiled to herself and blushed again. Oh, the indecency of it all . . . she should be chiding herself, she supposed, but her heart felt lighter than it had in weeks. Secretly, though she would never admit it, she looked forward to the night, when she would again be in his arms.

And what of Serennog? What of Payton?

She would talk to Devlynn, explain everything . . . surely there was a way to mend the rift between their castles. Both his father and her mother were dead, and Payton, perhaps he could find a peaceful way to satisfy his need for vengeance.

Geneva's words whispered through her mind.

In order for there to be peace and prosperity at Serennog

again, you will marry the Lord of Black Thorn. 'Tis your destiny.

She smiled to herself. Was it possible? Could she marry the beast of Black Thorn? Was it truly her fate? The thought was not unpleasant. Surprisingly it brought a warm feeling to her heart and when she thought of kissing him again . . . she quivered deep inside.

She looked at the oaken door to the chamber again.

Surely, now, after last night, he would trust her enough to let her out of this room, if not out of the castle.

She threw back the covers and climbed out of bed, humming softly under her breath, fearing that she was falling in love as she searched for the gold dress.

It wasn't on the floor. Nor were the borrowed boots.

She froze.

The damned knife!

No doubt Devlynn had discovered it upon arising. She cursed her luck and wondered if he expected her to stay naked within his chamber. Was that another way of punishing her? Of ensuring that she wouldn't leave the chamber?

Furious, she stormed through the room to the alcove between Devlynn's room and the chamber where Yale had slept.

Rounding the corner to the anteroom she stopped dead in her tracks.

All her silly dreams shattered in one moment.

She spied the dress hanging upon a peg, waiting for her.

Not the gold velvet gown she'd worn before.

Nay.

In its stead was her own dress, the gown Devlynn of Black Thorn intended her to wear to remind her of her sins:

Her mother's bloodstained wedding dress.

Chapter Twenty-six

"Bastard," Apryll growled as she wrapped the coverlet around her torso. So much for her silly romantic fantasies. The beast of Black Thorn had said he'd mete out his own kind of punishment and this seemed to be part of it, to wear the damned dress in which he'd first seen her, to remind everyone who saw her that she was an enemy, to mock her for thinking he had a grain of compassion in his sorry, black soul.

She heard the door open and, hauling the bloody dress with her, she found Anne, the serving maid, entering the lord's chamber. She balanced a tray on one open palm while the fingers of her other hand were wrapped around the handle of a bucket that she plopped into a corner. "Who brought this to me?" Apryll demanded, shaking the dress in her angry fist.

"I . . . I don't know," Anne said, her eyes rounding at the sight of the ruined gown.

"Did the baron ask that it be left here?"

"I said I don't know, m'lady," the girl repeated nervously as she left a tray of bread, cheese and dried meat upon the small table.

Apryll crossed the room, dragging the fur coverlet

and the damning dress with her. She stopped when
her bare toes were nearly touching the girl's boots.
"Am I to be locked in here all day? Is that what the
baron ordered?"

Annie blushed to the roots of her black hair. "I . . . I
only know that I am to bring food, water and a pail in
case you needs to relieve yourself." She cowered as if
she actually feared Apryll might strike her, the look on
her face evidence she would rather do anything than
withstand Apryll's ire.

"Fine . . . then tell the baron that I wish to see him."

"Oh, I can't do that!"

"Why not?"

"Because he is the baron," she replied, aghast. Obviously Apryll's suggestion that she speak with Devlynn was unthinkable.

"Well, then, can you talk to the steward, or the
priest?"

"Aye." She nodded emphatically, her braids bobbing around her ears.

"Then," Apryll said, her patience stretched so thin
she thought it might break, "Tell either one or both of
them that they are to tell the baron that I wish to speak
with him at once."

Anne nodded.

"At once," Apryll repeated as the girl backed to the
door, pushed hard and, as soon as there was a crack of
light from the sconces in the hall slid hurriedly out.
Apryll's fists clenched in frustration. Oh, this was insanity! Why would Devlynn make love to her all night
only to keep her prisoner in his room the next day? She
stalked from one door to the next, testing them, lifting
the latch and pushing against the heavy oaken planks
with her shoulder. All to no avail. The door to the hall-

way and the one leading to the chapel, as well as the door off Yale's chamber, were all locked, held fast. No doubt they had sentries posted on the other side.

Curse and rot the black-heart's soul! How could she have imagined she was in love with him? Oh, she felt every bit the fool she was. How silly she'd been to think that she could possibly be the beast's wife!

Blowing out her breath, she tried to form a plan. She had to get out of this prison of a chamber. She had to locate Payton. She had to return to Serennog.

And what then? Have the black-heart follow you? Oh, she would love to lock him away in *her* chamber. See how he liked that! She slid a glance at the bed and bit her lip. She *had* enjoyed the lovemaking.

*Love*making? Hah! There was no love involved in what they'd shared. 'Twas just the sex act between a man and a woman.

Her heart twisted at the thought and she called herself every kind of romantic ninny she could think of as she threw on the hated dress and everything it represented. But she'd wear it proudly. When she saw Devlynn again, she wouldn't so much as comment about the clothes.

When she saw him.

If he returned.

With a sigh, she flung herself into a chair and ignored the food. She wasn't hungry and her mind was racing with thoughts of escape. Again. Ever since she'd met the Lord of Black Thorn, she'd been on a mission to get away from him. Her fingers drummed against the arm of the chair. Where the devil was Devlynn? Why had he left her without a word? Was he looking for Payton? Or the rest of his army? How long was she to wait here? And for what?

Through the window she saw a sizzling fork of lightning split the dark heavens. A clap of thunder shook the walls of the castle.

Apryll shivered. Mayhap someone would take pity upon her as they had when Devlynn had locked her in the hermit's cell in the tower and release her. Or her brother would storm the castle and free her.

Disgusted, she remembered again Devlynn promising her that he would hand down his own kind of punishment. So this was it. He intended to mortify her, to make her squirm, as she would be the object of ridicule within Black Thorn. Her cheeks flushed at the thought, but she held her head high and tossed her hair over her shoulders.

Damn him to the very depths of hell, she would not break.

There was a light rap on the door. "Lady Apryll?"

Yale!

"Come in." She was on her feet in an instant.

She heard the sound of muddled voices as Yale spoke with the guard. A moment later the door opened and he was inside.

"Why are you in here?" he demanded. His eyes, so like his damnable father's, were worried.

"I'm being held prisoner."

"By Father?" Lines of concentration marred his smooth brow. His jaw thrust forward.

"Aye."

"But why? He likes you."

"It has nothing to do with liking," she said, though she doubted Devlynn cared a whit about her. Last night he seemed to care for her, but 'twas only lust, a moment's mistake; she was silly to think otherwise.

She took a seat near the fire and motioned Yale toward the other chair. "Eat some, if you like," she added, pointing at the tray of food Anne had left on the table.

Yale snatched up a piece of dried eel, plopped it into his open mouth and chewed thoughtfully, suddenly seeming more man than boy. "You did not answer my question. Why are you a prisoner?"

"Because your father blames me for some of the bad things that happened here."

"The fire."

"Yes . . . and kidnapping you."

"But it wasn't your idea. You didn't know about it," he protested.

"That's right, but how would you know?"

"The night I was taken. I was sleepy, aye, but I heard parts of conversations between Payton and the others. The conversations are . . ." He frowned, his small face scrunching as he tried to come up with the right word. "They are . . . like a fog, or a dream . . . I don't remember all of them, just bits and pieces that come and go."

"Because of the potion."

He lifted a shoulder. "It is all . . . fuzzy, but I am sure I heard Payton tell someone he knew you would not go along with a kidnapping so he did it himself. When I asked him about it later, he said it was part of the game."

"There was no game."

"Yes, I know." Yale swallowed the bite of eel and reached for another. "So, now, I will tell my father and he will release you. You will be free."

"It's not that simple, I'm afraid," she said, not daring to think of freedom.

"It should be." He stared at her as if he thought all

adults made life much more difficult than was necessary. "You saved my life, didn't you?"

She cringed. "I think not. My brother would not have harmed you."

His eyebrows drew into a knot. "Payton cares not for anyone but himself. Including you. He is evil, you know." With that, Yale popped the morsel into his mouth and sprang to his feet. All traces of his adult side disappeared. "If my father does not release you," he said with a naughty lift of one eyebrow, "then I shall do it."

"Nay!" She wouldn't let the boy risk his father's wrath. "'Tis something I will work out with the baron."

Yale's grin was that of a brash, wayward youth who considered himself invincible. "We shall see."

"Yale, do not!" she ordered as thunder rolled over the distant hills.

Feigning as if he held a sword in one hand and a dagger in the other, he spun on his heel, leaped over a small bench and rapped on the door in one swift motion. With a creak, the door opened. Offering Apryll a conspiratorial wink, Yale whispered, "I shall return."

"I have a confession." Miranda's voice was soft, her lips compressed, guilt shadowing her eyes as she ducked beneath the overhang of the armorer's hut, where Devlynn had been checking the stores of weapons.

His gut tightened. Was she going to admit that it was she who had betrayed him? "I'm not a priest."

"My sins are not against God," she said, the fingers holding the hood of her cloak in place white-knuckled as a drip of icy rain fell from the roof and splattered on the ground. Lightning flashed over the hills.

"What is it?" he braced himself.

She bit her lip. Closed her eyes for a second. Devlynn's heart pounded. "It was I who helped Lady Apryll escape from the tower. I betrayed you."

"And why did you do this?" he asked, but she didn't answer until a dung cart rolled toward the main gate. Devlynn watched as the cart-pusher called to the gatekeeper to open the portcullis. The sentry, who had a list of those who had been allowed in, started the winch.

"'Twas not that my loyalties weren't with you," Miranda said as a stray drop of rain slid down her nose. "But I could not stand to see a lady, a woman who reigned, be treated as a common prisoner."

"Should she be treated differently than a man should he have breached the castle walls? Remember, I did not throw her into the dungeon."

"I know. I have regretted my deed ever since . . . I . . . was misguided."

"By whom?" His eyes narrowed on his sister because never before had he known her to lie.

"By my own sense of pride and . . . what I wanted."

"Are you trying to tell me that you have plotted against me?" he hissed, his voice low. He grabbed her upper arm, fingers digging past the fine wool to her flesh.

"Nay!" She tried to yank her arm free as thunder smacked loudly.

"Listen, *sister*, I have sensed the unrest here at Black Thorn. There are traitors within the castle walls who helped Payton of Serennog. Are you one of them?"

"Devlynn, no! I . . . I only let the lady escape because . . . because . . ." She closed her eyes a second, gathered herself and shook her head. ". . . because she is all that I wished to be. Aye, Devlynn, I have envied you your station, have wished that I'd been born a man, that I would have been groomed to rule this keep, but I would not betray you."

"Other than to let my prisoner go free."

"Have I not confessed?" she said with a haughty toss of her head. Her cowl slipped to her neck.

"Confessed, yes. Atoned, no."

"Then lock me in the tower, brother, do what you will—"

"Mayhap I'll ship you back to your husband."

She blanched. Swallowed hard. "You would not," she whispered, and the sound was desperate; it grated upon his heart, for he had a soft spot for his sister. "Please, Devlynn. Anything else."

"Lord Devlynn!" The sentry's voice called over the drip of rain and the creak of wheels. "Sir Collin has returned . . . with prisoners!"

"What—?" Miranda was already flying across the bailey, mindless of the icy rain spitting from the sky.

"Wait—do not let them in—!" Devlynn yelled, but it was too late. The portcullis had already been raised, allowing the cart through, and twenty or more horses with riders clamored into the bailey. Some of the men upon the muddy steeds were bound. Others walked on leads. Collin, triumphant, was at the head upon his bay, his smile wide, his eyes bright. Blood stained one part of his tunic.

"Brother!" he cried victoriously, his eyes sweeping the crowd that had gathered. "I've captured the traitors. No more will those within the walls of the castle have fear! Black Thorn has been saved!"

Devlynn felt a tension in the air, more to do with those within the keep's wide walls than the lightning crackling in the air. He glanced at the faces of those Collin had taken prisoner. Some strangers, some men he'd trusted. The captain of the guard, Rudyard, sat stone-faced upon a brown horse. He stared straight ahead, refusing to acknowledge Devlynn, his arms tied to his body with a long length of rope.

"Oh!" Miranda cried when she spied Spencer, dirty and straight-backed upon a dun stallion streaked with mud. She mouthed his name as Collin dropped lithely to the ground.

"Where is Payton of Serennog?" Devlynn asked and felt the hairs on the back of his nape raise. Something was wrong here. None of his soldiers would meet his gaze. Devlynn's right hand curled instinctively over the hilt of his knife.

"Dead. Killed by his own men. We came upon his body in an old inn, the very one where he had kept Yale prisoner." With a wave to those who were with him, he clapped Devlynn on the shoulder, his hand gripping hard. "Come, let us go inside out of this weather. 'Tis time to celebrate with a mazer of wine."

From the corner of his eye, Devlynn saw the blade, a wicked little dagger that flashed bright in the gloomy day. "Now, brother," Collin whispered into his ear, "die."

Chapter Twenty-seven

A larm bells sounded.
    Thunder clapped.
Footsteps pounded.
People screamed.

Apryll threw herself at the door, her fists pounding on the hard oaken planks. "Let me out! Please. Someone!" Good Lord, what was happening?

Lightning sizzled, flashing through the window.

The door to the chapel was flung open. "Come!" Yale cried. "Lady Apryll, hurry!" He vanished into the closet and Apryll followed down the curved staircase and through the priest's alcove to the empty chapel. Through the open doorway she heard the sound of clanging, horses shrieking and men yelling.

Oh, God, she thought as she flew into the bailey and saw the melee of men in battle. 'Twas as if she'd stepped through the gates of hell.

Devlynn jabbed his elbow into his brother's side and swung 'round with his sword. Collin fell back, but his knife found its mark. Hot pain erupted in Devlynn's shoulder as his own sword found Collin's side.

His brother fell to his knees and pain tore through Devlynn's soul. *Collin! Why?*

"Get this man help," he yelled, but as Collin collapsed, his knife falling from his hands, Devlynn spied Rudyard break free of the fraudulent bonds restraining him, lift his sword high and kick his horse forward. The steed sprang. Rudyard swung hard, his deadly blade reflecting a blinding flash of lightning.

Devlynn ducked, his own weapon held high. Swords clashed loudly, the hilt of Devlynn's weapon reverberating in his hands. "Go to hell, you bastard!" Rudyard crowed, turning his horse so quickly it reared.

Zzzt!

Thwack!

Rudyard jerked. With a horrifying cry he tumbled forward. He landed headfirst in a puddle, an arrow protruding from his back. From the corner of his eye, Devlynn caught a glimpse of a woman in white. Apryll was running through the bailey, her white dress flowing around her, a long bow clutched in her hands. "Yale!" she was screaming. "Yale!"

Then he saw his son. Atop an empty cart, a sword in one hand, crouching as if he were going to slay the man at the other end of the cart, the soldier determinedly advancing upon him. Devlynn's heart stopped when he recognized Spencer.

No!

Devlynn ran, leaping over men writhing upon the ground, clutching wounds and moaning while blood seeped into the muddy ground and pooled around them. Thunder cracked. The wind raged and the fighting went on. Screaming, yelling, clanging, neighing, a horrid cacophony of sound while the stench of blood filled his nostrils.

Spencer advanced, wielding a mace in one burly arm, holding his sword in the other.

"Don't let this happen," Devlynn growled under his breath, either at himself or God, for it did not matter.

The boy backed up, slicing in the air with his smaller weapon, staring directly into the maw of death. Spencer's eyes glittered, his expression hard with battle. Devlynn leaped, climbing over the wheel of the wagon just as the soldier brandished his razor-sharp sword.

"Stop!" Devlynn commanded, pushing Yale over the side of the wagon, his sword crashing against Spencer's blade. But the big soldier swung his mace and as Devlynn stepped back, then lunged forward, his blade piercing Spencer's broad chest, a woman screamed and the mace crashed downward, splintering the sides of the wagon.

Yale! Where the bloody hell was Yale? And Apryll? God be with her. Twisting hard on his sword, he watched as Spencer dropped to his knees. Devlynn yanked out his blade and blood spurted, spraying the wagon. With a rattling breath and a bubble of dark liquid the big man fell forward while a woman squealed as if in agony.

He caught a glimpse of Miranda, her hair flying, her legs racing over the bloodied grass to the wagon. "Spencer, no! Oh, love, please, no, no, no!" She climbed over the wheel and fell upon the dying man. "Don't leave me," she cried, tears streaming from her face. "Don't leave me and Bronwyn. We need you." She was pushing his hair out of his eyes and cradling his head, but 'twas too late—the light in his eyes had dimmed.

Devlynn left her to mourn her hero, the traitor who had nearly killed his son, then he spied Yale and Apryll, standing together, the boy managing a crossbow and Apryll with her long bow drawn back, a deadly arrow aimed straight at the heart of a stocky man with a red beard, a man he didn't recognize.

"Call them off, Roger. All of them," she ordered. "And tell me where my brother is."

"I suggest you do as the lady says," Devlynn said and then, seeing that the fight had left most of the men, that those of Black Thorn, those who had lived and worked within the keep's walls, those whose fealty was true, seemed to have the upper hand, yelled, "All fighting is to stop. Now! Sentry!" he bellowed. "Ring the alarm bell!"

Roger dropped his weapon. "'Tis over," he admitted.

"And you shall be hanged for your treachery," Apryll charged. "Where is Payton?"

"Dead, m'lady," another man said. "Run through by Rudyard."

"Wh—what? Nay . . ." Apryll's face was suddenly whiter than the gown had once been. "Nay, he is alive . . . he must be." All of the fight seemed to leave her and she swayed for a second. Devlynn stepped forward, determined to catch her, but somehow she found the strength to stand. Tears ran down her face. "Those who have killed my brother and those who have carried out his vengeance against Black Thorn will come before me," she ordered. "Each and every man."

Devlynn turned to the men who still stood in the bailey, their weapons now on the ground or slack in their hands. "Enough!" He spied a group of traitors held at sword point by a few soldiers and several peasants and freemen, the butcher holding a meat cleaver high, the smith wielding a pipe, a sawyer gripping a broad axe. "Take them to the dungeons and have the physicians see to the wounds. We'll need bandages and . . ."

He felt a hand upon his shoulder. "You'll need a bandage," Apryll said, drawing her fingers back and showing him his own blood.

"'Tis not all," he whispered and pulled her close. "I think, lady, I need you."

"And I think you be confused because of the battle and your wound."

"What you think counts not," he said with a half smile as he wrapped one arm around Yale's shoulders. "I'm the lord here. You are my prisoner."

"Have I not earned my freedom?" she asked and he shook his head.

"Far from it, lady. For all your deeds, you've earned a life of servitude."

"What?" She threw down her weapons. "Of all the bloody, bullheaded, impossible—oh!" His lips crashed down upon hers and he kissed her as if his life would soon end. He felt her swoon against him, tasted the salty tracks of the tears she'd shed for her Judas of a brother, and realized that he would die before he would let her go.

Lifting his head, he said, "Marry me, Apryll of Serennog."

"But . . . I . . ."

"Let this be the end of the curse, let us join together for peace, and prosperity. Black Thorn and Serennog."

She bit her lip. Hesitated.

He stared deep into her eyes. "I love you." His voice

was only a whisper but it echoed through the chambers of Apryll's heart. Lightning sizzled through the dark night sky. "Marry me, Apryll. Take my heart and my life. Be the mother of my children. Stay with me forever."

Tears sprang to her eyes. Could she trust him? This emotion she felt welling up from the deepest part of her?

"What say you, woman?" he demanded and she felt a smile pull at the corners of her lips.

"Yes," she cried, flinging her arms around him. "Oh, yes, yes, yes!"

"Then let the banns be posted," Devlynn ordered. "Apryll of Serennog will become my wife!"

Epilogue

Lady Black Thorn heard the baby crying in the next chamber. Ah, she was a fussy one, her daughter. While the baron had the audacity to snore, Apryll pushed herself out of the bed and padded barefoot through the rushes to the antechamber where the infant was working up to lung-bursting screams.

"So when will you discover 'tis time to sleep at night?" Apryll whispered, pulling the tiny, dark-haired infant from her small crib.

The baby stopped crying and busily nuzzled at Apryll's swollen breasts. "In a minute, in a minute." She carried her daughter into the lord's chamber and settled into the bed again while the fire quietly burned and downstairs the castle was waking. A rooster crowed and somewhere down the hallway a woman was singing off-key. Tonight the castle would be open to celebrate the revels. Oh, so much had happened since last year's. One of Devlynn's most trusted knights was ruling Serennog and Sir Brennan and Father Benjamin were advising him.

Father Hadrian had slipped into the night upon hearing that Apryll was to marry Devlynn of Black

Thorn, and Geneva, poor woman, was still grieving Payton's death, though, Father Benjamin had reported, she seemed to be healing after nearly bleeding to death from the loss of her infant and the rape.

Dear God, how had such horrid things happened? Apryll wondered. How she'd misjudged her brother and the man who had become her husband. Serennog had prospered in the last year and though Apryll had visited twice, she now believed this was to be her home. Her destiny.

Mayhap Geneva's prediction had been right, though the sorceress had confided that she'd conjured up the whole idea, not so much to betray Apryll, but to satisfy Payton.

She glanced down at her babe, now suckling hungrily at her breast. Sweet little Rowelda of Black Thorn, a thing of mystery to her older half brother.

Devlynn stirred beside her, rolling over and opening one eye. "Again?" he asked and stretched.

"She is insatiable," Apryll said, lifting a brow. "Like her father."

"Aye, and her father is jealous." Devlynn scooted closer, kissed his daughter's head, then kissed Apryll's plump breast where a pearly drop of milk had collected.

"Uh-uh-uh," Apryll admonished, then smiled secretly. "Later."

Devlynn laughed and, despite his wife's warnings, kissed first the nipple and then her lips. "Tell me not what to do," he warned. "Or I shall have to punish you."

"And how would you do that, my lord?"

"Slowly," he said. "Very slowly. Until you beg for mercy."

She laughed as if the idea were preposterous. "Me? Beg? I think not. Now, I think that mayhap I would be the one who punishes you."

"Never."

"Hmmm. I have ways, you know." She shifted the baby to her other breast. "We shall see, husband."

"That we shall, wife," he promised with a wicked gleam in his eye. His fingers delved under the covers to trace the length of her thigh. "That we shall."

Turn the page for an exciting excerpt from
another historical romance by Lisa Jackson

SORCERESS

Available from Signet

North Wales
Winter 1273

*R*un, Tempest, run!
    Frigid air tore at Kambria's hair and whistled past her ears as she silently spurred her mount onward through the bare trees and snow-crusted ground. The poor mare was struggling, gasping for air as she gamely plunged forward through the scraggly thicket of yew and pine. Hot air plumed from the horse's nostrils and her hooves tore into the hard, icy earth, but her shaggy coat was covered in sweat, and despite all of Kambria's prayers to Morrigu, the Mother Goddess, the beast was losing ground.

Soon the hunters would be upon them. So-called holy men, dressed in black. Intent upon seeing their own twisted justice meted out upon her, they chased her with a wrathful, vengeful fire that no amount of reason or persuasion could dampen.

"Faster!" Kambria leaned over her mare's shoulders, hearing the poor horse labor, its breath whistling. Strong equine muscles began to flag. Her mission was surely lost. Nightfall was too far off. Even then, beneath the shroud of night, the hunters would track her, follow her, run her to the ground. There was no darkness deep enough to hide her.

"Give me strength. Lay your hands upon my mare," Kambria prayed as icy fingers of wind snarled her hair. Up ahead she caught a glimpse of another horseman darting through the frigid undergrowth. The dark riders were everywhere.

Even as she tugged on the reins and veered west, toward the mountains, she knew with a sinking heart that she was trapped. There would be no turning back, no circling around. The five horsemen had fanned out through the bare trees, cutting off all chance of escape, all roads returning her to her home, to safety.

Frantic, she pulled on the reins, guiding the mare to a narrow twisting path that climbed upward, through the lower hillocks toward a ridge. The territory was new. Foreign. Forbidden. But she had no other choice.

She heard their shouts.

Terror cut like shards of ice through her heart.

Tempest struggled, her hooves slipping, her flanks quivering, foam beginning to spot her gray, wet coat. "Please . . . you can do it."

Upward, ever more slowly, the beast ran on as snow began to fall, and Kambria felt a sharp cramp. She glanced down at her skirts, bundled high, and noticed the warm ooze of blood that dripped down her leg and splattered to the ground, bright red upon the frozen snow.

Her heart plummeted.

Not only would the blood leave a perfect trail—it would also strengthen the hunters' purpose.

"God's teeth," she said, placing the reins in her mouth and trying vainly to stanch the flow. From the corner of her eye she saw movement, black-robed figures upon fleet steeds climbing the ridge, flashing past a thicket of spindly trees. By the saints, they were upon her!

And all the while drops of blood spotted the ground, caught by the wind.

Somehow she had to stop this madness.

At the top of the ridge, she spurred her horse onward and the mare, finding footing, took off, cutting along a narrow deer trail. Heart pounding, skirts billowing, Kambria thought for a second that she would prevail, that her sure-footed jennet was more than a match for their bulkier steeds, which would scramble upon this narrow mountain spine. "Good girl," she whispered, barely believing her luck.

She prayed that the mountain would slow their steeds. If not, if they caught her, at least the dagger was safe; she had seen to that. A weapon possessed of great magick, the Sacred Dagger was destined to be in the hands of the Chosen One, as the age-old prophecy prescribed:

Sired by Darkness,
Born of Light,
Protected by the Sacred Dagger,
A ruler of all men, all beasts and beings,
It is he who shall be born on the Eve of Samhain.

The dagger could not fall into the hands of men with hearts of darkness, men like those who pursued her now.

As her horse galloped into the thin icy wind of the mountain, she felt a clutch of pain in her abdomen, a reminder of her baby, the child she'd had to leave behind. There was no pain like a mother's loss, but she'd had to see to the baby's safety, her child of Light.

At the crest of this hill, the trail split as neatly as a snake's tongue and, if she was far enough ahead, she might be able to tear off a bit of bloody clothing to lead her pursuers on the wrong course. She glanced over her shoulder and saw no one, none of the dark horsemen following.

Had she lost them?

Nay.

They would not give up. Their purpose was too strong. She dug her heels into the gasping gray's sides and wound through the trees. Blood sang through her veins when she caught sight of the fork in the path, one trail leading downward toward the village and river, the other following the backbone of these sheer mountains. Surely those behind her would expect her to take the lower path to the town. . . .

Suddenly her horse shied.

Stumbled.

Kambria's heart clutched.

She fell forward, nearly toppling over Tempest's bowed neck. Bristly black hairs from her jennet's mane stung her eyes and blinded her for a heartbeat. As the horse regained her footing and Kambria's eyes focused again, she saw him: a single dark predator upon a white steed. His head was covered with a black cloak, only the cleric's collar visible in the darkness, but she felt his eyes upon her, sensed his hideous intent.

She tried to pull her horse around, but it was too late. The others had closed in and she was trapped upon her panting mare.

Doom, it seemed, had found her.

"There is no escape for sinners," the horseman blocking the fork stated bluntly.

"I've not sinned."

"Have you not?" His dark eyes were slits deep in his cowl as he pointed a long, accusatory finger at the ground, where blood stained the icy snow. "Proof

of your perfidy, Kambria, descendant of Llewellyn,"
he said. "Of your heresy and adultery. You are a
harlot and a whore of the worst order, a daughter of
the devil."

She felt the other horsemen drawing closer, circling
her tightly, and for a second she felt as if she couldn't
breathe. The mare beneath her quivered and Kambria
laid a calming hand upon the frightened horse's
shoulder. Was there no way out? Could she force her
little mare to break through this ring of soulless men?
She turned her thoughts inward, to the strength that
lay deep in the marrow of her bones, the faith and
courage that had brought her this far. *There are ways
to defeat these monsters, means not physical, forces you
have only to call upon.*

As if he read her thoughts, the leader snagged the
reins from her hands and dropped to the ground.
"Dismount," he ordered.

When she hesitated, he nodded to one of the others. A large hooded man with shoulders as broad as
a woodcutter's ax hopped lithely off his bay, his
boots hitting hard against the frozen terrain. Though
she held on fiercely to the pommel of her saddle, it
was no use. The big brute of a man dragged her from
her horse and pinned her arms roughly behind her
back, causing her shoulders to scream in pain. She
felt the blood drain from her face but didn't cry out,
determined to confront the fury of these lying thugs
with a fire of her own.

The leader was the worst—a zealot who spoke of
piety and divinity but was, in truth, an abomination
to all of mankind.

He was known as Hallyd, and his cloak was but
a disguise to hide the legacy of evil he'd inherited
from his father, a man rumored to be half demon
himself.

Aye, she knew this man who posed as a priest by

day but was known to be quite a swordsman with women in the village by night. Had he not tried to bed her? Even threatened her when she'd refused him? But she'd seen the eerie light in his eyes. She could smell the smoky darkness of his soul. She sensed the yawning abyss of hatred that threatened to devour all light from the sky. She'd known what he really wanted, and she could not let it fall into his hands, even if she died protecting it.

If only the other hunters knew of his evil . . . but the men seemed all too willing to follow his orders as Hallyd gave a quick nod and they too slid to the ground, surrounding her.

Please, Great Mother, hear my prayer. If you do not save me, at least spare the life of my babe.

"Hypocritical spawn of Arawn," she whispered defiantly, "go back to Annwn, the underworld of the dead. May you never see the light of day again!"

He froze, thunderstruck.

"Silence!" Hallyd ordered.

"I know you," she whispered, holding his gaze. Even as he accused her of practicing the dark arts, beneath his Christian cloak and collar, he, too, was familiar with the old ways. Evil was apparent in the eerie, ethereal glow within his brown eyes—wild, determined eyes of a man who was not yet twenty years. "I know of your own sins, Hallyd, and they be many."

For an instant he hesitated.

"Harm me now and you will forever look over your shoulder, chased by your own guilt and my vengeance." As if to add credence to her words, lightning split the sky. The forest trembled.

"Mother of God," one of the men whispered nervously.

But the leader would not back down. Through lips that barely moved as the day darkened, he hissed,

"You, Kambria of Tarth, daughter of Waylynn, descendant of Llewellyn, are an adulteress as well as a witch. The only way to save yourself is to tell me where you've hidden the dagger."

She didn't respond, though in her mind she caught an image of a wicked little knife covered in jewels.

"You know where it is," he accused, leaning closer.

She spat upon his face, the spittle sliding down his cheek and neck, lodging behind his clerical collar.

Enraged, he yanked a rosary from a pocket, then forced it over her head, its sharp beads tangling in her hair. "For your sins against God and Man, you are hereby condemned to death."

She saw it then, the traitorous gleam in his eye. Oh, he was a fraud, a man with a soul black as the darkest night. He was doing this, sentencing her to die, to protect himself and his true mission. Her destruction had little to do with her, but all to do with his ambition to seize the Sacred Dagger.

"No amount of killing will save you," she said, then closed her eyes and began to chant, conjuring up a dark and deadly spell. She sensed the wind shift as it rattled the branches of the trees and swept across the icy ridge. Without seeing, she knew that thick clouds were suddenly forming, coming together, roiling toward the heavens, turning the color of aging steel. Far in the distance, thunder boomed.

"God in heaven," one man whispered, his voice raspy, "what is this?"

"Is she really the progeny of Llewellyn the Great?" another asked, and Kambria felt their fear.

"Ignore her cheap tricks," Hallyd said, though his voice was void of conviction. "She is using your fear against you."

"Save us all," the other man cried, falling to his knees and crossing himself.

Lost in her chant, Kambria barely heard their words.

Pressing fingertips to her forehead, she prayed, summoning the spirits, whispering for the safety of her child and the destruction of her enemies.

"Stop! Jezebel! Call not your demons!"

And yet her words would not stop, the prayers of the old ones springing from her lips.

"Nay!" the dark horseman cried, enraged at her calm, her inner peace. He wanted to see her fear, to feel her terror. He received no satisfaction from her serenity. "Tell me, witch!"

Through her fluid chant she felt his vexation swell, sensed the growing fear that he couldn't hide.

"Curse you, Hallyd, and may your darkest fears be known." Her eyes opened and she stared into the mask of rage upon his face. "Your black soul shall be condemned for all eternity and you shall live in darkness forever, the pain of day too much to bear. From this day forward you will become a creature of the night." She saw it then—the fear, causing the pupils of his eyes to dilate to holes dark as the blackest dungeon, black swirls that would never shrink. His would be a blindness not only of the soul but of all daylight. And he would be marked, the very ring of color of one of his eyes turning to a pale gray.

Roiling with fury, he curled his fingers into fists until every knuckle turned white.

But she would not be deterred. "Go back to the bowels of hell from whence you were spawned," she said, staring into his black eyes, dark mirrors that reflected her own image.

"Tell me where the dagger is," he railed. "Tell me, whore!" Enraged, he struck, his fist slamming into her face.

Her nose splintered. Blood sprayed over the earth, yet she didn't flinch.

When he saw she was unmoved, he said, "So be it. You are to die now. Do you hear me, whore? You cannot be saved. Go thee to Satan!" He shook her and more blood spewed from her body, streaking his white collar red, speckling his chin.

Jaw clenched, his pulse pounding at his temple, he reached into the voluminous folds of his robe and withdrew a sharp-edged rock.

In that instant, still chanting, she closed her eyes again and gave herself over to the Great Mother. In a heartbeat, she felt her spirit rise into the tempest of clouds. As she looked down, far below, she spied her body standing defiantly upon the jagged cliff, her skirts billowing. She watched from above as he hurled the stone with a fury born of fear. The rock crashed hard against her face, splintering her jaw, slicing her pale skin. Blood sprayed upon the ground as she stumbled back. Another stone smashed against her forehead and she fell, the group of men upon her, demons dressed in black pounding at her flesh.

There was no pain.

Only peace.

Her child, Kambria knew, was safe.

And vengeance would be hers.